DEATH AND THE LIT CHICK

G. M. MALLIET

Constable • London

CONSTABLE

First published in the USA in 2009 by Midnight Ink

This edition published in Great Britain in 2015 by Constable
1 3 5 7 9 10 8 6 4 2

Copyright © G. M. Malliet, 2009

The moral right of the author has been asserted.

A CIP catalogue record for this book
is available from the British Library.

ISBN 978-1-47211-772-4 (paperback)
ISBN: 978-1-47211-773-1 (ebook)

Typeset in Sabon by TW Typesetting, Plymouth, Devon
Printed and bound by CPI Group (UK) Ltd, Croydon, CR0 4YY

Constable
is an imprint of
Constable & Robinson Ltd
Carmelite House
50 Victoria Embankment
London EC4Y 0DZ

An Hachette UK Company
www.hachette.co.uk

www.littlebrown.co.uk

For my mother

Contents

Acknowledgments

My continued thanks to the staff of Midnight Ink for its thoughtful and inspired help.

Thanks also to Muir Ainsley and Scott Hockett, for reasoned and considered answers to preposterous questions. Any mistakes in this novel are entirely my own.

Author's Note

If you are familiar with Edinburgh and its surrounds, you may think you recognize Dalhousie Castle as the setting for this novel. While the stunning Dalhousie does exist, and shares certain features with my fictional Dalmorton Castle, it has not for centuries been, to the best of my knowledge, the scene of any murders. I have likewise altered many of Dalhousie's striking architectural features and its layout to suit my purposes.

The staff and guests of Dalmorton Castle live entirely in my imagination.

Cast of Characters

KIMBERLEE KALDER – Young, beautiful, and undisputed queen of the 'chick lit' genre, she courted trouble wherever she went.

JAY FFORDE – A literary agent, Jay wanted to acquire Kimberlee as a hot new property – a property that might prove too hot to handle.

LAURIE – Jay's assistant.

NINETTE THOMSON – Like Jay Fforde, a literary agent. Her client Kimberlee's success paid the bills; Kimberlee's defection to Jay would *not* fill the bill for Ninette.

WINSTON CHATLEY – A craggy writer of dark, brooding thrillers, but the thrill was gone: The anguished author was plagued with writer's block.

MRS JOAN ELKSWORTHY – an expat transplanted to New Mexico in the United States, where she wrote mysteries set in Scotland. Like many others, she was baffled and chagrined by Kimberlee's success – and more than a little jealous.

RACHEL TWALLEY – Organizer for the Dead on Arrival crime conference in Scotland, she said she never volunteered for murder.

LORD EASTERBROOK – A publisher who, like agent Ninette Thomson, had put all his eggs in the basket of Kimberlee Kalder's success.

MAGRETTA SINCOCK – A flamboyant, once-successful author. As she angled for a comeback, she viewed Kimberlee as both obstacle and threat.

DETECTIVE CHIEF INSPECTOR ARTHUR ST JUST – Dragooned by his Chief to appear at the Dead on Arrival conference, the shrewd detective found himself co-opted into solving a non-fictional crime.

PORTIA DE'ATH – A mysterious beauty, both criminologist and crime writer. St Just struggled to maintain his professional detachment in the face of his growing attraction to her.

B. A. KING – A publicist and firm believer in the maxim credited to P. T. Barnum: 'There's a sucker born every minute.'

ANNABELLE PACE – B. A. King's disgruntled client. A writer of forensic mysteries, she'd like to dissect B. A. King.

TOM BRACKETT – An American spy thriller writer with a mean streak and a covert past.

EDITH BRACKETT – Tom's downtrodden wife. The other attendees agree: The real mystery was why she put up with her ill-tempered husband.

DONNA DOONE – Aspiring author and event coordinator for Dalmorton Castle and Spa, she may have been sharper than her prose would indicate.

FLORIE MACINTOSH – A hotel maid, Florie had seen it all. Had she seen too much?

QUENTIN SWOPE – A reporter with several tales to tell.

DCI Ian Moor – From the Lothian and Borders police, an elfin man whose jolly demeanor belied a quick acumen.

SERGEANT KITTLE – Moor's gloomy sidekick.

Sergeant Garwin Fear – St Just's usual partner in crime solving. His thatching course in Shropshire is interrupted by murder.

Randolph – Dalmorton Castle's bartender, and keeper of its secrets.

Desmond Rumer – Earnest and attractive, he told the detectives about the real Kimberlee Kalder.

Robert and Rob Roy – St Just's old-fashioned fail-safe.

Elsbeth Dowell – Her tenure as maid at Dalmorton Castle was mysteriously cut short.

'God, protector of innocence and virtue, since you have led
me among evil men it is surely to unmask them!'

— SAINT-JUST

'Where both deliberate, the love is slight,
Who ever lov'd, that lov'd not at first sight?'

— MARLOWE

'A sad tale's best for winter; I have one
Of sprites and goblins.'

— SHAKESPEARE

Dalmorton Castle

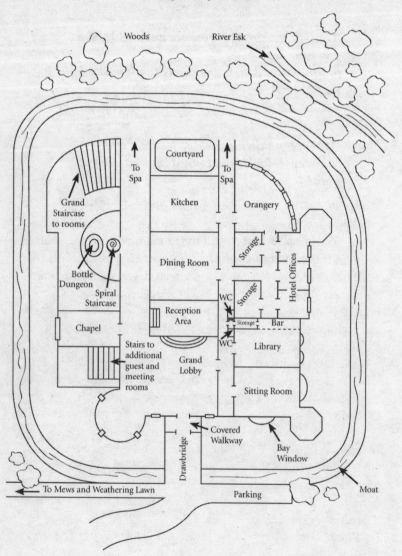

Woods

River Esk

Courtyard

To Spa

To Spa

Orangery

Grand Staircase to rooms

Kitchen

Storage

Storage

Hotel Offices

Bottle Dungeon

Spiral Staircase

Dining Room

WC

Storage

Chapel

Reception Area

Storage

Bar

Stairs to additional guest and meeting rooms

WC

Library

Grand Lobby

Sitting Room

Covered Walkway

Drawbridge

Bay Window

Moat

To Mews and Weathering Lawn

Parking

PART I: ENGLAND

i

'What do you think? Poisoned Pink, or Pink Menace?'

The young blonde woman of whom this question was asked adopted a pose of deep concentration, weighing the matter with all the deliberation of King Solomon presented with two feuding mothers. That the colors under discussion were nearly identical to the naked eye seemed to escape the notice of both women. The manicurist held the two small bottles aloft in the late winter sunlight streaming through the window of the trendy Knightsbridge beauty salon.

'The Poisoned Pink, I think, Suzie,' the blonde said at last. 'The other is so, like, totally last year. Positively no one in New York would be caught dead wearing it any more. Besides, Poisoned Pink sounds perfect for a crime writers' conference, don't you think?'

Suzie nodded, bending to her task and laying about with an emery board. *Give me an old-fashioned romance book any time*, she thought. *Barbara Cartland, now: There was a woman who knew which way was up with men and all. Lovely hair she had, too.*

'I'm getting an award from my publisher during this conference, you see. Did I tell you?'

Only three times.

1

Kimberlee Kalder, the blonde, paddled the fingers of one elegant, narrow hand in a bowl of soapy water as she lifted one elegant, narrow foot to examine the hand-woven gold brocade of her £900 ballet flats. 'And for that and, well, *other* reasons, I want to look, like, to die for.'

So there's another man at the end of all this effort, then, thought Suzie. *Thought so.*

'Not that I don't *always* strive to look, like, really hot,' Kimberlee went on. 'Image is, like, everything in this business, my agent says.'

'I'm certain he's right, Miss.'

'She, actually. At least, for the moment.'

Not really interested, Suzie asked politely, 'When's the conference, then?'

'This weekend. I head to Scotland tomorrow. My publisher is treating his most successful – well, in some cases, just his longest-lived – authors to a few days at Dalmorton Castle and Spa during Dead on Arrival.'

Seeing Suzie's look of mystification, Kimberlee said, 'That's a crime writers' conference held in Edinburgh every year. And, as I say, he'll be handing out a special award to his most successful writer: Me.'

'Me,' as Suzie well knew, was a favorite word in Kimberlee Kalder's vocabulary. That and 'I.' She was a big tipper, though – writing must pay bloody well.

'I always wanted to write a book,' said Suzie wistfully. 'Maybe I will one day when I have time. I'd write about me gran, during the war—'

Kimberlee just managed to stifle a snort of derision, although she didn't bother to hide the contempt that lifted her beautiful, chiseled mouth in a smirk. If she had a pound for everyone who was going to write a book when they could find the time – like they were going to pick up the dry cleaning or something when they got around to it. Really, people had no idea.

Cutting off the flow of wartime reminiscence, Kimberlee

said: 'No one cares about that old crap anymore. Don't forget – I want two solid coats of the topcoat. Last time my manicure only lasted two days. And watch what you're doing. You've missed a spot.'

'Must be all that typing you do,' Suzie said quietly. Kimberlee was her least favorite customer and there always came a point in their conversations when Suzie remembered why.

'What, me? Type?' said Kimberlee, as if to say, *I? Slaughter my own cattle?* 'I guess you've been looking at my publicity stills. "The Famous Writer at home, fingers poised over her laptop." But I have *people* who do all that. I mostly just dictate.'

Really? thought Suzie. *So what else was new?*

ii

News item from the *Edinburgh Herald*, by Quentin Swope:

Book lovers wait in thrilled anticipation of this week's Dead on Arrival conference, where fans and would-be authors gather to meet their favorite crime writers – in the flesh. Said writers will also be signing their books 'by the hundreds,' conference chair Rachel Twalley tells this reporter.

Among conference highlights is the anticipated appearance of hot young newcomer Kimberlee Kalder, who burst onto the crime-writing scene last year, quickly climbing the charts with her runaway 'chick-lit' hit, Dying for a Latte. *Kimberlee will be fêted before and during the conference by her Deadly Dagger Press publisher, Lord Julius Easterbrook, who must be thanking his lucky stars for leading him to Kimberlee. She may single-handedly have revived his moribund family publishing house.*

Other Dagger authors invited to push out the boat at Easterbrook's exclusive gathering at Dalmorton Castle include Magretta Sincock, Annabelle Pace, and Winston Chatley – the stars of yesteryear. Rumor has it top agents Jay Fforde and Ninette Thomson, and American publicist B. A. King, are also on the guest list, along with expat Joan Elksworthy, author of a detective series set in Scotland, and American spy-thriller novelist Tom Brackett. Also look out for newcomer Vyvyan Nankervis – a little bird tells me she's really Portia De'Ath, a Cambridge don, and the author of a delightful series of Cornish crime novels.

But it's our little Kimberlee who is stealing the other crime writers' thunder. Definitely, a publishing force to reckon with!

iii

Jay Fforde had come to the conclusion that the invention of e-mail signaled the imminent demise of mankind. Even though his agency website stated explicitly 'No E-mail Queries or Submissions,' every day his network server was nearly shut down by some berk trying to send him a 150,000-page manuscript by attachment. The ones that made it through went straight into his little electronic trash bin, unread. Even after fifteen years in the business, Jay was amazed at the number of people out there tapping away at manuscripts – each one, of course, a potential best-seller, according to its creator.

The phone rang. A carefully screened call had been allowed through the bottleneck by Jay's assistant. Jay picked up the instrument, first pausing to fling back a strand of the longish, sun-streaked fair hair that flopped in accepted head-boy style from a center part on his patrician skull. Many thought his wide-set eyes, high cheekbones, and sulky expression held a suggestion of Byronic decadence, a thought Jay liked to cultivate.

'Jay,' came a confidant, female voice. A trace of an American accent flattened what would once have been called BBC English, before regional accents became the new Received Pronunciation. Immediately Jay sat up a little straighter. The voice of a beautiful young woman who happened to be a wildly successful, selling-in-the-millions author was a potent combination for any agent.

'Kimberlee?' he said. Frightful name; it must come from her American side. Well, no one was perfect, although Kimberlee came close. 'What a delight to hear from you. How was the rest of the holiday?'

His assistant appeared in the doorway, carrying a sheaf of manuscript pages. Jay impatiently waved her away, miming for her to close the door behind her.

'. . . Bahamas are not what they were, but still – you should see my tan,' Kimberlee Kalder chirped on. 'I just heard you'll be at Dalmorton. How wonderful of Julius to include you. Of course, you rep what's-her-name, don't you?'

'Magretta Sincock? Yes. For a short while longer, at least.'

'Oh *really?*'

'Yes. Damned shame about her books and all, but tastes change, and poor Magretta will keep turning out the same old thing. I mean, seriously, how many women can there be out there married to some guy who – surprise! – turns out to have shoved his three previous wives overboard during their honeymoon cruise? Anyway, Easterbrook thought it would be a good opportunity to mix business with a little pleasure.'

'Good,' she said, lowering her silky voice to a purr. 'I do think it's time you and I had a serious discussion, too, don't you?'

Jay's heart took flight at the words. If he could land Kimberlee Kalder as a client, well . . . He'd be running the agency in a year. The Troy, Lewis, Bunter, and Hastings Agency would become the Fforde Agency at last. And he could ditch his other clients, beginning with Magretta. Who would need *them*?

Reluctantly, he tore his mind away from empire building. Kimberlee was saying something about train connections and reservations at the castle.

5

'You'll have to call today if you want to get near the castle spa,' she told him. 'They'll be booked solid from the moment this crowd of scribblers arrives.'

'I'll tell you what, Kimberlee. Why don't I book a massage for you while I'm at it? My little treat, courtesy of the agency. I insist. What's that you say?' He picked up a pen and jotted notes as she talked. 'All right. So that's a black mud envelopment treatment, an Aromapure Facial, a hydro pool session, and a sun shower treatment.' Feeling like a waiter, he asked, 'Will there be anything else?'

He rang off awhile later, Kimberlee having run out of special requests. Almost simultaneously, the door to the outer office swung open again.

'That was Kimberlee, wasn't it?' said Laurie. 'She wouldn't identify herself, but the bossy tone is unmistakable.'

'Yes. She's ready to dump Ninette and come over to the dark side.'

'I suspected as much. You can tell her from me you can catch more flies with honey—'

'Before I forget, call Dalmorton Castle, will you, and book her into the spa for these treatments.' He handed her the list. Laurie glanced at it and sniffed.

'She doesn't want much, does she?' Laurie tucked the list in her pocket and began tidying his desk, gathering files, tapping papers ruthlessly into line against the antique mahogany wood.

'If you move that you know I'll never find it again,' said Jay.

'That's what I'm here for, Jay. To find things for you.'

Jay smiled absently. Laurie always made him think of the redoubtable Miss Lemon, Hercule Poirot's fiercely competent secretary, foil to the well-meaning but dim Hastings. She placed a stack of papers before him.

'Magretta's late again with her rewrites. She's getting worse, I think.'

Jay was pulled back from a daydream of yachts, Caribbean

beaches, and ski chalets in Val Claret. He sat up, shoving the stack of papers to one side.

'Give her a few more weeks,' he said. 'It doesn't matter anymore, does it?'

iv

A few blocks to the west, Ninette Thomson was worried. Kimberlee Kalder, her megastar client, as she supposed they would say in Hollywood, was sending out all the well-known signs of a writer in flight to a new agent. Increasingly ludicrous demands – an espresso machine, for God's sake – temper tantrums, insistence on impossible terms from her British and American publishers for her next book, over-turning all the carefully negotiated – and extremely generous for an unknown author – terms of the contract Ninette had painstakingly organized for her. Demanding Ninette take the new book when it was ready to a larger publisher, despite a contract option that stipulated she could *not* do precisely that.

Honestly, thought Ninette. It was worse than dealing with the commitment-phobic, hormone-blinded male. You always could tell when they had one foot out the door, headed for another woman's bedroom, if you knew the signs. Which Ninette, fifty-four and the survivor of countless 'summer' romances, felt certain she did.

She stood, stretching the tension from her shoulders. She had to get home and pack for this castle fandango. Good of Easterbrook to include her, really, although she knew Kimberlee Kalder was the only reason. She, Ninette, certainly wouldn't have been invited for the sake of a Winston Chatley or a Portia De'Ath. She turned away from the large, modern desk that stood in front of the floor-to-ceiling window in her office. More and more, Ninette had started working from home – less temptation to frequent the wine bars that way – but she remained reluctant to give up the fantastic view and, more importantly, the prestigious address of her London office. Sometimes the only indicator of a good agent that a writer had to go by was the address. But the expense! The expense would have driven her down and out long ago if that wonderful manuscript of Kimberlee Kalder's hadn't shown up in her slush pile two years ago.

Wonderful, she reminded herself, meaning saleable, meaning marketable, meaning the only things that mattered in today's publishing climate. Every day Ninette turned down manuscripts that were wonderful – wonderfully written, insightful, sad, funny, groundbreaking, heartbreaking, whatever. And not one of them met the blockbuster, plot-driven standards that were becoming the byword of the industry: less character, more plot.

Fewer and fewer publishers were willing to take a chance on an unknown writer. But Ninette, after years in the business, could sense a best-selling winner, and had persuaded Easterbrook to take that chance on Kimberlee.

The last truly fine writer she'd taken on, knowing for certain she'd never make a fortune, but not caring, had been Portia De'Ath, who was now selling at a decent little clip. Winston Chatley once fell into the same category...

But it was Kimberlee, damn it all, who was paying the bills.

Now the silly, greedy little twit thought she could do better. Imagined a different agent, a different publisher, would bring in even more than the ridiculously large amount the first book had brought her already.

Kimberlee Kalder suddenly thought she didn't need her, Ninette Thomson.

Well, we'll just see about that now, won't we?

V

Winston Chatley was having tea with his mother in their narrow row house in a small, hidden mews in Chelsea. The fashionable part of Chelsea had grown up around them,

leaving them stranded like shipwrecked survivors clinging to a valuable piece of real estate they couldn't afford to
sell. Winston thought of them as on an island of desperation
surrounded by a sea of clamoring, mobile-phone-chatting
yuppies.

Where would we move? Winston would ask his mother
when the subject arose.

Somewhere smaller, in the country, Mrs Chatley would
reply, in her increasingly vague way.

*You need to be near the best treatment available, not stuck
in some backwash village,* Winston would say. *Besides, I like
the city.*

We'll manage, then.

They had had the identical conversation so often it
amounted to a comforting ritual. For his mother, Winston
suspected it was just that.

Winston worried he'd need home care for her eventually.
For him the best thing – maybe the only good thing – about
being a writer was that he was home most days. But she was
fast reaching the stage where she'd have burned the house
down if he didn't watch her constantly. What really needed to
happen was for Winston to sell the house, use the proceeds to
put her in a home, and use whatever was left over to buy that
remote country cottage.

The idea had never seriously settled on him and would have
horrified him if it had. This house was all she knew of home,
of warm familiarity. It would kill her to be moved.

And so they circled around the topic. But today, his mother
reverted to another familiar line of questioning.

'So, how is the new book coming?'

If there is one question a writer fears more than any other,
it is that, for the answer calls upon more skills of invention
and creativity than the actual writing of any book.

She beamed at him in anticipation of his answer. That
Winston was an ugly man, combining the worst features of

Abraham Lincoln and Boris Karloff into a homely yet surprisingly engaging whole, she had never really noticed. She loved Winston with all the devotion and sublime lack of awareness of a golden retriever nursing an orphaned bloodhound pup. She herself was beautiful and never seemed to see the craggy, bumpy planes of Winston's face. It didn't matter: He was hers.

'It's fine,' he said at last. 'The first fifty pages are really quite good, I think.' He neglected to mention he had been stuck at page fifty-one for perhaps the last three months, and was growing more certain those pages would soon join the ever-growing pile of fifty-page beginnings in his bottom desk drawer.

'Do you think Ninette Thomson is really doing the best job for you?' Mrs Chatley asked, with one of the stunning reversions to her old self that kept him alive in hope for her condition. 'I keep reading in those publishing magazines of yours about this Jay person.'

'Jay Fforde?' Winston asked. Did she seriously think that was an option? Jay was far out of Winston's league, a star agent dwelling amongst the Lotus Eaters of Hollywood and Pinewood. Winston had a realistic enough assessment of his gifts to recognize that they didn't translate well to the cinematic.

'I couldn't leave Ninette, mother. After all these years, it wouldn't be right,' he said. 'More tea?'

vi

Joan Elksworthy said, 'I'm surprised you didn't just stay in Edinburgh with the conference so near, Rachel.'

The two friends were splashing out on afternoon tea at Fortnum & Mason's – a rare, guilty indulgence. They had seen each other seldom in the decades since they'd been girls at school together. Rachel had married a Church of Scotland minister, Joan an American who had carried her off to Washington,

D.C. When she left the brief marriage, she retained the name and remained in the United States – moving to Santa Fe to write her crime stories. The only sign she was sometimes homesick was that she chose to set all her books in the west of Scotland.

'Didn't I say? I had to fly up to London to stay with my daughter's infants. She's got legs, you know,' said Rachel.

Joan interpreted this correctly to mean Rachel's daughter was again having trouble with her legs. Varicose veins, most likely, from the three stone of extra weight she carried around since the twins arrived, but Joan would have stabbed herself with one of the tearoom's lovely pudding forks before saying so.

'I see. You *had* to come down, did you?' she said.

Rachel Twalley smiled. 'Can I help it if they're the world's most beautiful – not to mention gifted and intelligent – grandchildren?' A waiter approached to verify they had enough hot water in the pot, then glided soundlessly away. Rachel looked around her at the white tablecloths and glittering glassware, sank further back in her plush chair, and sighed. This, indeed, was the life.

'I'll be taking the train Thursday to Edinburgh,' Joan said. 'Should we arrange to travel together then?'

Rachel shook her head.

'Can't. I have to head back straightaway – even though most of the work for the conference is done. I'll never volunteer for this sort of thing again, I can tell you that. What with the program, registration, sponsorships, coordinating everything with the hotel – getting volunteers for all that is well nigh impossible these days. Then there's all the usual internecine squabbling. I should have known: The village fête last time took years off my life.'

'I wish you were staying with us at Dalmorton Castle,' said Joan. 'We could've treated ourselves to the mud cure, you and I.'

'I wish, too. I've always wanted to wallow in mud – in a

11

manner of speaking. But I have to be on the ground at the Luxor, rallying the troops, who only lurch into action when someone is keeping an eye on them. I must say, it was jolly nice of your publisher to arrange all this for you. I've heard Dalmorton is *such* a lovely place.'

'It's all in lieu of bigger advances, you watch. I can't imagine why I'm included, to tell you the truth. Kimberlee Kalder is all that's on Lord Easterbrook's mind these days.'

'Humph,' said Rachel. 'I don't care if I never hear the name again.'

Joan smiled. 'The cozy mystery is dead, haven't you heard?' She waved an imaginary (pink) flag. 'Long live Chick Lit.'

'I tried to read that thing of hers,' Rachel said, adding hastily, 'I didn't buy it, never fear, I got it from the library. It was just absurd. Pink, and silly. "Will he call, or won't he?" Romance via mobile and e-mail.' She sniffed. 'Not the way things were in *my* day. And what is it with the shoes, anyway? If I'd spent that kind of money on shoes my Harry'd have shown me the door *tout de suite* and no mistake, minister's wife or no. As for plot – the whole thing seemed more an excuse to skewer people she didn't like. Which seemed to be everyone.'

'But you read the whole thing,' said Joan. It was a gentle question. Why shouldn't Rachel have read the whole thing? She'd have been nearly alone among the women – and many of the men – of the English-speaking nations had she not.

Rachel, crinkling her face apologetically, admitted, 'They are sort of like chocolates, those books. Actually, more like swallowing a box of licorice all-sorts. But I do try to move with the times. I don't exactly *approve*, mind.'

'Well, if there's one thing these books do prove,' said Joan, 'it's that men haven't improved one bit since we were girls.'

Rachel nodded somberly. 'Have you met Kimberlee Kalder?'

'Once.'

'Really? And what's she like?'

Joan hesitated, toying with her butter knife. It went against her grain to disparage a fellow author. In the latest incident, Joan's American publisher had approached Kimberlee about writing a blurb for the back cover of Joan's latest book – since Joan had been instrumental in bringing Kimberlee to the attention of the Americans. But Kimberlee had flat-out refused. As the publisher reported later, Kimberlee's exact words were, 'There's nothing in it for me, so why in hell should I?'

'What is Kimberlee Kalder like, you ask?' Joan looked straight at Rachel. 'Pure poison.'

vii

Lord Easterbrook sat at his desk, staring at a spreadsheet on his monitor, scrolling back and forth with his computer mouse to read the numbers in the outer columns. He accidentally struck the wrong key and the whole thing disappeared. He let out a bellow that set the eighteenth-century glass rattling in the windowpanes.

His youthful assistant, well-used to these technical emergencies, came rushing in – a pretty girl in her mid-twenties, dressed in black and white. A no-nonsense type whose crisp demeanor nicely kept Easterbrook's querulousness at bay. She'd become adept at coping whenever he threw his toys out of the pram. Now she deftly tapped at Easterbrook's keyboard until the vanished document reappeared.

'Haven't I told you then?' she said. 'Stay away from that delete key and you'll be fine.'

'I was never near the blasted delete key. Print the infernal thing out for me, will you? On good old-fashioned paper. Oh, and tell my wife I'll be late.'

'Yes, sir.' And the young woman went to do as she was told. Her great-gran was the same way: She'd never quite resigned herself to any invention introduced since the telephone, and even that she thought was full of 'rays,' whatever that meant.

13

Left alone five minutes later, Lord Easterbrook perused the rescued document, now safely consigned to paper. On the mend, he thought, on the mend. His was a tiny press, its prestige and respectability owing more to longevity than anything like profitability. Who, after all, would expect to turn anything like a real profit on a house specializing in crime novels?

Rumor had long had it in the City that Easterbrook simply kept Deadly Dagger Press on as a rich man's hobby. Like those fools knew anything, he thought. But then, Kimberlee Kalder had come along, rising from the submission pile like – well, like Venus rising from the sea. That his assistant, not he, had recognized the potential at once was something he often conveniently forgot. Thanks to Kimberlee, silly name and all, Dagger was, to continue the metaphor, afloat.

Not that Easterbrook had ever actually *read* Kimberlee's book. The balance sheets were the only required reading on his night table.

But what the deuce was taking the girl so long with the next manuscript? he wondered now. It's not as if she were writing *Pride and Prejudice*, for God's sake. The last time they'd spoken on the phone she'd been decidedly cagey about that. 'Wasn't quite ready,' she'd said. 'A bit more of a rewrite on the end, I think,' she'd said.

It was balderdash, of course. She was out shopping for a new agent, and a new publisher, if the rumors from the publishing trenches were true. Which was why he'd had the sudden inspiration for this pre-conference gathering, and the little award to keep her happy. A chance to talk with her in person.

The personal touch, yes, that's what was needed.

He looked at the figures, mostly black now instead of red.

Leave Dagger, would she, and break her contract? Well, we'd just see about that.

If the personal touch didn't work, there were always other means.

viii

In a beautiful flat high above the Thames, Magretta Sincock stared at the screen of her own computer with none of the complacency of Lord Easterbrook, just across the water in his counting house. She reread the e-mail several times, blinking in disbelief. Perhaps it was spam, a cruel hoax? But the return e-mail address indicated clearly enough it was from Ludwig's, her American publisher. And the body of the e-mail said clearly enough that, regrettably, they would not be picking up the American rights to her next manuscript. But they wished her well in her future endeavors.

Well, that at least was something, after thirty bloody years, thought Magretta. That well wishing certainly made all the difference.

They were dropping her by e-mail. Not in person, saving someone the airfare to London. Not even with the minor expense of letterhead and airmail postage. They were dropping her. *Her.*

After a very long while, Magretta got up from her desk and walked to the French doors of her aerie. Barely feeling the blast of cold, she stood looking down at the brown river, churning up a whitish foam as it eternally snaked its way through London. Anyone looking up from the ships below would have thought they were seeing a large tropical bird perched on the balcony, bedecked in an array of green plumage. Magretta's large red crest of hair would have added to the illusion.

The conference in Edinburgh, to which she had so been looking forward, she now viewed with dread. They would all know, all her fellow scribes, everyone connected with this wretched industry. Probably knew before she herself was sent that miserable e-mail, bad news traveling faster in the publishing world than in any other. She'd have to call her agent.

But he should have called me. *Jay must have known this was coming. This was all his fault. If he'd kept his mind on his job* . . .

Still, she had to go show the flag, since Lord Easterbrook had invited her. She at least could still count on her British publisher.

Couldn't she?

ix

St Germaine's had been in existence so long it was the one restaurant everyone in Cambridge, rich and poor alike, had heard of. The ruder the *maître d'*, the wider grew its fame, and the more wealthy patrons schemed and plotted to secure a reservation.

There were exceptions to the reservation rules, but only the owner, Mr Garoute, knew what they were. Solving the murder by poisoning of the restaurant's *sous-chef* and thus saving St Germaine's from certain financial ruin was clearly top of his list. Mr G. always, therefore, held a table open for DCI Arthur St Just, knowing the unpredictable schedule of the Inspector, and he always greeted him with rapturous cries of joy – cries that would have astounded his business competitors, who only saw Mr G.'s flintier side.

It so happened today was St Just's birthday, a fact he himself had nearly forgotten until his sister's birthday card arrived that morning, and which fact he found somewhat depressing once he'd been reminded. Dinner at St Germaine's was his effort to shake off the pall of being forty-three – a boring age with neither a here nor a there to it, he thought.

To make matters rather worse and himself grumpier, his new Chief Constable, Brougham – her motto was, predictably, 'A New Brougham Sweeps Clean,' and she was given to using terms like 'Crime Management,' which set St Just's teeth on edge – had conscripted him into giving a presentation in

Edinburgh as part of her 'Reach Out!' public relations campaign. He was to speak at a crime writers' conference, for God's sake, on the subject of police procedure. Rooms at the conference hotel already being sold out, his sergeant had booked him a room at Dalmorton Castle for the weekend. St Just grinned, wondering how the Chief was going to like it if she saw *that* bill.

Once St Just had been settled behind a hastily assembled fortress of gleaming glassware, cutlery, table linens, and menus the size of Moses' tablets, he took a moment to survey his surroundings, peering about in the dark, candlelit room like a mole adjusting to daylight. As he was just emerging from his last case, which had lasted many hectic weeks, that was close to describing how he felt.

Mr G. always took into account St Just's preference for an unobtrusive table away from the action, where he could sit and indulge his penchant for people-watching.

To his right: An animated young couple, perhaps celebrating some sentimental anniversary of a first meeting, the young man resplendent in what may have been his first suit, she beautiful in the way all twenty-somethings in love are beautiful, irradiated by the glow of first infatuation and a little too much make-up.

To his left an older couple, perhaps in their late thirties, provided a contrast, a living tableau of aggrievedness, warning of the dangers that might lie ahead for the young lovers. The older pair sat in a sulking silence, their meal eaten mechanically, with little evidence of pleasure. Their thoughts might have been on absent lovers or the terms of their imminent divorce. Or even, thought the detective, on murder.

At a far table in the opposite corner from his a woman sat, her head bent over a sheaf of papers as she waited for her companion. She made the occasional note in the margin of a page using a Montblanc fountain pen – St Just could just make out the white six-pointed star on the cap. But by the time St Just had finished his first course, she was still alone and he was growing alarmed. It was no way to treat a lady, for a lady she clearly was, and St Just's sense of outrage at this cad-like behavior on the part of her missing companion almost could not be contained. St Just generally disliked dining alone in public and rarely did so, which was why he was glad to have Mr G.'s discreet little table at his disposal. Unthinkable then, for this woman to be treated so shabbily by a husband or companion.

Still, the woman herself did not seem perturbed by this social disgrace, calmly setting aside her papers as her meal arrived, and only reverting to them again once her coffee had been brought. Most people, women especially, he felt, would have hidden behind a book the whole time, lacking the *savoir faire* to dine alone. He found her self-possession fascinating, and he began committing her details to memory for later rendering on his sketch pad. She was not a classic beauty, he decided. Still, it was hard not to stare at her. Maybe this was where all those years of surveillance training paid off, he thought wryly. But she did seem oblivious. Probably, she was used to being stared at.

She looked the type of woman who had found her style years ago and kept it: long dark hair pulled back, with escaping tendrils feathering an oval face, darker brows framing somewhat hooded eyes, an apparent absence of make-up aside from deep red lipstick against translucent, marmoreal skin. He was to learn that she always wore long earrings that accentuated her long white neck; this evening the earrings were silver and spun like wind chimes whenever she moved.

Her companion never arrived and she seemed in no hurry to leave. St Just, wanting to extend the time he had to observe her (as he thought, unobtrusively), ordered a second coffee that would keep him awake into the wee hours, trying to recapture in his sketchbook the angles and planes of this lovely creature's profile.

He would have been chagrined to know that while Portia De'Ath noted with amusement the tall, barrel-chested man staring at her with wounded eyes, she herself slept that night like a baby.

PART II: UNITED STATES

i

'What is it now, Annabelle?'

B. A. King, publicist and former literary agent, studied his new manicure, while reflecting on the problems of having a former lover as a client, especially a lover/client like Annabelle Pace. The chief problem was that there was never a decent out, not that decency was a quality B. A. prized too highly.

'Don't use that tone with me,' came a voice over the phone at a volume calibrated to shatter B. A.'s whiskey glass. 'You've got me signing books in some godforsaken town no one ever heard of in a store no one can find. I drive around for two hours and when I *finally* get there, ten people show up and half of them thought they were there for Patricia Fucking Cornwell. The other shoppers skittered around me like I was harboring the Ebola virus. You call this a promotional tour?'

B. A. sighed heavily. *How many times?* 'It's not the readers here in New York you need to cultivate,' he said patiently – for him. 'It's the people in the heartland who never heard of you. Name recognition comes by increments. There is no such thing as overnight fame.'

'Tell that to Monica Lewinsky. I want you to cancel the

20

rest of this tour. Whether you cancel it or not, I'm not show-ing up.'

'That will certainly add to the fund of goodwill you've been building up with the independent bookshops. Listen, Annabelle. You've only got two more days and then you have to get on a plane to Scotland anyway. If you think they haven't heard of you in Iowa, just imagine the reception you'll get in Scotland. But that's exactly the point of getting yourself out there. So you will become better known by the people who've never heard of you yet. Do you follow me?'

Somewhat mollified, or rather, somewhat deeper into the wine bottle she'd ordered from room service, Annabelle said, a wheedling note in her voice: 'You will be there, won't you? You did promise.'

'Of course, darling Annabelle. Your invitation to Easterbrook's little fling is something I'll be busy exploit-ing to the fullest. It's quite an honor he included you, you know. You're the only American on the list. Well, apart from Tom Brackett and his wife. And, I suppose, Joan Elksworthy – she lives here now, even though she's from Scotland or somewhere.'

'Well, that's four of us, even if you don't count Kimberlee Kalder,' said Annabelle. 'She's half American, I've heard. In fact, I've been hearing too much about her lately. She must have one hell of a publicist.'

'Not at all, Annabelle. Some books sell by word of mouth.'

He felt somehow it would be wisest not to mention that his main – his only – interest in being in Scotland was the opportunity it afforded him to talk with Kimberlee and see if he couldn't woo her into his stable. Not that Annabelle wasn't perfectly aware of that. Yet another of the pitfalls of having a former lover as a client: She simply knew him too well.

'What exactly is that supposed to mean? *My* books sell by word of mouth.'

He supposed she had a point: For grisly autopsy scenes it

was hard to beat Annabelle and her 'plucky, zany, forensic-scientist sleuth,' as Lord Easterbrook's marketing department would have it. And maybe the mistakes Annabelle rather famously made in writing about police and medical procedure caused the pros to snap up her latest for a good laugh.

'What's that you say? We're losing the signal.' A near impossibility, since he was on a land line, but hopefully she wouldn't recall that.

'See you on Thursday, then,' he shouted into the phone. 'Bye!'

He hung up hastily, just in time to miss the next salvo.

It was time to get rid of Annabelle, he decided. One way or the other.

ii

Further down the coast, in Washington, D.C., warmed by a fire of piñon wood imported from the Southwest, Tom and Edith Brackett were discussing the upcoming conference over a scotch and soda (him) and an herbal tea (her).

'I have a bad feeling about this,' said Edith. 'Do we have to go?'

Tom looked at his wife, annoyed. He had to keep reminding himself to try to be nicer to her, a resolution forgotten almost as soon as it was made. But, really – no matter how often they traveled, the little ninny always had an attack of nerves just before a trip. If anything, she was getting worse. And . . . couldn't the woman do something about that hair? Was it really necessary to try to make some kind of virtue of turning gray? When he thought of the pretty woman he had married twenty years ago, he couldn't believe the dried-up wreck she had become. It never occurred to him that marriage to him for twenty years might have had something to do with it.

'How, bad feeling?' he asked, with exaggerated tolerance.

He began repeatedly smoothing his mustache, a sure sign of his irritation, but Edith forged ahead.

'Not about the conference. About the castle. Look at this.'

She thrust a travel magazine across at him, indicating an article illustrated with color photos; the headline read, 'The Haunting of Dalmorton.' The castle, filmed at night, battlements illuminated, rose like a dragon out of a fog-shrouded, medieval moat.

Tom scanned the first few paragraphs, then burst out in coarse laughter.

'You're talking about the ghost? The "Woman in White" seen walking the halls? For God's sake, Edith. It's a bunch of crap they make up to give gullible tourists like yourself a cheap thrill.'

'But I—'

'I'll tell you this for free. If I'm going to start believing in ghosts I'm not going to start with a hoary old cliché like that. "Woman in White" indeed.'

He knocked back the dregs of his drink and held out the empty glass to his wife.

Edith took the glass from him – it would not have occurred to her to suggest he get his own refill. She was miffed, however; long experience of their marriage told him that. She withdrew, but with an expression that told Tom the retreat was only temporary. She handed him his fresh drink, then sat waiting in what would have looked to an outsider a companionable silence, her eyes tracing the familiar pattern in the Aubusson carpet at their feet. Then it came:

'I don't mean the ghost will come and . . . cast a spell or something. Try to frighten us. But – just look at this place. The photos give me the creeps. It has a *bottle* dungeon, for God's sake. Think of all the poor people who suffered and died there.'

'Think of all the publicity I won't get if I don't show my face. It's an honor to be invited, Edith. Hard as it is to believe, the old tightwad is voluntarily loosening the purse strings at last. I have to go. If you really want to stay here—'

'No,' she said, in a still, small voice tinged with panic. She had a morbid fear of abandonment that Tom exploited to the full. Some idiot story about being left behind by her family – he couldn't be bothered to recall the details.

Edith brought out the worst in him, he thought irritably. He would no more leave her behind than he would fly to the moon. She served as his personal valet, and after twenty years of having her at his beck and call he could hardly dress himself.

'We've not been apart in twenty years,' said Edith, 'I'm just saying – be careful. Be careful, that's all, Tom. It's just a feeling I have . . .'

Tom smiled, a smile that generally remained hidden behind an expression of intense self-satisfaction. His was otherwise an unremarkable face that a shaved head and Van Dyke beard did nothing to render memorable. His years in the spy trade may have taught him too well the value of blending in.

'Don't be stupid. No ghost has ever gotten the better of me yet. Editors, yes. And agents. B. A. King, that fatuous jerk, is going to be there. And that nitwit who wrote the chick lit mystery that sold by the truckload.'

'*Dying for a Latte*? I know. I read it.'

'*Edith*. You didn't.'

'I often read your competition,' she said defensively, always alert to warning signs of a quarrel. Tom with a wounded ego was not a man to be crossed. 'I have to keep up on trends, you know.'

'That is going above and beyond the call. I hope you held a book burning afterward. Anyway, what did you think?' he asked.

'About the book? Like the reviews said: It's a bright, frothy *roman à clef* with dark undertones. It's set in a major magazine publishing house and it's transparent which house it's meant to be. The main character comes across as a nitwit, all right, but I wonder if that's also true of the author. Certainly she did a fine job of filleting the fashion magazine industry.'

'All in all, I'd say, forget the ghost,' said Tom. 'There's a *real* woman to be scared of.'

PART III: SCOTLAND

CHAPTER 1

Book People

Donna Doone was at work on her novel, happily oblivious to the futility of writing a detective story set in prehistoric times.

She was at her desk in her little private office at Dalmorton Castle, staring at a computer screen that stared back, somehow accusingly, with the manuscript on which she had secretly been working for two years, stealing a few minutes from her employer wherever she could.

She had chosen to set her romantic-suspense crime novel in the Paleolithic era, something she was sure had never been attempted before. She was only just now beginning to appreciate why. But, she reminded herself, there were best-selling books with cat sleuths, pie-baking sleuths, psychic sleuths – pie-baking, psychic, quilting, archaeologist cat sleuths, for all she knew. Why not a crime novel featuring a Neanderthal detective, the first amateur detective in history? Or prehistory, as it were. It did away with the need for anything like a working knowledge of legal or police procedure. It also largely eliminated the need for scenes where teams of crime scene technicians swooped in with fingerprint kits and swabs and whatnot. Somehow, Donna didn't feel modern-day forensics were her strong suit.

She was certain, however, that she was striking just the right note with her dialogue, which she muttered aloud, reading from her screen:

> '*Why you think Batmo kill him, Ugmay?*' asked Desirooma, deep brown eyes beneath her low, overhanging brow crinkled with concern, but filled also with that sullen, come-hither look that always made Ugmay's blood pulse with desire. He dropped his club to kiss her, hardly but gently.
>
> '*Me no know, but find out. Look, see scratches on Black Rock? He no fall, he push. Only bad man like Batmo do this. Me find. Me kill.*'
>
> He kissed her again, pregnant with animal longing.
>
> '*Ugmay, you no fight Bad Batmo alone,*' she flushed, some time later, readjusting the bison pelt around her broad, work-coarsened shoulders. '*Here, eat nuts and berries I gather for you today as Sun Goddess light fire in sky.*'
>
> '*You good number-five wife, Desirooma,*' said Ugmay.

Donna plunged bravely on, sending Ugmay and Desirooma off to report the suspicious death of Gonzola to their tribal chief. She was interrupted by a hesitant tapping on her door. Quickly, she hit the 'save' and 'close' commands on her computer, bringing up in place of *Caveman Death* a spreadsheet of hotel reservation statistics. Only then did she call out, 'Come in.'

A small red head appeared around the opening of the door.

'They're starting to arrive. The book people.'

'Be there in a minute, Florie. Be sure to alert reception.'

Florie nodded, thinking as she shut the door that Donna had overdone the perm again. Her head was a perfect round ball of tight curls, as if she'd pinned one of the loofahs from the spa to her head.

Taking care to first turn off the computer, Donna walked down the hallway connecting the set of offices that constituted the administrative area for the spa and hotel. At reception, a young clerk stood chatting with one of the many bridal consultants who organized the weddings that took place in the castle's old chapel nearly every day. This weekend, nuptials had been put on hold because of the group from the writers' conference, but on Tuesday there would be another giddy bride and groom. The castle increasingly was becoming a romantic destination spot, with Scottish law, unlike English, still favoring hassle-free weddings. Donna had heard one American refer to Scotland as the Las Vegas of Europe, and she supposed they weren't far wrong. In any event, it meant a thriving cottage industry for the castle, and steady employment for Donna.

'Just until I sell my manuscript,' she reminded herself.

From reception she walked up the stairs leading to the grand entrance hall, and from there into the sitting room to check on the preparations for afternoon tea. She heard from outside the crunch of tires on gravel. The velvet-covered window seat offered a view below of the front entrance to the castle. Donna settled herself comfortably to observe the various guests arriving by taxi or limousine.

An inveterate crime-novel reader, Donna found she could recognize nearly all the authors, even Magretta Sincock, whose publicity photo on the back flap of her books hadn't changed in thirty years. Seeing Magretta in person for the first time, Donna felt a pang of sympathy: Magretta must have added three stone since that early photo, and seemed generally to be having trouble climbing out of the taxi. She wore lipstick of a virulent orange, recklessly applied, and

28

looked very much old and diminished, despite the cinemato-
graphic splendor of her outfit – a flowing affair of puce green
silk. Why, wondered Donna, did women with red hair always
think any old shade of green flattered them?

Magretta began capering her way over the drawbridge, but
halted at the sight of another arrival – a stork-like, dour man
who Donna thought bore a striking resemblance to photos she'd
seen of Abe Lincoln. As the man drew closer, she saw this was
Winston Chatley, his undertaker's countenance easily recognizable. He wrote those dark, serial-killer thrillers. Not really
Donna's cup of tea.

Winston's arrival was immediately followed by that of a
woman in a taxi whom Donna knew to be Joan Elksworthy,
who wrote those lovely cozy mysteries set in Scotland. Donna
began a mental head count: Still missing, among others, was
Annabelle Pace, who wrote novels about a female medical
examiner that, to Donna's taste, were just a touch too grue-
some. There were things, after all, that were just not quite
nice to think about.

Behind Joan Elksworthy, in a limousine, came what might
have been the male complement to Magretta, the sartorial
salt to her pepper, a man dressed somewhat in the style
of a carnival barker. Altogether not a nice type, thought
Donna, and undoubtedly the worst sort of American:
loud.

Another limo crunched up the drive, this one stopping
to dislodge another sort altogether, one of those upper-
crust stalwarts of the British Empire she thought had died
out with the Boer War. This, she felt, must be Lord Easterbrook.

Next, another posh man she didn't recognize, very young
and handsome and golden in a Great Gatsby way, sleekly
upholstered and spit-polished.

Yet another limo, this one causing a bit of a jam at the
foot of the castle moat. The ensuing hubbub heralded the

arrival of what was unmistakably Kimberlee Kalder, whose lovely image had illustrated countless displays in every major bookstore for the past year. It didn't seem possible, thought Donna, but Kimberlee was even prettier in person, her skin with the kind of natural glow that could never be achieved by mere spa visits. She wore a black suit with a pink shirt and matching pink high heels, colors she had made her own and seemingly forced upon half the female population of British twenty-somethings. She walked with a model's runway slide, her body tipped slightly backwards as if she were walking downhill, her hands hanging straight at her sides. Her driver brought up the rear, carrying her bags.

Donna Doone sniffed, her lips folded tightly together. A right proper little madam and no mistake, this Kimberlee. Judging by her limo driver's face, he would be glad to see the back of her, too.

Why were writers so often *difficult*? So . . . ambitious . . . bound to cause upset. . .

She recognized the next woman to arrive, too. This, emerging gracefully from a taxi, was Portia De'Ath, who had won all those awards for her first book. Set in Cornwall, it was – lovely. Lovely-looking woman, this Portia was, too, with her sleek dark hair tied back by a scarf. Tiny thing, she was. Rather, a tall thing with a tiny waist and slender hips. Gym or genetics? Perhaps a bit of both. Donna glanced down at her own padded hips and sighed.

As Donna watched, Portia shot Kimberlee a look that was none too different from that of the limo driver. Apparently Portia had also made the acquaintance of the Pink Princess of Publishing.

Let's see . . . Donna counted on her fingers. That agent, Ninette Thomson, and that spy writer Brackett and his wife were still to arrive, and – Who was this?

A tall, well-built, dark-haired man was emerging from

a taxi. He took one look at Portia and stopped dead in his tracks, a look of stunned amazement on his face.

Now *that* would bear watching. Donna felt she hadn't spent years helping stage weddings without becoming sensitive to love in bloom.

This big fellow was coming down with a very bad case, indeed.

CHAPTER 2

Alive on Arrival

Portia De'Ath believed in premonition, if that was the right word for the free-floating anxiety that heralds something about to spin horribly out of control. The problem was, of course, the feeling was always too vague to be acted upon in any preventative way. Only in twenty-twenty hindsight did it seem that precisely this or that disaster had been foreseen.

The entire trip up from Cambridge had been like that: Nothing felt *quite* right. For a bad start, she and Gerald had quarreled as he drove her to the station – a minor squabble, soon forgotten, but an increasingly frequent occurrence. Of lesser moment, but adding to her discomfort, she'd worn all the wrong clothes for the March weather, which, to spite the forecasters, had turned as balmy as spring. The glassy blue sky held just a smudge of gray cloud, like a small scattered army. Since the rail network apparently followed the same BBC forecast as Portia, her train compartment was overheated, and the window stuck shut. She'd also forgotten to pack the new P. D. James she'd planned to read over this weekend, which left her somewhat at the mercy of her serendipitous travel companion, Kimberlee Kalder.

Kimberlee, of course, looked like an illustration for a magazine article on travel tips for the trendy, her sleeveless pink top perfectly suited to the climate. She wore gravity-defying high heels; diamond studs too big to be real flashed from the lobes of her ears, and evidence of rude good health

DEATH AND THE LIT CHICK

shone from her luminous face. Despite a somewhat pointed jaw that leant a sly, ferrety cast to her features, Kimberlee was a showstopper.

She had appeared in the carriage just as the train pulled out, pulling a checkerboard-pattern Louis Vuitton bag like a dog on a leash, and carrying a matching computer bag slung over her shoulder. Greeting Portia with a girlish shriek of recognition, she'd deposited herself on the seat opposite, then stretched out her legs like a bored leopard, also taking over the place beside her. She pointedly ignored other passengers as they peered into the compartment from the corridor, looking for a spare seat.

'You're going to this soirée at Dalmorton, of course,' Kimberlee said, talking into a compact mirror as she checked her flawless make-up. She had pale blue eyes and straight, white-blonde hair that positively shouted 'plundering Viking ancestors.' She now gave a vigorous toss of her head in a gesture that Portia came to realize was habitual, and probably designed to show her natural highlights to advantage. As Portia ruminated on the genetic heritage that blessed or doomed us all, Kimberlee continued:

'I saw your name in the conference program. I can't *tell* you how, like, surprised I was to learn the true identity of the author of the Vyvyan Nankervis novels was none other than Portia De'Ath. The very same writer with whom I happen to share an agent *and* a publisher. Why ever did you keep it such a secret?'

Portia shrugged. 'Self-preservation? I'm at Cambridge as part of a fellowship program. Not quite a "don", as the *Herald* would have it. Trust me, the real dons would want to know why I'm spending time writing crime novels when I'm supposed to be writing a thesis that's the last word on recidivism.'

Kimberlee creased her lovely, vacant face with an effort at understanding. Her blue eyes blanked on 'recidivism,' but after some apparent internal struggle she decided not to ask.

'Oh, surely not,' she said instead. 'Would it, like, have mattered – like, seriously – if they'd known?'

Like, how to explain, thought Portia. The 'they' of their conversation being eccentric Cambridge academics, there was no telling. All Portia knew was that life for a female visiting fellow at St Michael's was tough enough without sticking pins in the eyes of her mostly male comrades. Comrades who would be deciding her academic future very soon.

'Oh, right, I suppose I do see what you mean,' Kimberlee went on. 'It's the same old story: Crime writers just aren't taken seriously, for they all hand out laurels to Ruth Rendell. You'd think we were drug dealers. Still, crime writing pays, for some of us; those ivory-tower types are just jealous, living in hovels, most of them. I wouldn't give it another, like, thought.'

Portia gazed levelly across at her companion, delighted by the mixed metaphor and wondering if she herself were seriously included in that 'for some of us' remark.

She was already regretting her promise to moderate a panel at the Dead on Arrival conference, not least of all because, as Kimberlee had said, the conference sponsors had chosen to 'out' her without her permission. Clearly they were blissfully unaware of the pains to which she'd gone to keep her secret vice a secret. And yet: She had felt that a long weekend in Scotland might be a rejuvenating reward for the soul, a plunge into cold water after the steaming sauna of academic life.

She had been at St Mike's two years, a fleeting nanosecond in the glacially slow-moving world of academic research. But a fair amount of her time was taken up not with the penal system but with a dark-haired fictional detective of the Devon and Cornwall Constabulary named DCI Nankervis. What had begun as a lark had become nearly a full-time job, requiring more and more hours devoted to correspondence with agents and editors, in addition to the writing itself, of course.

Generally, she avoided book promotion like the plague it was, but this offer from Lord Easterbrook had sounded too good to pass up – all expenses paid for three nights at the fifteenth-century Dalmorton Castle while she and her fellow authors appeared on panels at the nearby conference in Edinburgh.

Kimberlee, apparently quickly bored by any problem not her own, indicated they had reached the limit of her interest by immersing herself in *Vogue*. After awhile she dozed off, the magazine landing with a resounding 'thunk' on the carriage floor.

By now they were leaving the Satanic mills of the industrial revolution behind, heading into lush terrain as the train neared Scotland. Huddled piles of sheep sped past the window, white dots against a green-gray landscape. Portia anticipated the moment when the sea would open up on her right, offering an endless horizon dappled with fading sunlight. She recalled that Rosslyn Chapel, that supposed site of Masonic mysteries, was not far from Edinburgh, and didn't wonder at the myths that clung to the area.

Eventually the train chugged and screeched its way into Edinburgh's Waverley Station, waking her companion. Portia helped Kimberlee muscle her luggage onto the platform, but when she turned to offer to share a ride, Kimberlee was nowhere to be seen. Minutes later, on reaching the taxi ranks, Portia was dumbfounded to see her – or at least, the back of her white-blonde head – speeding off in a limo. Suddenly the rumors Portia had heard of Kimberlee Kalder, Overnight Sensation, began ringing true.

Bemused and more than a bit annoyed – so much for the sisterhood of writers – Portia hailed a small taxi brightly decorated with an advertisement for jeans, a taxi imaginatively and exuberantly driven by a large, gray-haired man with an apparent death wish. He sped away from Edinburgh and hurtled like a bullet toward the outskirts, passing increasingly small and picturesque villages on the way. They looped under a bridge and zipped past the mildly curious gaze of a large herd of cows.

The driver accelerated on a final curve, and Dalmorton Castle came suddenly into view, perched dramatically on a small rocky mound and surrounded by a moat. She'd been prepared for this by photos from the castle's website, but not for the sudden reality. They had slipped the bonds of the modern world. The castle stood as it had for centuries – gray and austere, its dark drum tower and arrow-slit turrets starkly outlined against a blue-moonstone sky.

The castle was effectively sitting on its own little island, Portia realized. What had she been reading recently – something about how one lost touch with the world on an island, for an island was a world of its own. Then she remembered: The words were from *And Then There Were None*. And Christie had called the world one 'from which you might never return.'

'Cor,' said the driver.

'Yes,' agreed Portia.

They arrived at the drawbridge that spanned the moat – *a moat, for heaven's sake* – before which other conveyances were depositing little knots of people. Another little knot had gathered just inside the castle entrance.

Magretta Sincock stood about fretfully, no doubt waiting to be recognized. Portia, who knew her slightly from previous conferences, cast around her mind for words to sum up Magretta's style. She seemed overall to be aiming for an earth-mother-slash-brothel-madam look, with armorlike bracelets and brooches that suggested something unearthed at a Celtic dig. Her bouffant hair was a frizzy halo of geranium red, which she seemed to think showed to best advantage against shades of green. Today it was a billowing dress cinched at the waist by a wide Friar Tuck leather belt and a matching felt hat. A green boa scarf fluttered in the quickening breeze.

With a final rakish toss of her boa, Magretta attached

herself to a blonde, urbane young man who greeted her with evident reluctance, dodging her questions about print runs before making his escape into the castle. Kimberlee Kalder having already sloped off with the only available bellhop, Portia was left standing with a small, nut-brown woman with gray hair cut in the shape of a German helmet. She introduced herself as Mrs Joan Elksworthy, recently of New Mexico, formerly of Scotland.

Heads together, one gray and one dark, the two women began walking companionably over the drawbridge, stopping briefly to inspect the rope-and-pulley arrangement that raised the bridge in case of invasion. They continued through an arched stone walkway into the castle proper before descending a short flight of stairs to the reception desk. Here they were greeted by a round, bubbly woman, tightly spandexed, who introduced herself as Donna Doone, the castle's event coordinator.

'I'm here to make sure things run smoothly for our distinguished guests,' she chirped. 'I am so *thrilled* to have all of you here. I'm a writer myself, you know.'

Cautiously, they shook hands all around – cautiously because Donna had the air of an author about to produce her unpublished manuscript for their delectation, there and then. As Portia stood back to admire the ancient room, a large green presence fluttered to her side.

'Now this,' Magretta Sincock pronounced, 'is more like it.'

Her arm swept round to encompass the wood paneling, the rough-hewn fireplace, the stone stairway, and the weapons and armor ranged against the walls. An outsized painting, its varnish alligatored with age, depicted one of the many hopeless but heroic battles of Scotland's calamitous past.

'The perfect setting for a murder, don't you think?' said Magretta. '*So* inspiring. For one's *books*, I mean, of course.'

Magretta's words made Portia vaguely uneasy. But, really, what were the odds anyone would actually be *murdered* at a gathering of murder mystery writers, when you really thought about it? Surely these people all batted out their hostilities on their keyboards.

The hotel receptionist called her over a few moments later and Portia stepped up for her turn at the registration desk. As she followed a porter up the main staircase toward her room, she never noticed the large man from Cambridge who stared after her, transfixed.

CHAPTER 3

Walkabout

DCI St Just's room was on the top floor of the castle, and, while small, it more than lived up to the themes of plunder and pillage introduced by the main rooms below. To his delight, it proved to be one of the corner rooms featuring a turret. The turret itself had been transformed into a writing nook, complete with antique desk, lamp, and phone.

He began to unpack, laying out his kit in the marble-tiled bathroom, and folding his clothes into a beautiful old rosewood chest of drawers, on top of which rested several brochures describing the amenities of the hotel. A glossy blue tri-fold advertised the full-service spa.

He ran a hand down the back of his neck. He'd badly wrenched it once subduing a high-spirited villain, and after a month of pain-filled, sleepless nights, his wife had given him a certificate for a spa massage. He'd let the certificate expire; to him there was something decadent, something *un-English*, about such self-indulgence. Beth had asked him about it a few times. He wished now he'd at least had the kindness to lie and say he'd used her well-intended gift.

Beth had been dead three years now.

That wasn't possible, was it? Three years?

Poor Bethie.

His reaction to that lovely dark-haired woman – he'd over-heard the clerk call her Ms De'Ath – filled him with guilt, much like that spa certificate. He and Beth had never had the conversation where each spouse releases the other from the obligation of prolonged mourning in the event of the death of either. He and Beth had thought they'd live forever. They'd joked about having walker races when they reached the old people's home together.

He had never in three years given a thought to remarrying, but not for want of well-meaning friends, usually happily married women, who saw his single state as an affront to nature. A good-looking, intelligent man in possession of a steady job, a weekend home, and a good pedigree must be in want of a wife. Or famous words to that effect. They had waited a decent interval – eight weeks – before the invitations started pouring in. It was not from lack of respect for Beth, he came to realize, but more a case of supply-and-demand economics. These friends liked nothing better than to invite him to dinner and spring an unattached female on him. None of these arranged matches had 'taken,' of course. In fact, under the rapt gaze of these matchmaking friends, most of the women had seemed as uncomfortable as he.

Sadness settled over him like a monk's cowl. He simply was not in the market for a wife, and the whole concept of dating – dreaded word – struck him as both ridiculous and terrifying. Beth had been all he'd ever wanted. Her death had been the defining loss of his life. He wasn't going to allow the gods a second chance to destroy him.

Looking for a diversion from his thoughts – any diversion – he pulled out of his suitcase the conference brochure that had arrived the other day through the post. It was printed in pitch black and shrieking red, the bulleted points illustrated with little dripping bloody daggers.

He settled at the desk in the turret and began flipping through the pages. Among the scheduled topics were 'Fifty Ways to Leave Your Agent' and 'Print on Demand, or, First Let's Kill All the Editors.' They were also to be treated to 'Is PoD the KoD?' *What on earth?* This was followed by the equally opaque 'Time to Deep-six the Chix?' He stopped to read the description: 'Is it Women's Literature, or is it Chick Lit? Some in publishing circles feel it's time to nix the chix – chick lit that is. Hear what publishing experts see as the future – or not – of this hot genre!'

He continued to struggle through the recondite schedule, trying to get a feel for what his audience might expect from him. On Sunday, they were to be treated to 'Cat's Meow or Dog's Dinner?', apparently a discussion of which animal had a greater impact on sales of crime novels. St Just would have thought neither. At least a parrot might prove a useful witness to a crime.

As an appetizer before the luncheon break, there was to be a session by one Annabelle Pace on 'Every Which Way: Detection via Blood Splatter Analysis.' His own session, he saw with dismay, had been titled, 'Bad Boys.' He sighed, reading the description: 'Top cop DCI Arthur St Just discusses police procedure in nabbing the baddies. Hold *your* fire as he fires off tales of his most famous nabs.'

This was dreadful, even worse than he'd imagined. Who did they think he was? Eliot Ness?

He heard a tentative knock on the door. He opened it to find a woman with an exceedingly permed head of hair who introduced herself as Donna Doone.

'Just checking to make sure everything's all right,' she said with a bright smile. 'I see you did get upgraded to one of the lovely turret rooms – I made a special point of putting you in for one when I saw your name in the program. The famous detective here at Dalmorton? Too thrilling. Free upgrade, never fear.'

Without invitation she bustled in, parked herself on the canopied bed, and surveyed the room. She was wearing, St Just could hardly help but notice, an extremely tight-fitting and low-cut dress in a shiny fabric more suitable for a night at the opera. While he found the woman's familiarity a bit startling, St Just was used to this kind of thing. Women trusted him, children trusted him, dogs and cats followed him home.

Nodding at the brochure, Donna Doone said, 'Chronic, isn't it? Are you signing up for any of the excursions? You won't want to miss the Vaults in Edinburgh. They're like an underground village, really. Haunted, you know.'

'I hadn't thought about it, in—'

'I must say, I've been looking forward for weeks to having all of you here. Have you seen Kimberlee Kalder yet? And Winston Chatley – now, there's a dark horse if you like. And Joan Elksworthy with those Scottish books – so lovely, you forget they're about murder. Still, I don't think they're as unrealistic as the pathologist capers that Annabelle Pace writes . . . But as a writer myself I know how difficult this can be. Reality, I mean.'

Politely, wondering if she was planning to stay the night, St Just asked her what she was writing.

'It's an historical mystery set during prehistoric times.' She hesitated. 'I could use some advice on the forensics, you see.'

He didn't doubt that for a moment.

'I'm not really an expert in that area . . .'

It certainly explained the red-carpet treatment he was getting. What could he tell her, though? Mercifully, she had skipped ahead to another topic.

'Have you seen the castle grounds yet? Do let me give you the Cook's tour.'

He started to refuse, worried he was incurring some kind of indebtedness, for clearly she was after advice for this novel of hers – advice no one alive could provide. Still, his legs wanted a stretch after the train ride.

Also, it might be the only way to get her out of the room.

The grounds of the ancient fortress consisted of acres of wooded parkland nestled near the banks of the River Esk. St

Just and Donna walked slowly, savoring the unusually warm but windy day, as she pointed out the flora and fauna and the golf course in the distance. Snow dotted the grounds like melted ice cream.

Eventually their walk brought them to a mews and weathering yard near the castle. Dalmorton, she explained, boasted a collection of hawks, buzzards, falcons, eagles, and owls – all medieval weapons of choice until the invention of the gun. The birds passed expert eyes over St Just, like connoisseurs assessing the contents of a butcher's display cabinet.

He and Donna stepped into the aviary, where the cages looked barely strong enough to resist the birds' wire-cutter beaks. St Just instinctively kept his distance. He was being closely scrutinized by one ferocious-looking buzzard when a woman feathered in a vivid shade of green flew in. He placed her in her late fifties, with a hairstyle that owed much to the influence of Maggie Thatcher, who in photos always appeared to be standing in front of a large balloon.

'There you are, Miss Doone,' the woman trilled. 'I've been looking all over for you.' She waved her boa about to indicate the width and breadth of her search. 'My room doesn't have a turret. I specifically asked for one of the turreted bedrooms.'

'I say, I have—' St Just felt a sharp little elbow in his ribs.

Donna Doone said, 'Magretta. Miss Sincock. I'm afraid all room arrangements were made at the direction of Lord Easterbrook. I can't change them without his authorization.'

Magretta was letting fly a salvo of protest when a brisk figure in brogues came bustling along the path and into the aviary. An Alice band in a fabric of Native American design held the chopped gray hair framing her betel-nut face, browned and scored from too many years in the sun; turquoise stones in intricate settings adorned her ears and wrists. The woman stopped with a friendly cry and introduced herself as Mrs Elksworthy of Santa Fe. Donna took the opportunity to glance at her watch and detach herself from the group.

'Cocktails,' she threw over her shoulder. 'Seven o'clock. Tomorrow, don't forget, is the awards dinner. Smart dress code, everyone!'

If she'd hoped to escape, she was mistaken. Magretta maneuvered a U-turn and churned off in Donna's wake.

Mrs Elksworthy said conversationally, 'Magretta lives in her own little Ruritania. Has done for years.' Her eyes were a startling lake blue against the ravaged desert of her complexion. 'As if we could forget that blasted dinner. What was Lord Easterbrook thinking – bound to cause trouble. I gather you're new this year?'

He nodded. In the distance, they could see a young man strolling the grounds by himself, his hair streaked nearly white by the sun. A golden-haired boy, indeed. Perhaps strutting was a better word: St Just was reminded of a peacock looking for a mate.

'That is Jay Fforde,' Mrs Elksworthy informed him. 'Agent to the stars.'

'A nice-looking man,' St Just commented.

Joan Elksworthy again gave him the benefit of that disquieting gaze.

'He would surely agree. Anyway, Jay represents the turretless Magretta Sincock, among others, including me.' She turned to him. 'They couldn't get anyone from Lothian and Borders Police to do a little talk about police procedure?'

'For some reason they asked for me.'

'Then you're being modest. I'm a friend of the conference organizer. You must be very well known indeed for her to have asked specifically for you.'

Together they left the aviary and crossed the weathering

lawn. He found Mrs Elksworthy to be a comfortable woman, the type probably most at home in a world of herbaceous borders, potting sheds, and bedding plants. Except he imagined in Santa Fe the herbaceous borders might be replaced by rows of cacti. She carried about her a no-nonsense, captain-of-the-hockey-team aura. Such as she, reflected St Just, had seen Britain through the Blitz.

They followed a sign pointing to the Old Spa area, which proved to be a room lined with antique photographs of large, stern-looking ladies from the turn of the last century wading, fully clothed, like hippos into the steaming bath waters. From there he and Mrs Elksworthy ('Call me Mrs E, everyone does') walked up a stone staircase to an area housing the modern-day indoor pool and spa. The azure pool water sparkled invitingly under recessed lighting.

It was as they walked down the hall toward the main part of the castle that St Just noticed an ancient wooden door to the right. A small plaque on the wall next to it read: Bottle Dungeon. The door opened at his touch with a satisfyingly ominous creak.

'After you,' said Mrs Elksworthy, hugging herself in a mock shiver.

A spiral stair led down to an empty, stone-walled room – empty except for a metal railing at the top of what appeared to be a literal hole in the ground. St Just eased his way down the narrow steps, Joan Elksworthy at his heels. A cold, musty smell assailed their nostrils. They peered over the railing, from which point they could look far down into the cell. It was windowless, about ten feet square. A posted brochure to one side of the barricaded opening contained a diagram illustrating that the little prison cell featured such amenities as a latrine and a ventilation shaft. St Just spotted the shaft high up on the wall, but it emitted no light.

'"Prisoners were lowered into the dungeon by rope",' Mrs Elksworthy read aloud from the brochure, '"and the score marks of the ropes can still be seen in the stonework. Once in, there was no escape through the eleven-inch thick walls.'

'How perfectly dreadful,' she said. 'And right here, practically in the dead center of the building. You'd think the screams would have kept everyone awake at night.'

Surely she was right – the prisoners must have disturbed the other denizens of the castle. But then St Just realized that the remoteness of the dungeon, off what then must have been a little-traveled hallway at the bottom of the castle, probably muffled the cries.

Anyway, he realized, the poor ragged, emaciated sods were probably too weak from injuries, torture, hunger, and thirst to do much yelling. In his imagination, he heard their cries echo faintly off the stone walls. How many had languished at the bottom of this pit, suffering lingering and horrible deaths by starvation in this literal hellhole?

'I doubt the victims were in much condition to scream by the time they were thrown in here,' he told her. A small shudder of revulsion lifted his shoulders. He felt a sinking of the spirit, much as he had felt looking at the leper holes in the porch of a medieval church at Englishcombe. The long creep of centuries added weight to the fetid air.

Joan said, 'Let's get the hell out of here.' He didn't stay to argue.

'The hotel brochure also mentions a priest's hole,' Mrs Elksworthy said as they emerged into the main hallway. 'This place has everything, doesn't it?'

From the registration area below, they could hear Magretta putting the staff through its paces. They dared a peek down the stairs. Magretta was pounding one bejeweled fist on the countertop for emphasis.

'If, as you say, there are no turrets left, which I do not for one second believe, I shall have a room with a view. The closed outdoor pool does not count as a view. I came to Scotland to see the mountain vistas and by God, I shall.' She stamped one small, green-shod foot.

'Madam, I am sorry,' said the clerk. 'I can only repeat, the last turreted room went to Miss Kalder. Perhaps she would be willing to organize an exchange.'

'Perhaps pigs will fly,' muttered Joan Elksworthy.

As there were in fact no mountains near the castle, St Just could only wonder how the staff was going to cope with Magretta. He and Mrs E – she really seemed to prefer the more informal mode of address – carried on into the sitting room, where waiters bustled about replenishing the afternoon tea service. The pair stood near where Donna Doone had sat earlier, overlooking the front of the castle. A limo was now disgorging a broad-shouldered, pugnacious-looking man and a woman, presumably his wife. St Just somehow was put in mind of photos of Gertrude Stein and Alice B. Toklas from the 1930s. He had never been sure what black bombazine was, but felt fairly certain this is what the woman might be wearing – there was something altogether faded and old-fashioned in her appearance. She hovered several feet behind the man like a paid companion.

'That,' said Mrs Elksworthy, 'is Tom Brackett, the spy novelist, and his wife. I always forget her name. Tom claims to have been a real spy once. Or at least, he doesn't bother to deny the rumors – good for sales. Spy novels . . . not really mysteries, are they? Oh, and this woman just now arriving. That's Ninette Thomson. She's an agent.'

Another taxi pulled up, and it proved to be the last one of the day. It disgorged a woman of perhaps forty years with graying brown hair, plainly dressed in a nondescript dress of muddy brown.

'No idea,' Mrs Elksworthy said. 'She looks like she's been dragged through a hedge backwards, doesn't she? Oh, wait, that's Annabelle Pace. My, she's put on weight.' She lowered her voice confidingly. 'Occupational hazard for a writer,' she informed him. 'Writer's butt. I grew as big as a barn writing *No One Here but Us Dead*.'

Mrs Elksworthy excused herself after one cup of tea to finish unpacking. St Just stayed on as long as he could, and ate and drank as much tea as he could hold, hoping this Ms De'Ath would appear. She never did.

CHAPTER 4

Darkness Falls

Portia De'Ath had spent the afternoon in her room, going over her notes for her work in progress. The castle's romantic setting so far wasn't helping as she'd hoped. She'd devised a plot of what had seemed at the moment of inspiration to be devilish ingenuity. In execution, it was turning into a sea of red herrings.

But it was seven the next time she looked at her watch. She'd missed the start of the cocktail hour and would have to rush to change for dinner. She emerged from the bathroom a few minutes later in a fusion of steam and lavender scent, wrapped in one of the hotel's plush white terrycloth robes. Quickly, she slipped into a travel-proof black jersey, accenting it with gold jewelry at her neck and ears, and headed downstairs.

At the Dungeon Restaurant, festively decorated with weapons and suits of armor, she was briskly led by a hostess to a table for two near Tom Brackett and his wife – too briskly for Portia to stop her. She had encountered the pair at a previous conference and had spent much of the time wishing she could kidnap Edith away from the man.

Her agent Ninette Thomson, this night foreswearing her usual animal prints and leggings in favor of a simple black dress, joined her moments later. Portia now realized that at another nearby table sat her disappearing travel companion, Kimberlee Kalder, and a handsome blond man whom

Ninette introduced – rather frostily, thought Portia – as Jay Fforde, agent. Ninette treated Kimberlee to an accusatory glance that could have done service as a steak knife. Kimberlee smiled sweetly back, scanning both women with expertly kohl-lined eyes. If Kimberlee remembered abandoning Portia at the train station – in fact, if she remembered her at all – it was clear that now she only had eyes for Jay Fforde.

Ninette and Portia studied the menu, eavesdropping the while. Kimberlee seemed to be the topic of several muted exchanges going on around them. Heads also kept turning in the direction of an unremarkable woman who sat alone, wearing an unfortunate dun-colored polyester dress. Portia finally recognized her from years of seeing her photo in bookstore advertising displays – Annabelle Pace. Annabelle, who wrote tales about an oversexed forensic pathologist – Canadian, Portia rather thought. Despite the fact the author's research on forensics had been criticized as laughably slipshod at best, the books generally lingered several weeks on the best-seller lists. Although, Portia realized, she hadn't seen the name Annabelle Pace in those lists for some time. Annabelle was looking decidedly ill and drawn – far older than her publicity photos, at any rate.

Other people recognizable as conference attendees began straying in, including Magretta Sincock, dressed now in a peculiar green the color of decomposing celery. Thankfully she had left any matching hat in her room. She stood surveying the restaurant, apparently captivated by its barrel-vaulted ceiling. Portia had a suspicion she was holding this pose until most of the diners registered her presence. She also suspected Magretta was waiting for one particular pair of eyes to notice her. When Kimberlee Kalder finally did look up, Magretta did a staged double take and danced across the room, gushing hallos, a wizened but game Peter Pan. If Magretta had hoped politeness would demand she be invited to sit, it was a short-lived hope.

DEATH AND THE LIT CHICK

The pair gave her a dismissive, chilly greeting and resumed their conversation under her nose.

A somewhat subdued Magretta nevertheless threw back her shoulders and marched over to Tom Brackett's table, a move Portia doubted was any more inspired. Her effusive greeting did not include Tom's wife, although it was possible Magretta didn't actually register the woman, who had an eerie ability to blend into the walls.

'I am so pleased to meet you at last,' Magretta warbled. 'I am. . .' and she drew herself up to her full five feet, in heels, '. . .well, as of course you *must* know, I am Magretta Sincock. It is odd, is it not, that two such *famous* writers have never met?'

Tom put down the knife with which he had been sawing at something and surveyed the little hand being offered him, as if he had never seen such a thing before. He extended one large paw in Magretta Sincock's direction, then suddenly seized the hand tightly, holding it in a grip until Magretta let out a little squawk and began, ever so slightly, to buckle at the knees. Finally, silently, he released her. Magretta Sincock stood wavering, stoically masking the pain. The other diners exchanged alarmed glances, no one quite knowing what to do. Kimberlee Kalder laughed.

'Well, best be off,' Magretta said at last, in a bright, strangled voice, her face nearly as red as her hair. 'I've so enjoyed our little chat.' Bowed but unbeaten, she walked, slightly staggering, over to Annabelle's table, where a similar performance was repeated, minus the wrestling match. Annabelle took her hand gingerly and asked her to join her, 'one star of yesteryear to another.'

'Oh, *God*. Don't remind me,' said Magretta, flapping a napkin into her lap.

'I suppose it's marginally better than calling us washed-up has-beens. . .'

'Not by much. Wait until I get my hands on that loathsome

little toad of a reporter.' She paused. 'I hear you're just back from Iowa.'

'Kansas or Iowa or *some*where. Goddamn publicists. I've seen bigger crowds at a salad bar.'

'Been there,' said Magretta. 'Just me, three store clerks, and a homeless man who tried to follow me back to the hotel.'

'Who is your publicist?'

'B. A. King,' said Annabelle.

'Ah,' said Magretta.

'I wonder what Tom Brackett's doing here anyway,' Annabelle said after a moment.

'He doesn't have to come, that's certain. He seems to get plenty of publicity without leaving home.'

'It would probably be better for his career if he stayed put, actually. I doubt he'd have as many fans if they'd seen his performance tonight with you.'

Surreptitiously, Magretta shook out her still-aching hand. But her resentful gaze slid over not to Tom, but to Jay and a simpering Kimberlee.

'I see the world hasn't changed since I was a girl,' said Magretta.

'How so?'

Scarcely bothering to lower her voice, Magretta said:

'It's not whom you know, but whom you sleep with.'

'Roger that.'

CHAPTER 5

At Third Sight

The conference began in earnest the next day, and St Just, along with most of the authors, was bussed into Edinburgh, feeling rather like royalty on the way to open a chain store in the provinces. The air was cold and the road glazed with frost, the warm spell of the day before a fast-fading memory.

The coach deposited them at the Luxor Hotel, where they were issued name badges and set loose to mingle, clash, or – in St Just's case – hope to escape notice altogether. He'd stayed in his room the night before, ordering room service, but he'd met most of the others at breakfast. The one person he wanted to see, of course, had not been there.

An opening session was scheduled within the hour in the hotel's main ballroom, and participants had begun to gather outside its double doors, some sitting on the floor with coffee cups, like mendicants in a church porch. Many had opted for comfort in jeans and spandex, while many had gone in – oddly, St Just thought – for the pinstriped captain-of-industry look. Most had mobiles attached to their ears.

Old acquaintance were reuniting, standing back to admire and comment on how well the other looked. But underneath it all – all the back-slapping and the faces wreathed in smiles – St Just picked up the occasional impression of a past slight or grudge being dusted off for a closer look.

Donna Doone squeezed her way out of an opening in the crowd to join him, dressed today in a sequined, low-cut white jumpsuit that inescapably called to mind Elvis: The Vegas Years. Mrs Elksworthy also materialized from somewhere, just as Magretta Sincock came steaming into view. Today she had assembled a costume the color and texture of a putting green, with a feathered cavalier hat and a leather belt slung gunslinger style around her ample hips.

'Oh, look,' she said, pointing with her glass of orange juice. 'Rachel Twalley.'

'Yes, she's a dear friend of mine from school days,' said Joan Elksworthy, following Magretta's direction, then adding, 'Oh, my.' They all looked over at Rachel, who stood wrestling with a cascading sheaf of papers and an empty stapler, casting aggrieved glances at the burbling entourage now forming around Kimberlee. Her harried manner suggested a woman tired of all work and no glory.

Magretta went on: 'She writes, or rather wrote, Regency mysteries with a corgi sleuth, owned by a Princess Royal – or was it a dachshund owned by Bonnie Prince Charlie? Anyway, I suspect she agreed to arrange this rave-up in an attempt to keep her name alive before the public. At least she'll be listed in the program for *something*.'

Ignoring the frosty reception these comments were getting from Joan Elksworthy, Magretta went on:

'But historicals are doing rather well now. I'm thinking of going in for one myself. What would you say,' she said, turning to St Just, 'to a spunky heroine who escapes human sacrifice in ancient Gaul, only to find that she has the ear, along with other parts, of the great Caesar, helping him resolve potentially embarrassing political scandals?'

'It's a . . . novel idea,' said St Just, not daring to steal a glance at Mrs Elksworthy.

'You think it's rubbish, of course,' said Magretta, catching him off guard with her unexpected acumen, 'but I tell you, publishers are looking for a hook, however stupid. Is that Quentin Swope, I wonder? The one who wrote that simply *libelous* article in the *Edinburgh Herald*? I have a word or two for *him*.' Magretta slid the strap of her purse over her shoulder and swooped off in a flutter of molting plumage.

The eddying crowd gradually pushed them in the direction of the sellers' room, where books representing the fevered output of the gathered were offered for purchase, along with apparently in-demand mystery paraphernalia such as sloganed T-shirts and cat bookends. St Just was becalmed near Annabelle Pace at a table selling collectible crime novels. He was turning to comment on a first-edition Chandler when he saw she had struck up a conversation with Winston Chatley on her other side. Sensing some old chemistry or affinity there, he held back.

He began idly looking for the books of authors he recognized from the castle, reading the little biographies on the back jackets and marveling at the revealing choices of author photo. Magretta, in a hazy black-and-white studio shot clearly decades old, was recognizable mostly by her rigid, unchanging hairstyle. Head propped on her hands, she smiled at the potential buyer with the coy, come-hither look of an old-time movie vamp. Most of the other authors had adopted a friendly grin, or, in the case of the thriller writers, a grimace suggesting a minor bowel obstruction. Tom Brackett glared out at the world with a fierce sneer on his lips.

Kimberlee's book was impossible to miss, and not only for the sheer volume of copies available for sale. The thick glossy cover was coated in a garish shade of hot pink; its title, *Dying for a Latte*, was set in a jagged black font meant to resemble knife blades. The subject was illustrated by an androgynous, prone victim with a black stiletto heel sticking out of its back and a woman's stocking tied garrotte-style around its neck. In its outstretched hand was a martini glass filled with something St Just hoped was meant to represent one of those designer cocktails rather than blood.

The latte of the title was nowhere to be seen but perhaps that oversight was explained in the narrative.

A scene ripped from today's headlines, thought St Just. He picked up the book and leafed through it rather furtively, like a man in a lingerie store shopping for his wife's Valentine's Day gift. The story seemed to be about – as much as it was about anything – a young woman in a low-level publishing job with a tiny apartment, a shoe fetish, an unlimited clothing budget, and a philandering boss she finds dead of a gunshot wound. St Just flipped back to the front cover at that point, wondering what had happened to the shoe, the stocking, and the martini glass. Shrugging, he flipped through a few more pages. Ninety percent of the book seemed to be taken up with the protagonist yakking about either this shooting or, in equal measure, her ex-boyfriend with her two 'gal pals' and a gay decorator. These breezy discussions generally were held over cocktails in one trendy nightspot or another. Midway through, the heroine accosted the ex-boyfriend and gave him a good bollocking. Henry James it was not.

'A Kimberlee Kalder fan? You?'

The low, honeyed voice at his side startled him so the pink horror of a book nearly flew out of his hands. He blushed, as if he'd been caught reading porn.

'Who, as they would say in America, would'a thunk it?' the soft voice added.

He turned toward the speaker. Looking down, his eyes met a blue gaze the color of the sea at midnight. He felt as if he'd again slipped sideways through a time warp, for it was the dark-haired woman from St Germaine's restaurant, the one he'd glimpsed again yesterday. Since he thought it was doubtful she'd remember him, he was reluctant to mention their former 'acquaintance,' for reasons of pride or whatever that he didn't care to examine too closely.

He closed the book and replaced it carefully with its ghastly pink sisters.

'Just curious,' he cleared his throat, smiled. 'There's been so much talk.'

'Hmm. Oh, about the book, you mean?' she smiled mischievously, a smile to light any room. A smile he decided instantly he wanted to – had to – see every day of his life.

Whatever it took.

He'd learn to tell jokes, memorize joke books, if that's what it took, to make that smile appear.

He didn't care who this woman was.
He didn't care where she came from.
He didn't care if she snored.
St Just was a goner.

CHAPTER 6

Stirrings

'Yes, I suppose,' continued the vision. 'The *roman à clef* always arouses a certain amount of curiosity, at least among the people who think they might have been portrayed in it.'

He stood transfixed by that curious blue stare.

Make her keep talking, he thought. *About anything. It doesn't matter. Don't let her leave.*

His brain, at least the part that connected to his tongue, refused to obey.

She'll think I'm an idiot, he thought frantically. *Say something!*

Providentially, she seemed not to have noticed she was talking to an idiot.

'But in this case, once the lawyers were through pecking at the *Latte* manuscript, I hear there wasn't any real meat left. Assuming there ever was. I've only read a few excerpts.'

'You said, *roman à clef*,' he managed to croak.

She nodded.

Doing great there, Arthur, he thought. *She probably knows what she just said.*

'I mean,' he went on, stopped, tried tearing his eyes from her face and found he could not. 'What I meant was, the author worked in publishing?'

'Apparently. Magazines. All the more surprising since Kimberlee seems barely able to spell or construct a sentence that does not contain the word "like". Although the spelling

58

may be the typesetter's fault. You can never be sure. My last book had the word "pratmatic" sprinkled throughout.'

The Kimberlee remarks were said without rancor. She was merely reporting her observations.

She. She must have a first name. Must find out name, telegraphed his brain.

'You're—' he started.

'Although,' she was saying, 'perhaps that's no longer a requirement in the publishing world. Spelling. Well, I'd better get a move on,' she said, starting to turn away. She had a smile like a lightning strike. 'It was nice talk—'

'*No!*' he nearly shouted.

She turned back, looking stunned, as well she might.

Jesus!

'I'm sorry. What I meant was. . .'

She was of course connected with the conference – what else would she be doing here? – but he could hardly ask her where in the castle she was staying, could he?

'I meant to say, it was nice talking with you.'

Nice and lame, a phrase he trotted out ten times a day. Then he rescued himself by adding:

'My name is Arthur St Just, by the way.'

'I know.' Smiling, she stuck out her hand.

She knew? She *knew* who he was? Merciful heaven. He was so flattered he nearly missed taking the small white hand she proffered. Her skin was as soft as a newborn's.

'Bye now,' she said.

Spellbound, he slowly raised one hand in an answering wave. 'Bye.'

He had somehow lost all interest in these books and their authors. Sidling his way, crablike, out of the crowded seller's room, he leaned against a Grecian column to watch the milling multitude, which continued its amoeba-like splitting into ever-changing groups. Apart from the large Kimberlee Kalder cluster, there were others centered around perhaps six authors who St Just gathered were to be much praised and emulated for their sales figures. These focal points included Tom Brackett. But the mother of all groups had collected around the handsome young agent, Jay Fforde, who was beginning, rather frantically, to eye the exits.

Just then, a commotion could be heard above the generally deafening noise level, and the words 'stars of yesteryear' carried clearly across the room. Magretta had apparently brought to bay the author of the *Edinburgh Herald* piece.

'I mean really, how *dare* you print such libel,' Magretta said, in her now-familiar clarion tones. 'Quentin, I demand a retraction.'

The offending reporter, much like the agent, seemed to be seeking escape. St Just was stirred to pity. Quentin sported an assortment of metal studs in his ears and hair moussed into wilted maroon spikes. Against Magretta's own swirling red locks, one would have thought that corner of the room had caught fire.

'Look, I can't print a retraction for something like that. I mean, it's not like I really said anything much, did I? Stars of yesterday – it's a compliment, like. Depending how you look at it.'

'Yester*year*. Yester*year*. I've told you how I look at it. You said quite enough, my young man. I'll have you know my fans are legion. *Legion*. I can promise you'll be hearing from them, as will your editor and publisher.'

If there is one thing the young cannot stand to be reminded of, reflected St Just, it is that they are, in fact, young. A mulish look rumpled Quentin's face.

'Look, I'll tell you what. I'll make it up to you, like. How's about you give me an interview? I'll plug your latest book, give you a leg up, like.'

A moue of distaste settled over Magretta's features. *A leg up, indeed*. Still, Quentin had learned enough in his short time in the company of crime writers to know that the offer of an interview – any interview, anywhere, with anyone – was an irresistible siren call.

She tipped back her head and eyed him from half-closed lids, a queen considering a stay of execution.

'When?' she demanded.

'What's wrong with right now?'

Kimberlee Kalder, having disengaged from her fan club, materialized at St Just's side, likewise watching the proceedings.

'Magretta – such a silly old moo,' she said, beaming at him. She tossed her head like a shampoo model, swinging her gleaming hair into slow-motion action. 'I've come to rescue you. A good-looking man like yourself shouldn't be, like, left at the mercy of this crowd.'

He demurred. She persisted. St Just was quickly persuaded that persistence was her calling card.

'Don't be shy,' she said. She now twirled a strand of the white-blonde hair around one finger, giggled up and down the scale, and gave her head another toss for good measure. 'Cultivate the fans – that's *totally* what these conferences are for.'

St Just smiled feebly. 'I don't have fans. I'm a cop.'

She paused, mid-twirl. 'Then whatever are you doing here?'

'It's rather a long story.'

She emitted a girlish squeal and, with an expression of mock horror, threw up her hands and said, 'The Bill! Ooh! I surrender!' There was more in this vein, and then, rescue mission forgotten, she giggled again and spun off in search of her publicist, who 'was supposed to be arranging an interview with the *Scotsman*. I don't know what I pay him for. How am I supposed to finish this book if I have to do his job, too?'

As she strode away on champagne-stem heels, a bedraggled Annabelle Pace crossed his line of vision, carrying a plastic bag bulging with about a dozen books.

'You've been shopping, I see.'

She nodded. 'One has to keep up with trends, however appalling they may be. I never thought I'd say this,' she added, 'but "poor Jay".'

Nodding in the direction of the besieged agent, she said, 'He doesn't need this grief. He certainly doesn't need the money, nor the publicity. I wonder why he's here at all.'

'Looking to recruit new talent?' said St Just.

'You're joking, right? He's probably got more successful clients than he can handle now. Besides, agents never come to these things looking for talent. But would *you* turn down a free holiday?'

Splinter groups were now forming around people Annabelle identified as late-arriving publishers and magazine editors.

'They're trying to get on the publishers' lists or finagle a book review,' Annabelle informed him. 'Oh! See that gray-haired man, the toff who looks like Ian Richardson? That's Julius Easterbrook, the publisher. My host and yours, in case you haven't yet met him.'

Watching the sycophantic crowd, and thinking of the hundreds of books he'd just seen at the booksellers' stalls, St Just said, 'It's a funny business you're in. Constantly writing about murder.'

'Are you wondering, in your professional capacity, if we're ever tempted to take it that *one step further* – cue sinister harpsichord music?' asked Annabelle. 'The answer is no. Writers are observers, not doers, Hemingway being the rare exception. We don't, as a rule, engage in anything so . . . proactive as murder. Especially crime writers. Completely lacking a spine for that sort of thing, I would have said.'

'But you're forgetting,' he replied. 'Crime writers are people, too.'

She looked about them. In one corner, an author was whinging to his publisher about the 'puny print runs' for his book, 'which would otherwise have been a best-seller.' In another, a woman surreptitiously added a tot of brandy from a hip flask to her morning coffee. A scruffy-looking man in an overcoat was taking down one of the booksellers, who had apparently committed the mortal sin of forgetting to stock the author's books.

'Only in the most *elastic* sense of the term,' she told him.

Annabelle soon left him to discuss contracts, and St Just began walking about, sipping his juice and trying to look as though he belonged. He'd never known how to 'work' a room, which often left him at the mercy of whatever bore latched onto him, but he had learned how to move quickly and purposefully through a crowd so as not to be waylaid. As he did so, he came across Magretta, enthroned in an armchair, interview with Quentin Swope under way. She was apparently just wrapping up a defense of the mystery genre, and the enduring fascination of reading about others being done to death in outrageous and implausible ways.

'Would you not say it is true that good writers can no longer find a platform, especially in America?' St Just heard Quentin ask. 'That they're being ignored in favor of the few, reliable blockbuster writers?'

'Not at all,' Magretta replied frostily. 'The blockbuster writers like Kimb – I mean, these newcomers, some of whom are here with us today, will be forgotten in twenty years' time, you mark my words. While the carefully crafted suspense novel, such as I write, will, like the pyramids, withstand the test of the ages.'

Registering that Magretta had actually failed to answer the question, St Just strode briskly past, gathering odd scraps of conversation as he went.

'You have to have a corpse by page fifty-seven. Page seventy at the absolute outside.'

'Says who?'

'Why, so says everyone. It's the industry standard.'

'Industry *standard*? What are we writing here? CliffsNotes or crime novels?'

Another group, this one dominated by a man in green golf slacks. Surely a soul mate for Magretta, or her lost twin.

'Prologues are so last year. Did you read that pointless, winding thing in Magretta's last book?'

Or, perhaps not.

A few steps further brought him to a redoubtable woman sporting a pince-nez and a brocade waistcoat.

'The murder has to take place in the first five pages. Otherwise, the readers lose interest.'

'Are they suffering from attention deficit disorder, or what? I mean, surely these decisions depend on the requirements of the story one is trying to tell.'

'I'm telling you. Monique's last book didn't have the murder until page twenty. The returns positively *flooded* back to the publisher.'

'That's just ridiculous. The book didn't sell because it was rubbish.'

And a bit later:

'Fifty? Honey, she's sixty-five if she's a day. Hell, her author photo is practically a daguerreotype.'

Another group was discussing the famous Hercule Poirot.

'All those giant marrows,' said one. 'I mean, really. One can't escape the symbolism. And Miss Marple, with her knitting—'

Just then the conference organizer, Rachel Twalley, whizzed by, an hysterical gleam in her eyes, just avoiding a collision with a ginger-haired man in granny glasses.

'Have you ever noticed how serial killers always think in italics?'

One conversation he overheard that later seemed significant was when his orbit brought him past Tom Brackett and Lord Easterbrook, Tom leaning in confrontationally, hands on hips.

'It's not blackmail if no money changes hands,' Tom hissed at the older man.

'Extortion, then. And I've had enough of whatever you choose to call it. If Kimberlee goes, everything's changed. You must realize that. I may well be bankrupt next year.'

'Don't give me that crap. You've got more money than Croesus.'

St Just missed the rest of the conversation, a jam having formed in earnest near the ballroom, resulting in some genteel shoving and elbow-pushing. The throng eventually swept St Just through the door and deposited him inside, where Rachel Twalley and several other dignitaries were arranged on a dais behind a long, cloth-covered table. The seated audience members alternated between rubber-necking and studying their programs as intently as scholars decoding the Dead Sea scrolls. St Just, finding a seat near the back, hoped no one would hold him responsible for 'Bad Boys.'

Rachel stood and bustled to the podium, rather in the unto-the-breach attitude of a suffragette about to chain herself to the gates of Parliament. Gripping the microphone as if it were a lifeline attached to a rescue helicopter – 'Testing! Testing! Can you hear me in the back?' (St Just felt sure they could hear her in the North Pole) – she launched into her opening remarks.

'The crime novel, once the poor stepchild of literature, has at last been crowned, thanks to all of you who gather here yearly to raise the fallen flag and rally the troops to the side of the immortal Agatha, the inimitable Ngaio, the sublime Dorothy – our Great Softboiled Ladies of Mystery – and their hardboiled cousins: Hammett, Chandler, and Cain.'

She mined this vein for some twenty minutes longer. St Just, losing the thread – along with, he was sure, many others – looked about him in time to see Tom Brackett plod in, his wife several steps behind, carrying his briefcase. There was a little jostling hubbub at one of the doors and then Magretta shot through the opening, immediately followed by Kimberlee

Kalder. Kimberlee's entrance was accompanied by a certain amount of fuss that made St Just think her delayed appearance, probably like Magretta's and Tom's, had been planned in advance. Her presence sent a flutter of whispers into the air like gulls startled by a sudden noise.

Signaling to Kimberlee to remain standing, Rachel trilled, 'There has been a last-minute change in the program that I know will *greatly* please all of you aspiring young authors in the audience. Kimberlee Kalder, best-selling author of *Dying for a Latte*, has generously consented to hold a Q-and-A session on how to break into the chick lit mystery market.'

This announcement met with a small ripple of applause and comment, some of it puzzled (*What in hell is chick lit?* one elderly woman with a hearing aid demanded loudly) and Kimberlee remained standing as necks craned to see her. She smiled, offered a lofty wave, then approached the podium, uninvited, a queen heaving her way through a swarm of courtiers. She had learned the orator's trick of maintaining a drawn-out silence before beginning to speak, first gathering all eyes to her.

'They say I am the new Jane Austen,' she began. 'Certainly I've sold more copies of *Latte* than Jane ever sold of *Persuasion* in her lifetime.'

A murmur of unrest rose from the assembly.

'As if,' whispered a middle-aged woman seated to his left.

'Blasphemy!' hissed another behind him.

'Who is "they"?' demanded another.

Unabashed, Kimberlee weathered on. Edith Wharton was mentioned, and George Eliot. St Just looked around to see how everyone else was taking this. By now several loud, incredulous snorts had erupted from various quarters of the room. Many heads were bent in heated discussion, and at least one member of the audience – the woman with strong opinions on Poirot's marrows – had had enough. With rather more commotion than was strictly necessary, she headed for the door.

The rest – especially, he supposed, the aspiring authors Rachel had mentioned – remained in their seats, entranced.

The buffet lunch proved to be a doughy mutton pie and a plain salad of lettuce and tomato, innocent of dressing, followed by oatmeal biscuits from a packet. Seeking out a quiet table, St Just noticed Donna Doone had now attached herself to Winston Chatley, handing him several dozen pages of typescript, presumably of her manuscript, which he politely pocketed. Magretta Sincock gave St Just a flirtatious wave, clashing with his naked salad greens as she sailed by.

Mrs Elksworthy appeared at his elbow and asked him to join her.

'That Tom,' she said as they pushed through the melee near the buffet table. 'How rude to sit there snorting like a sow throughout poor Rachel's speech. But Kimberlee was worse. Why didn't she just hire a trumpet player to announce her entrance? "Tips on writing *chick lit*", indeed.' She drew out a pause with staged emphasis, her customary sang-froid having apparently deserted her. No one could doubt chick lit was in for a thrashing. 'After all, what can there be to say? Keep your pencils sharpened?'

They passed Kimberlee sitting at a large round table with a flamboyantly dressed man Joan identified as B. A. King. St Just was in time to hear Kimberlee say, 'You stole it. I want what's mine or I promise you, you'll pay.'

'You're crazy,' King hissed back. 'I don't know what you're talking about.'

He stood abruptly and left. Sensing an opportunity – for what, St Just wasn't sure – more and more people began to gather around Kimberlee, like pilgrims drawn to a shrine. Most held copies of her book open for signing. Unfazed by either the crowd or the heated conversation with King, Kimberlee smiled serenely, taking veneration as her due.

But St Just noticed the touching scene of homage seemed to induce a vein-popping anger in both Magretta Sincock, who struggled to hide it, and Tom Brackett, who did not.

It is a jolly good thing that looks can't kill, thought St Just.

CHAPTER 7

A Sight to See

By breakfast time on Saturday, the gloves were starting to come off.

As St Just descended to the Orangery, anticipating a vast Scottish breakfast of eggs, bacon, sausage, black pudding, tomatoes, and mushrooms, he thought of Dr Samuel Johnson, who had declared that all epicures would choose to breakfast in Scotland. Life was probably happier, thought St Just, before we knew the calorie and cholesterol counts for everything.

He carried with him a copy of that day's *Edinburgh Herald*. Yesterday's conference was featured prominently in the Life section.

Magretta Sincock, bellowing his name, waved him over to her table.

'You saw it then?' She snapped a napkin into her lap. 'That cheeky little creep.'

'What, in the paper? I haven't read it yet,' said St Just. 'Is anything wrong?'

'Wrong? *Wrong*!' said Magretta, her voice throbbing with emotion. She fairly grabbed the paper out of St Just's hands and vigorously shook it open at the fold, like a farmer wrestling a bit onto a stubborn horse.

'First the little pillock gives a synopsis of my latest book that *reveals who the killer is*.' Magretta scanned the page columns until she found the relevant paragraph. 'Here it is:

"Since the most inattentive reader will be able to guess it, anyway, I shall save you the trouble of reading this tedious rehash of the plot of her 1984 *Mystic Murder in the Mirror*." Of all the bloody *nerve*.'

St Just looked to where she pointed, her finger trembling with outraged indignation.

'I say, Ms Sincock, that is a rum deal. Quentin didn't directly reveal the killer by name, though – there's that to be grateful for, I suppose. Anyway, I'm sure your new book is completely different from any of the older ones.'

A look crossed Magretta's face so fleetingly he might have missed it, but it told him she had indeed recycled an old, successful plot, quite possibly unaware she had done so. That possibility was the *bête noire* of any prolific writer who had been at the game a number of years, he supposed, and Magretta must have been churning them out for decades. However – and worse, from Magretta's point of view – Quentin Swope had gone on in his article to again sing the praises of 'the enchanting Kimberlee Kalder.'

'He didn't even mention he was going to interview her,' sniffed Magretta.

'In all fairness, would you have expected him to mention it?' asked St Just.

Magretta's look said all that needed to be said about her expectations. She sighed theatrically.

When St Just later read the review more closely, he wondered what Magretta had done to the man to provoke such a response. It was even worse than the bits Magretta had been able to bring herself to read aloud. Swope had indulged himself in a lengthy harangue about the dying mystery market, a setup for subsequent paragraphs that cast Kimberlee Kalder in the role of publishing's darling, one who had come up with a 'bright, fresh slant that threw open the mullioned doors and windows and let some much-needed air into the cloying atmosphere of the stately home murder, not to mention the tedious predictability of the woman-in-jeopardy novels of Magretta Sincock.'

St Just looked across the room to Kimberlee Kalder, that darling of publishing. She wore a low-cut blouse in her signature pink, this time with a white skirt so tight he could practically read the fabric care instructions through the material. At one point, Lord Easterbrook came over to offer obeisance. Kimberlee, nodding her elegant, narrow head, again seemed to take this as her due.

St Just watched, thinking thoughts about absolute power and corruption.

A tour of Edinburgh Castle had been scheduled for that afternoon, mainly for the bored spouses of conference attendees. The writers quickly dubbed it the Desperate Spouses Tour. Nonetheless, during an endless session on 'Where Have All the Profreaders (sic) Gone?' Portia had decided to sign on, and at the appointed hour she boarded the waiting coach.

She called Mrs Elksworthy over as she came down the aisle, indicating the free seat next to her. Ninette was already seated opposite, fixing her make-up. It seemed many had the same plan of escape. Of the people from the castle, only Edith Brackett, technically a spouse, was not on the spouses' tour. St Just also was missing, Portia noticed. Jay Fforde, walking down the aisle with Kimberlee, loudly informed the coach in general that he had had to get away from 'those lunatics, springing at me from every corner' – one unpublished author, it seemed, had literally followed him into the men's room, waving a manuscript.

'*And*, it was a female author.'

Mrs Elksworthy, waiting until Jay and Kimberlee were safely past, asked Portia, 'How old do you think Kimberlee Kalder is?'

'I'm never good with ages,' said Portia, 'especially when it's someone younger.' She took her program from her purse and looked up Kimberlee's biography under 'K.'

'She can't be more than twenty-seven or -eight. It says here she wrote a column for the *Sheffield Bugle* before the column was picked up by the *City-Central*. I remember reading the *City-Central* column – a bad habit, like chewing gum. Anyway, somehow that led to a job with *Belle de Jour* magazine. It was there she began writing a book. She denies *Latte* is a *roman à clef*, but I don't know whom she thinks she's kidding. The rest, as they say, is history.'

'Indeed,' murmured Mrs Elksworthy. 'To be the golden girl. I wonder, though . . . is it a blessing or a curse?'

'I suppose I'd like to try it for a week and find out.'

Flipping through the program, Portia next happened upon the biography of Magretta, accompanied by a photo easily twenty-five years out of date.

'This is interesting,' she said. 'Magretta worked for the *Sheffield Bugle* at the start of her career, the same as Kimberlee.'

'Kimberlee must have come along years later, though,' said Mrs Elksworthy.

'Hmm.'

Portia had stopped by the booksellers' stalls that morning and bought several books; one was by Magretta Sincock. She'd stood in line to have it signed, in a show of solidarity against the Quentin Swope interview. As the coach began its climb up Castle Hill, she flipped past Magretta's scrawling black signature to the last chapter of the book. After a few minutes, she dropped it in her lap. The secretary had committed the murder, and Portia realized Quentin was right – the secretary had been the culprit in an earlier Magretta book. Could she have deliberately set out to reproduce the success?

Portia had also given in to curiosity and bought Kimberlee Kalder's book. She began skimming, then reading it more slowly. The first chapter was lively, written in a captivating, rapid-fire, youthful voice. It was indeed full of text messaging and obsessive ponderings about weight and shoes and men, and was calculatedly aimed at the world's twenty-or-thirty-somethings. But it was polished and assured. Portia found it hard to believe it was Kimberlee's first novel.

She put the book aside as the coach neared Edinburgh Castle. The magnificent castle, like an enormous ship beached on a rock, was at the moment cast in bronze by the pale glow of the sun. It once had housed the muddle-headed Mary, who had given birth there to James VI before her life of bad choices was extinguished by the executioner's axe.

'You go on, dear,' said Joan Elksworthy. 'I should have realized – my legs won't be able to take that climb.'

So Portia made her way alone up the Esplanade and to the Portcullis Gate, where she escaped for a moment the stinging wind that swirled around the Castle ramparts. Pausing at a small iron wall fountain identified as the Witches' Well where over three hundred women accused of witchcraft had been burned at the stake (*plus ça change*, thought Portia), she came eventually to the Upper Ward, the main part of the Castle in medieval times. It still housed the tiny, Norman St Margaret's Chapel.

From the ramparts Portia gazed out on the magical view: New Town to the north, spread far below between the Castle and the Firth of Forth, and to the east, Old Town, a maze of winding streets below roofs that, from her eagle's nest, appeared no larger than postage stamps.

A somber tour of the War Memorial, and then Portia headed back to the coach, haunted by the photographs of too many too-young faces.

A sudden fall of shadow caused her to look up. The heavens were now threatening a storm, with swollen gray clouds rolling in against a darkening sky. The sun seemed to bob like a fluorescent orange ball on the horizon, and the wind whispered of either rain or snow. The gray-yellow sky was like a bruise. It put Portia in mind of paintings she'd seen of nuclear winter.

Thunder rumbled in the distance as she scurried back to the coach, just missing the first drops of what proved to be a major storm.

The night looked set for quite a bit of drama, thought Portia. She voiced the idea of skipping the awards dinner, thinking the time better used on writing or reading. But Mrs Elksworthy persuaded her to go.

And the night *was* filled with drama, only of a kind Portia couldn't have imagined.

CHAPTER 8

It Was a Dark and Stormy Night

'I think I can fairly speak for everyone when I say, "Thank God that's over".'

It was just nine o'clock and the dinner had ended. Annabelle was sprawled in one of the leather chairs in front of the library fireplace with its serpentine grate, studying the effects of lambent firelight on her glass of brandy. There had been a bit of a crush to get to the bar, as the writers had quickly drunk all the wine allotted them at dinner by Easterbrook.

'The old skinflint,' was Annabelle's comment. 'Some awards dinner. Hard enough to get through the speeches drunk, let alone sober.'

The Dalmorton staff had transformed the barrel-vaulted dungeon-slash-dining room for the event. Three large tables replaced the smaller individual ones, an arrangement Portia thought amounted to putting all the zoo animals together in three cages. She wondered if Lord Easterbrook knew the kind of tension he might be creating by singling out one writer from his list. Most awards, after all, reflected some kind of vote. This was simply a private reward that might have been handed over privately.

Several local Scottish dignitaries, including the local mayor, had been collected for the festivities, arriving importantly in a limousine from Edinburgh. Quentin Swope, wearing a tuxedo T-shirt, had also somehow wangled an invitation, along with Rachel Twalley.

Once again in keeping with sod's law, St Just arrived in the dining room too late to secure a seat next to Portia. This night she was dazzling in a long, blue velvet dress; she had smoothed her hair into a gold net at the nape of her neck, and a blaze of sapphire earrings dropped nearly to her shoulders. She looked, he thought, like a *châtelaine* from another century. He took a seat between Mrs Elksworthy and Annabelle, who wore something long, dark, and drapey that could have been called into service as a *burkha*. Donna Doone trotted in several minutes late, wearing a bugle-beaded red dress that made her look rather as if she'd just escaped a Victorian bordello. The Bracketts arrived last, Tom ordering his wife into the chair next to Annabelle. For the next hour, as Tom worked his way steadily through the courses, he spoke to no one. At one point Rachel tried to volley some pleasantry in his direction, to which Tom – after an appraising, up-and-down stare – did not reply.

They got through the rest of the meal, their aimless chatter and industry gossip magnified by the room's vaulted roof. When the waiters began bringing coffee and dessert, Rachel Twalley rose and began reading from her prepared welcoming speech, which bore an uncanny likeness to her opening remarks at the conference. The evening bore all the hallmarks of the usual interminable awards dinner, in fact, until Lord Easterbrook stood to announce it as his pleasure 'to honor Kimberlee Kalder for writing the best debut novel Deadly Dagger Press or any other publisher has seen in decades . . . or perhaps, ever. Kimberlee Kalder came from obscurity' (here a dark frown creased the perfection of Kimberlee's brow) 'and rose quickly to become the brightest star in the Deadly Dagger galaxy' (the frown disappeared, and the mouth widened in a catlike smirk). 'To prove how highly we honor our successful authors, I am pleased to present Kimberlee this evening with a bonus cheque for thirty thousand pounds.'

A collective gasp came from every corner of the room.

Portia remembered it later as more a howl of outrage, but that may have been Magretta's contribution to the chorus. Kimberlee rose from her chair, dressed in what looked like a white satin slip, and gave an unconvincing show of surprise followed by a long thank-you speech that managed to thank no one or smooth any feathers. Midway through, Tom Brackett walked out, followed by Edith.

When it was over, Portia turned to Mrs Elksworthy.

'Whew. I don't know about you, but I could fancy a brandy.'

'I could fancy several. It might stimulate my thinking on how I might have spent my bonus cheque if one had ever been offered. *Bonus cheque* – whoever heard of such a thing?' Joan Elksworthy's cheeks held a high color, her face an angry expression.

St Just, who had been sidling up on the pair from behind, planning his ambush, was just about to seize the moment when Rachel Twalley approached.

'Would you both like to join us for a drink?' Portia asked.

St Just nodded as Rachel said, 'I thought you'd never ask. A quick one, though, and then home to my husband. Really, sharing a table with Tom was the last straw for me tonight. That man is so *spiky*. I can see why he writes spy novels. Not a word out of him, even under torture.'

'He really was a spy once, wasn't he?' said Portia. 'That's always been the scuttlebutt.'

'If you told me he'd spied for the Russians and they'd refused to let him defect to Moscow, it wouldn't surprise me. Anyway, I heard him inform Edith just now that they were meeting someone in the sitting room, so let's take over the library.'

The library was fashioned in the style of a gentleman's drinking club, all wing chairs and roomy, rumpled sofas, with shelves of crumbling leather-bound books lining the walls. It was sited next to the sitting room at the end of a long hallway, past display windows of clothing, sporting goods, and high-end souvenirs. The library contained a service bar, which was technically in operation twenty-four hours a day, or until the last guest was rendered unconscious, whichever came first, which had made it a natural meeting place throughout the conference. One seating group centered round a wood-burning fireplace; another was clustered near a panoramic window offering a far-ranging view of the castle park. Individual chairs with side tables dotted the corners of the room. Faded Persian rugs were strewn about the vast floor.

Their party, which grew to include B. A. King, Ninette, and Winston – Donna Doone having returned Cinderella-like to her castle duties, with a promise to join the group later – ran into Magretta at the door to the library, waving a sheaf of stationery headed with the Dalmorton crest.

'I'm taking a drink up to my room to work on my new novel.' Her eyes glistened dangerously. 'Research, you know. *Some* of us have to work for a living.'

She cantered off on high heels, green shawl billowing like a sail behind her.

'What's there to research?' wondered Annabelle. She threw back her shoulders, and, puffing out her considerable chest, mimicked: 'Details, details! Verisimilitude is of course important! But people are the same in every age, don't you think? It's the – universality – of the naked human condition, its tawdry hopes and blind ambitions, that I por*tray* in my books.' Laughing guiltily at Annabelle's pitch-perfect imitation, the group began placing orders with the bartender. There was some muttered grumbling that Kimberlee – and Lord Easterbrook – should pick up the tab.

Lord Easterbrook was nowhere to be seen, but Jay Fforde and Kimberlee entered, shoulder to shoulder, and quickly commandeered the view overlooking the grounds. They sat throwing significant glances at each other, backlit in a yellow nimbus cast by the castle floodlights, in a pose that invited no interruptions. Beyond this romantic tableau, Portia could see a strengthening storm whipped by wind; intermittently the room's arched and mullioned windows rattled gently, lending a constant rumbling undercurrent to the buzz of conversation. The wind stepped up its mournful chorus as it moved through the distant trees – a chorus punctuated by shrieks as it skirled through the chimneys and wound past the castle battlements.

Everyone else, including Rachel Twalley and the local dignitaries, drifted into small groupings by the fire (St Just again lost the scrum to sit beside Portia). Before long the talk reverted to the apparently inexhaustible topic of Amazon.com rankings. And from there, Kimberlee being preoccupied safely out of hearing range, the conversation turned to the chick lit trend.

'I don't get it, I really don't,' grumbled Annabelle. 'What exactly is the attraction of crime stories where the heroines teeter around New York and London in stiletto heels swigging martinis and coffee with a mobile glued to their heads? Besides, I never thought a mystery could make any sense written in the first person, present tense.'

'It is rather an interesting technique, though,' said Winston in his deep, melodious voice, 'once you stop noticing how ruddy intrusive it is.' Winston sat folded into his chair, legs and arms jutting in all directions. He put Portia in mind of a grasshopper. 'In comparison, how would you characterize Magretta's work? Romantic suspense?'

'Womjep,' supplied Mrs Elksworthy, leaning in to the group. 'Woman in Jeopardy. As different from Kimberlee's stuff as can be imagined. All creaking staircases and shadowy figures. The heck of it is, Magretta Sincock was the lodestar in the Dagger constellation for a very long time. But – at least to hear her tell it – every word is conceived and produced only by painstaking labor. Kimberlee makes it all look too easy.'

'That local reporter seems to think books like Kimberlee's

are the wave of the future,' said Annabelle. 'Sadly, I think he may be right.'

'Quentin Swope?' asked Ninette, pushing back the heavy fringe over her eyes. 'I saw him just now joining Tom in the sitting room, weighted down by hair gel. Hard to imagine what Tom might have to say about chick lit.'

'Hard to imagine Tom inviting anyone to join him. Harder still to imagine anyone accepting the invitation,' said Annabelle.

'I suppose he's hoping for some positive publicity out of Quentin,' said Winston. 'And I, for one, did accept the invitation – hoping for the same, I don't mind admitting.' He stood. 'I should be getting over there.'

'Judging by what happened to Magretta this morning, that might be a dangerous game,' said B. A. King. 'She should leave publicity to the professionals.' He stood, shooting the cuffs of his dinner jacket. 'I think I'll join you, Winston. Can't hurt to know what's in the pipeline.'

'I wonder,' said Winston, 'if the reporter isn't hoping for an "in" to the book publishing world. If ever I saw someone likely to have an unpublishable novel in his bottom desk drawer, it's Quentin Swope.'

'I rather think it's part of Edith's job to keep that type away from Tom,' said Mrs Elksworthy.

'What an odd couple they make,' said Annabelle. 'She and Tom.'

'Without a doubt,' said Mrs Elksworthy. 'The miracle is that anyone as unpleasant as Tom Brackett managed to attract a mate in the first place. And yet those two have been together a donkey's age, content to all appearances. At least, Tom seems content. Edith merely seems flattened into quiescence.'

'The spy who loved me,' said Winston.

'I've also heard he was a schoolteacher,' said Annabelle, 'which is tremendously difficult to imagine, unless it was in a juvenile detention center. And that he was an actor at one time, but I think that's a story that's become mixed up with a screenwriting stint out in Hollywood. Certainly I've heard most often he was a spy, presumably for our side.'

'He was just bloody rude to Rachel Twalley tonight,' said Winston. 'Not to mention poor Edith. Anyone for another drink before I go?'

Portia thought Winston seemed unusually nervy this evening – unlike the mellow, somewhat melancholy self he most often projected. Probably more of the fallout from Kimberlee's award, she decided.

Donna, having just rejoined them, may have noticed the shift in mood, too. She suddenly asked the group, 'Did I tell you the bar used to be part of a priest's hole? They converted it when the hotel opened.'

'Converted?' said Annabelle. 'No pun intended, I presume. I read somewhere the castle has the requisite ghost, too.'

'The Lady in White. Oh, yes, indeed,' said Donna. 'Most thrilling. It's a woman killed by a jealous wife while her husband was away. Or was it the wife who was killed? I always get it mixed up. Anyway, this had to have been . . . oh, I don't know. Sometime during the Crusades or later. She wanders the halls in a white gown – or so they say. I've not seen her. They do say only those who die young become ghosts. I think it must be true – they've left behind so much unfinished business.'

This led to a swapping of macabre stories of ghosts and hauntings, on which Joan Elksworthy seemed to be an expert. From there, the conversation crisscrossed Scottish history and then, by some strange byway, arrived at the merits of Meryl Streep. Was she a great actress or merely a talented mimic?

'Oh, please,' said Annabelle. She flattened her voice, shrieking a perfect imitation: 'The dingo ate my baby!'

Everyone, laughing, took a turn trying out the phrase.

St Just stole a look at his watch. It was early – just past

9:30. He had sat for the most part in silence, listening, and observing the others – one in particular. A crack of nearby lightning caused him to look over to the window. Kimberlee had slipped out of the room at some point; Jay sat alone, apparently lost in thought, staring into his drink.

St Just, with a glance at Portia as he stood to leave, sighed. He just missed seeing her fleeting look of disappointment at his departure.

Portia left the group around a quarter to eleven as the party was winding down. Rachel Twalley and the Scottish dignitaries had departed long before – Donna Doone had left the library briefly to activate the button that would close the drawbridge behind them.

Portia stole a peek into the sitting room where Tom and Edith, Quentin Swope, and B. A. King sat watching the telly. She waved them goodnight as she passed.

Walking upstairs, Portia saw a figure she couldn't make out just ahead of her, at the curve of the staircase. Oh, my, she thought, grinning to herself. The famous shadowy figure of Magretta's novels. Whoever or whatever it was, she saw it pass by an angular form that could only belong to Winston Chatley.

At that moment, the lights went out. Disoriented, Portia stumbled, grabbing at the railing just in time to keep her balance. The darkness seemed to stretch ahead forever as she stood frozen, unable to decide whether to go up or down.

Great, she thought. All that's missing is Bella Lugosi creeping down the hallway.

She heard, faintly, a man's voice saying, 'Kimberlee?'

Soon afterwards, the same voice was at her elbow.

'Are you all right?'

The flare of a lighter hissed into life and a ghostly, disembodied face, lit from beneath, appeared – the face of a gargoyle.

'Winston?' she said faintly. 'Yes, I'm fine, thanks. Power outage, it looks like.'

'Damn!' The lighter went out. 'Sorry, the metal gets too hot. I can't keep it lit very long. What do you want to do? Go up or down?'

'Do you think you could bring up some candles from the dining room?'

'Good idea,' he said. The lighter shot into flame again as he started down, calling, 'Kimberlee, can you hear me?' He turned back to Portia. 'That's odd. She was just here. Wait for me.'

He returned perhaps ten minutes later, his features again lit eerily from underneath, this time by candlelight. Black shadows played under his dark eyes. Portia had called out Kimberlee's name once or twice in the meantime, but had gotten no response.

Winston handed one candlestick to Portia and they continued up the stairs. They had reached the hallway of the next floor when he asked, 'Where has Kimberlee gone?'

'I don't know,' said Portia. 'I couldn't see or hear anything and she didn't reply when I called to her. I assume she found her way to her room somehow.'

Just then a door off the hallway creaked open. St Just peered out, wearing one of the hotel's white bathrobes over blue-striped pajama bottoms, a book under one arm.

'I've just been trying to read by the fire,' he said. 'It makes you wonder how our ancestors weren't blind by the age of thirty.'

'Most of them were dead of battle, disease, or childbirth well before that became a problem,' she said. Seeing the cover of his book, she added, '*Baudolino*? How are you enjoying that?'

'I've been reading it for two years now,' he said. 'Every time I get to chapter three I get interrupted by something at work. Then I have to start over.'

Just then there was a rumble of thunder followed shortly by a brilliant flash of lightning. The trio having moved into the room to escape the cold of the hallway, Portia crossed over to a window and looked out into the night. She saw Donna Doone far below, moving across an inner courtyard. What on earth could she be thinking, to be out in such a storm? In the light cast by the moon Portia could see she was holding a candle, long extinguished by the wind.

'Do you want to join me for a drink?' Winston asked St Just. 'Maybe just until the power is restored?'

St Just shook his head, stifling a yawn.

'I'll just finish the chapter and be asleep again in ten minutes. It was only the hubbub that woke me up.'

They wished him good night and continued making their slow way down the hallway, the wind outside wailing as it whipped around the turrets.

Suddenly, Portia didn't want to be alone in her room.

'I think I'll go down and find a book to read,' she told Winston. 'I forgot to bring anything with me and the only reading material I have is the conference program.'

'Bound to cause nightmares,' he said, nodding somberly. Then he gave her one of his sudden sweet smiles that took the edge off his saturnine looks. She smiled back.

Just then they both noticed a dark apparition hovering at the foot of the main staircase. As they approached, the specter resolved itself into Donna Doone.

'The bartender says we're all trapped inside,' she told them. 'The drawbridge over the moat is run by electricity, you see.'

'Don't the ropes work mechanically?' asked Winston.

Donna shook her head. 'That rope-and-pulley thing is there only for show. But they think they'll have the generator working soon. What's odd is the backup system seems to have blown as well. Meanwhile, it's eat, drink, and be merry in the bar, but I've had a sufficient amount. I'll see you all tomorrow.'

'A wise choice,' said Winston. 'I'll say good night to both you ladies. If you'll both be all right?'

In the library, Portia found only semi-darkness, with the fireplace relieving the gloom. The scene had shifted somewhat, which was a problem when she later tried to reconstruct the entire evening in her mind: She was not entirely clear who was where, talking to whom. Ninette sat alone on the sofa where Kimberlee and Jay had reigned earlier. She thought she saw Quentin in a distant corner; Annabelle was talking with Mrs Elksworthy. The topic was herbal remedies of the American Indian tribes.

'Root cabbage for asthma, of course. Nothing else works as well.'

Portia greeted the two women, explaining her mission, and found her way over to the nearest wall of books. B. A. King sidled up as her eyes scanned the available titles. The selection ran heavily to musty histories and memoirs of the more obscure members of the Scots Guards. With a sinking heart she heard B. A. ask her about the Fisher murder case, the investigation of which Portia had been involved in when she first arrived at Cambridge.

'There are those, you know, who feel the butler really did do it,' said B. A.

'I know. There are those who feel the earth is flat, but they're wrong. The husband did confess just before he died, were you aware?'

Grabbing a book at random (it later proved to be a battered copy of *Ivanhoe*) and smiling sweetly, she turned quickly to leave. There was something about B. A. – a whiff of the snake-oil salesman clung to him, not to mention a more noticeable odor of whiskey.

At the entrance to the lobby she waited for her eyes to adjust to the gloom. There was no fireplace here to light her way, the vast room seemed to swallow up the candlelight, and everywhere the windows were mere arrow slits set high in the stone walls. She began feeling her way toward the main stairs.

The staff had by now set out candles on the table in the corridor, creating a beacon of light surrounded, however, by pitch darkness. It was as Portia stepped into the shadows she saw – or thought she saw – a figure in white walking away from the door of the bottle dungeon. The figure seemed to disappear into the door at the end of the hallway – an impossibility. Portia shook her head, really regretting the after-dinner brandy now. As she stood peering into the darkness, she sensed a movement behind her. Swinging around, she saw Jay. She could hear at a distance the rest of the library party, rowdily bidding the bartender a good night.

It was then a scream cut through the dark silence. Without visual cues, to Portia the sound seemed to come from everywhere at once. She saw Jay turn in her direction.

Then Magretta came flying out of the door leading to the bottle dungeon. She screamed again when she saw Portia and kept running, surprisingly light on her feet. Portia called after her.

'What is it, Magretta?'

Magretta's voice carried across the darkness, words tossed over her shoulder as she continued hurtling pell-mell up the main staircase.

'Kimberlee!' she cried. 'It's Kimberlee! And she's dead!'

CHAPTER 9

Death's Door

There was little doubt it was Kimberlee Kalder, and less doubt she was dead. She lay on her back at the bottom of the bottle dungeon. Even in the flickering and feeble light of the candle, Portia could see the poor girl's head and neck were twisted at an impossible angle. Her right leg seemed to have snapped just before the knee. She was in her stockinged feet, but in the corner of the horrible little cell where she had died was one of her black, pointed shoes, crouched like a rat. She was wearing the white dress she'd had on that evening for the awards dinner.

But something about the scene was wrong – Portia wasn't sure what. Something was missing or something had been added.

'What is it?'

Portia jumped, nearly shouting at the voice behind her. Mrs Elksworthy was at her shoulder.

'It's Kimberlee. She's dead. Go fetch DCI St Just, would you? Quickly. Have him call the local police and then get him down here. Top of the stairs, the room two doors down on the right.'

Magretta's screams could still be heard, now coming from a floor far above.

'Then for God's sake go and see if you can calm Magretta.'

Mrs Elksworthy seemed frozen to the spot. Portia had seen this kind of reaction before, even in sensible souls, such as

Mrs Elksworthy appeared to be. Especially in sensible souls, to whom the chaos of violent death was an abomination.

'Joan,' Portia said sharply. 'You have to help me.'

Nodding slowly, Mrs Elksworthy started backing up the stairs, her eyes holding Portia's.

'Hurry!' Portia urged. At that Joan turned and ran as quickly as her short legs and the narrow, worn steps would allow. Anxious not to disturb what was clearly a crime scene – there was no way Kimberlee could have just fallen over the banister; it would have been nearly as high as the bottom of her rib cage – Portia crept back up the spiral stairs to the wooden door at the top. Mrs Elksworthy and St Just had just arrived at the foot of the main staircase, both illuminated by candles.

'The local police are on the way,' he said. 'Are you all right?'

Portia nodded absently. 'Think so.' Looking up, she could see every guest on that side of the castle had been alerted that something was amiss. They all seemed to be leaning over the landing banister. All except Tom.

'She's been murdered, Arthur,' Portia said quietly. Her familiar use of his Christian name struck neither of them as odd. 'There's no way she fell.'

St Just, following her gaze to the row of horrified eyes watching them from the landing, turned to Mrs Elksworthy. 'I'll need you to keep everyone out of the way until the police arrive. Will you do that?'

Mrs Elksworthy, who seemed to have aged a decade in the last few minutes, nodded.

'Nothing to worry about,' Portia heard her telling the little assembly a bit later. 'Just an accident, I'm sure. The police will have it sorted in a minute.'

'It will take a lot longer than a minute,' murmured Portia to St Just, following him back down the bottle dungeon stairs. She watched as he, in his turn, looked over the railing and took in the scene.

'Stand here a bit closer with that candle,' he said. 'Mind the wax, though.' He stooped to examine the railing.

'There are what look like fresh marks here in the wood, possibly scratch marks made as she fought off her attacker, or possibly made as her attacker hefted her over the railing. I'll make sure forensics examine those nails of hers. They would have made good weapons, if she got the chance to use them. What do you think?'

He turned to Portia, who was staring intently at the body, with all the clinical detachment of a SOCO.

'Robbery?' he asked.

She shook her head.

'Something was added, or taken away.' The words ran like a mantra through her head. Something . . . missing? Turning, she held her candle aloft to examine the floor around them. In the corner a bit of cellophane glinted, perhaps part of a sweet wrapper – nothing more. 'Damned time for us to lose the lights, don't you think?' she asked. 'It's dark as pitch down here. And she didn't have a candle, unless it's some-how hidden by her body . . . Wait. That's what's missing. She could never have found her way down here in the dark with-out breaking her n – oh, sorry. But you can see what I mean. She didn't fall down the stairs and pop over the railing to end up in the bottle dungeon. Maybe she made it this far on her own steam and then there was a struggle. Or she was pushed down the stairs and someone heaved her body over the rail. She wasn't a large person; it's just possible that's what happened.'

'We'll see what forensics has to say,' said St Just. 'Oh, for pity's sake.'

'What?'

'We're forgetting, there's no way in here with the draw-bridge up.'

She looked at him.

'Try calling them on your mobile,' she said. 'They'll have to get across the moat somehow and break in through one of the lower windows.' Then, noticing his look, she said, 'What?'

'Do you always plan ahead for emergencies like this?'

'It's just that I was photographing the lower windows yesterday. The stonework is fascinating. What we really need is the fire department with a ladder.'

'What we really need is a portable generator. And a land line. Mobiles weren't designed for stone walls thick enough to withstand a siege,' he said. 'One thing's nearly certain: It was an inside job. There's no way anyone could have got in from outside, not without getting soaking wet and leaving tracks like a badger, at any rate.'

They heard the sound of sirens wailing somewhere off in the distance, growing steadily louder as emergency vehicles peeled up the road. St Just and Portia again walked up the stone stairs, nearly colliding with Donna Doone at the top. 'Is there no way to get that generator going?' he asked her, fruitlessly punching numbers into his mobile.

She shook her head.

'Robbie says the battery's depleted or overheated or it froze at some point or something. He's got a call in for a portable replacement, but if you ask me, it's Robbie should be replaced.'

'It can't be lowered manually, the bridge?'

She sighed in frustration. 'Winston asked the same thing. You would think that would be an option, wouldn't you? It used to be, but the rope was damaged and never repaired.'

Portia, meanwhile, walked over to one of the windows at one side of the drawbridge. An ambulance and two police cars, a panel of lights flashing across the top of each, were pulled up outside. Five policemen were on the lawn, staring helplessly across at her. Not knowing what else to do, she waved and then with her forefinger and smallest finger, mimicked someone talking on a telephone. One of the men, small and white-haired, sprinted over to his car; minutes later the phone rang at the reception desk. St Just ran over and picked it up.

'Yes, it's murder,' Portia heard him say as she approached. 'Is fire on the way? Good. You'll need a ladder and some way to winch up a portable generator. Yes, I know, it's incredible they didn't realize. A fuel-generated power source would have prevented it.'

So it was that half an hour later, the hotel guests, who by this point had gathered in Mrs Elksworthy's room, as having the best view, were treated to the sight of firemen wading waist deep in moat muck over to the base of the castle, carrying overhead a ladder up which they proceeded to climb, and gaining entry through one of the lower, unused bedrooms. Two men carrying a generator in a sling followed behind; it was hoisted knapsack-style by the two men at the window. St Just, Portia, and Donna were there to greet them.

'We'll need the guests' cooperation,' said St Just. 'Everything that isn't powering that drawbridge will have to remain shut off.'

Donna went to find Robbie and his maintenance crew. Some time later, to the sound of faint cheering from Mrs Elksworthy's room, the grind and moan of the drawbridge coming down could be heard.

'DCI St Just of the Cambridgeshire Constabulary,' he said, and held out a hand to the Scottish DCI, resisting the temptation to bend at the knees to meet him on a more level playing field. Ian Moor was an elfin man who must just have passed the height requirement for acceptance onto the force. He wore a handlebar mustache that looked pasted on but undoubtedly was real – two dramatic white swoops that cupped either side of his round face. It was a face mobile and alive with an expression of happy anticipation; his eyes twinkled with evident pleasure at having a brand-new case to solve.

St Just pulled out his wallet and opened it with a reflexive snap. Moor took the leather holder from his hand and stared at his photo ID with the gimlet eye of a museum curator presented with a suspicious artifact. Then, ostensibly satisfied, he closed the wallet with deliberate care before handing it back.

'Cambridgeshire. Lovely town, Cambridge. The wife and I went there on one of those charabanc tours one summer. Boring place, really, isn't it?'

St Just smiled. For one thing, he hadn't heard anyone use the word charabanc for twenty years.

'Sometimes. When the students aren't around, certainly it can be a quiet place.'

Moor grunted. 'Not Scotland Yaird, then.' He gave St Just a beatific smile. 'Worse luck for us. With their help, we could have wrapped this up by teatime.'

The Scottish policeman looked around at the crowd again gathering at the top of the stairs, like children spying on the grown-ups' party.

'These would be the crime writers, then?'

'Yes.'

'And you, Sir. You're a writer, too – in your spare time, perhaps?'

'Not I. A happy life for me. I'm here to deliver a talk at the conference being held at the Luxor in Edinburgh. Anyway, the young woman over there' – and he indicated Portia, standing by the hall table, a ghostly apparition surrounded by candlelight – 'she was among the first to find the body.'

The two men, now joined by another whom St Just took to be Moor's sergeant, walked over to Portia. The policeman introduced himself as DCI Ian Moor and his far more subdued companion as Sergeant Kittle.

Portia nodded. Kittle had a face like a ruined monastery. A perfect character for my book, she thought reflexively.

'Portia De'Ath,' she said. She made as if to offer a handshake, but Moor hadn't paused for the formalities. He continued on through the door into the bottle dungeon and down the stairs, where they all – except Portia, who, at a signal from Kittle, held back – followed him to the guardrail. The three policemen stood looking at Kimberlee's body, flung like a rag doll at the bottom.

'Bloody hell,' said Moor. 'How are we going to get a team down there?'

He turned and looked back up the stairs at Portia.

'Who is she?' he asked her.

'Kimberlee Kalder. A writer.'

'A successful one?'

'Very, in the US especially, but also here.'

'Jealousy?'

St Just noticed Portia seemed to have no trouble following DCI Moor's rather telegraphic mode of questioning.

'Maybe. She earned a lot, and very quickly. She was quite young and had become a multimillionaire with her first book. The rest of the writers here, nearly all of them, have toiled for years – decades – with far less success. Kimberlee also didn't go too far out of her way to ingratiate herself with the others.'

'I don't know . . . That's a far-fetched motive for murder,' said Moor.

'I think you'll find that within the culture of this group, it's not at all far-fetched,' said Portia.

'But,' said St Just, speaking more to himself than the others, 'why kill her here, at the conference? Rather a public choice . . .'

'Maybe because something happened here,' said Moor.

'The award,' said Portia, who proceeded to tell him about the night's dinner.

'It was an extraordinarily tactless thing for Easterbrook to do,' she concluded. 'There was already some feeling that his long-time writers were being neglected, chucked out, and/or replaced. And God knows, if anyone needed the ego boost of an award – not to mention thirty thousand pounds – it wasn't Kimberlee.'

'Ms De'Ath noticed something that's undoubtedly

important,' St Just told Moor. 'There is no means of producing light – no candlestick or lighter – on or about the victim's body. At least, so far as we can tell without moving the body. Kimberlee either came down here before the lights went out—'

'Or she came down here with someone who had a light,' Moor finished for him.

'There's no handbag, either,' said St Just. 'She had one at the dinner. Some small, sparkly thing like women carry in the evening.'

'An evening bag,' offered Portia.

'Right. An evening bag. She may just have left it in her room. She's still wearing her jewelry. . .'

Portia again spoke up. 'You can forget robbery as a motive. I never saw her with jewelry of any value. What she had on tonight – still has on – is costume jewelry, enameled. Of a good quality, but not real jewelry. That's a nice watch she has on, though, and she's still wearing it.'

DCI Moor, who only just now seemed to wonder how this civilian had injected herself so thoroughly into his case, turned deliberately to St Just to ask his next question:

'Did she generally carry anything else worth stealing? Large sums of money?'

'I wouldn't know,' said St Just. 'I have to agree with Ms De'Ath here. It doesn't look to me as if she had anything on her worth stealing, apart from the watch. And wearing that dress, it's unlikely in the extreme she could have anything hidden on her person.'

DCI Moor scratched at the slight growth of white stubble on his chin. 'The storm is going to help us,' he said at last.

'How so?'

'The road was near to impassable earlier tonight. It was really chucking it down, and for ages. No one came here by car, I'd wager. We barely made it through ourselves.'

'You are thinking one of the staff, or one of the guests in the hotel. . .?'

Moor nodded. 'And you agree?'

'Someone could have come in on foot through the woods, over the grounds . . . but it's doubtful,' said St Just. 'For one thing, there's too big a chance of being seen – nearly all the rooms have a prospect. They'd be soaking, besides.'

Moor nodded.

'We're lucky in other ways. Sometimes we have the haar this time of year, working to the advantage of the villains. Making them harder to spot, you see.'

At St Just's questioning look, he explained:

'It's a fog – dense as foam, it is – that comes in from the North Sea. You could hide your granny inside the haar and she'd not be found for days. Who is here besides the crime writers?'

'The staff, mainly,' said St Just. 'Lord Easterbrook took over the place for the writers, exclusively. He also invited a couple of writers' agents, and a publicist.'

'How many people are we talking about?' asked Moor.

'The Easterbrook party? About ten or eleven of them.'

St Just turned to Portia for confirmation.

'And someone brought Quentin Swope, the reporter,' she said. 'He got stuck here by the storm, I guess – by the drawbridge's not working. I saw him sitting with the group watching the telly just before we lost the lights. Oh, and Rachel Twalley, from the conference – she left earlier, with a contingent of Edinburgh nobs. Donna Doone, the hotel's event coordinator, closed the drawbridge behind them. Lucky escape for Rachel, that.'

'How well do you know these people?' asked Moor of St Just.

'I've known them for just a few days, during the conference.'

'And you?' Moor asked Portia. 'How well, for example, did you know this Kimberlee? Can someone spell that for me, by the way?'

Portia complied, adding, 'I knew her hardly at all. She was on the train with me from London. Friendly . . . to a point.

But she slept most of the way, so there was little time for confidences. Actually, I didn't gather the impression Kimberlee was given to confidences. As to the rest of them: We've all more or less bumped into each other before on the circuit – seen each other at conferences and things.'

'But not Kimberlee?'

She shrugged.

'Kimberlee was what you call an overnight sensation. I don't know how well the others knew her. Kimberlee and I share, or shared, an agent – Ninette Thomson – who may know her fairly well. At least she may have known her for some time – not quite the same thing, is it?'

Portia added that they were all scheduled to leave tomorrow.

'Today, rather. Sunday,' she said.

'No,' said Moor.

St Just also shook his head. 'No one goes anywhere for the foreseeable future.'

Moor turned to St Just, indicating the stairs.

'Come along, Cambridge. You may as well lend a hand so long as you're here.'

St Just hesitated. 'I have virtually no authority here. You know that.'

'Of course. None, really.'

This last came out as 'noon rally' to Portia's ears. She looked mystified for a moment, then St Just saw the penny drop, and smiled. He had a sudden nostalgic turn for 'Agnes the Cook' – an ancient, ribald Scottish lady in a nursing home in Cornwall who had been a key witness in a case of his the year before.

'But then,' Moor went on, 'the suspects won't know that until it's too late. I say what goes on in my patch and I say you're helping us with inquiries – I'll square it with your Super, never fear. And you being a Sasannach is something I'm willing to overlook. Have to make allowances sometimes, you know.'

This last was said with a smile to take the edge off – barely. St Just knew it wasn't worth arguing that he was hardly a Saxon. He lived in England and that was enough as far as Moor was concerned.

St Just suddenly did not fancy any lag's chances up against Ian Moor. There was more going on behind that jolly Father Christmas-mustachioed façade than met the eye.

For that reason, he didn't bother to ask why Moor didn't first have him, St Just, checked out for rogue-cop tendencies: He felt certain the Scottish detective was already planning to do just that.

By now they had reached the top of the bottle dungeon stairs and entered the hallway. They could see across the lobby and through to the drawbridge where, in time-honored fashion, three workmen were standing around chatting, presumably 'supervising' the work of the one doing the actual work, a man displaying an impressive buttock cleavage at the top of his jeans. Repairs on the drawbridge mechanism were apparently continuing.

One of the hotel's maids appeared near the reception area, handily carrying a tray that had to be half her body weight. Apparently the beleaguered guests were to be provided tea to calm their nerves. She – St Just recalled her name as Florie – seemed to register the same workman's phenomenon; as she passed down the hallway, St Just heard her fume, 'Lazy sods. *Three* women would have had that fixed already – but for this we bring in reinforcements.' She strode toward the drawbridge as if to drop off this opinion on her way.

Moor turned to St Just.

'Who knows? With your help, maybe we'll all get to go home just that wee bit sooner.'

'All except for the murderer,' said St Just.

'Yes.' Again, the twinkle that was nearly a wink. Moor did seem to be a man who enjoyed his work. 'Except for the murderer.'

CHAPTER 10

The Game's Afoot

The investigation began with a search of Kimberlee Kalder's room, Inspector Moor first having directed his team to collect statements from everyone in the castle, staff and guests alike. But St Just also heard him say the guests were the real focus, and he couldn't but agree with that strategy. With sexual assault to all appearances ruled out, along with robbery, it was hard to see how the staff were involved, barring a complete lunatic having gotten past the hotel's human resources department.

'Tell them they are not to go back to their rooms until we give them permission to do so,' Moor concluded his instructions. Donna Doone was dispatched from her current occupation of fluttering anxiously about the lobby to find the best place to interview witnesses. Eventually they settled on two of the hotel's small meeting rooms on the second floor, the St Andrew and the round-walled Sir Walter Scott.

Donna having provided them a passkey, the three men – DCI St Just, DCI Moor, and Sergeant Kittle – entered Kimberlee's room, knowing they couldn't do much before SOCO arrived but take a visual survey.

St Just thought he would have known it was Kimberlee's room without having to be told. Clothes were strewn everywhere, in a lacy black and hot pink explosion that looked, somehow, viral against the red tartan décor. Not just a blouse or two draped over a chair, either – it was as if the entire contents of a woman's boutique had been tipped into the room. Many items still wore their price tags. He took a peek at one, being careful of prints, and winced at the triple-digit cost.

He walked over to a small desk by the window. He imagined that daylight would reveal a spectacular view encompassing the castle grounds and forest, the swollen banks of the normally placid River Esk, and the river pasture beyond. Just then a shaft of moonlight revealed a deer emerging tentatively from a screen of trees. Something or someone must have frightened it awake. St Just watched until it retreated safely back into the forest.

He looked down at the desktop. It held a room service tray with a bottle of wine, two unused glasses, and the leavings of assorted kibbles – cheese, biscuits, and the like. In addition, the desktop was littered with all manner of detritus: little pots of make-up, manicuring equipment, and a small, strange device of metal and rubber that Moor later identified for him as an eyelash curler ('I've got four teenage girls at home. I haven't seen the inside of the upstairs bathroom in ten years but I could spot an eyelash curler at forty paces'). Little jewelry, but what there was, as Portia had pointed out, was good quality. Her evening bag was there, no doubt with Lord Easterbrook's cheque inside. No manuscript, St Just noted. No laptop, either.

But wasn't Kimberlee supposed to be working on her new book? He mentioned this lack to Moor, currently investigating the contents of Kimberlee's wardrobe.

'I have never,' said that redoubtable Scotsman, 'been able to understand how anyone, man or woman, can tolerate these things.' He held out, draped over a pencil, a frilly pink thong edged in black.

St Just pointed out the relative lack of anything like writerly equipment.

'No laptop. No manuscript. No paper, except the handful

of letterhead provided by the castle. There is a Montblanc fountain pen over there on the dresser.' Automatically he thought of Portia and his first sighting of her at St Germaine's. He supposed an expensive fountain pen might be the celebratory purchase of a writer on making his or her first sale.

'I'm not really surprised,' said Moor. 'She was here on a holiday of sorts, wasn't she?'

St Just, nodding, still wasn't sure what to make of it. Would a writer travel anywhere in the world without something to write on? *Portia will know*, he thought.

'Maybe there's a notebook, at least, in her purse,' said St Just. 'I don't want to rummage around in there until it's been dusted. There's a mobile phone on the desktop, buried under the make-up gear – we'll need someone to look into that, of course.'

He again looked across at the dresser, where copies of Kimberlee's book lay scattered about. There was also a romance book of the bodice-ripper sort, by one Leticia-Anne Deville, titled *When Summer's Passion Lingers*. It didn't immediately strike him as Kimberlee's kind of book, but he would have been hard put to say what Kimberlee's type of book may have been. He picked it up, using his handkerchief. Then he saw something from the corner of his eye.

'Oh, wait,' he said, crossing the room. 'She was writing something, after all. But it's a letter. She'd evidently been using one of these books as a surface to write on, rather than the desk.'

He held up a note on castle stationery, written in a round, childish script that just avoided having its 'i's' dotted with smiley faces.

'So this may have been what she had been doing between leaving the bar and going for her fatal excursion to the dungeon,' said Moor. St Just and Portia had filled him in as best they could remember or knew of Kimberlee Kalder's movements of the night before.

'Possibly,' said St Just. 'She could have written it earlier on, of course. Whenever it was, she was interrupted.'

He began reading aloud, with as deadpan a delivery as he could manage:

'"Dearest Darling: What agony – to see but not *be* with you! Only awhile longer and the charade ends! But you are right, my dearest. We must play it cool, especially in front of the wrinklies. This must remain our secret . . . must make sure he doesn't suspect . . . clever of you to think of a way. But – so soon! Patience! – we'll be united in love forever!!! First I have to—"'

'The letter breaks off in mid-sentence.' St Just turned the page toward Moor. 'Perhaps she ran out of exclamation marks. It almost sounds like something Magretta would write, actually.'

Moor grunted.

'A love letter.'

'Or a suicide note.'

Moor widened his eyes.

St Just said, 'I'm joking. Kimberlee was the least likely person in the world to cheat everyone of her presence. It is, of course, a love letter.'

St Just reread the note to himself, frowning.

Sergeant Kittle, on his hands and knees at the moment, looking under the bed, said, 'Maybe a London boyfriend she was planning to meet up with later. Otherwise, why write a letter? Why not just tell him to his face, for heaven's sake?'

'No,' said St Just. 'She talks about the "agony" of seeing him. He's here. Remember they're all writers, this lot. Probably she saw the opportunity to write a longing, soulful love letter as too good to pass up. It's a dying art in the days of the text message, one would imagine. Maybe the whole thing is just some writer-type exercise, a limbering-up activity that she meant to throw away. "Must make sure he doesn't suspect." Make sure who doesn't suspect?'

'Someone at the conference, presumably,' said Moor.

'Or even, someone she just doesn't want to get wind of what's in the air. Fear of spreading gossip.'

'I suppose that's possible,' agreed Moor. 'But, just by the way, there's nothing there to indicate that letter wasn't addressed to a female.'

St Just regarded him thoughtfully.

'It's not impossible, of course,' he said. 'But if you'd ever met her you would know how unlikely that is. Insofar as Kimberlee Kalder was able to direct her attention outside herself, I'd say her inclinations were heterosexual – rather insistently so.'

'Did she travel here alone, do we know?' asked Kittle, now shooing the dust off his knees.

'Ms De'Ath said they traveled up together, but I didn't get the impression that was by prearrangement. If Kimberlee got on the train alone, someone still might have traveled 'with her,' but in a different compartment. Or the same someone, traveling on a different train altogether, or by car or plane, could have met up with her here. In either event, Kimberlee and whoever it was may have made a point of not being seen traveling together – from the tenor of that letter that's certainly what they would do.'

Again, he read the short letter aloud.

'So, we agree,' St Just said, 'the Dearest Darling to whom this is addressed is here at the conference, but she is asking him – or rather, agreeing – that he should make himself scarce and pretend they don't know each other well – at least, in front of the wrinklies and "him". I have to say she seemed quite taken with Jay Fforde and made no secret of it.'

'Right,' said Moor. 'And it sounds as if she's cheating on someone else by seeing Jay. Someone here at the hotel?'

'We should be so lucky,' said St Just. 'That would narrow the field considerably. Let's see. . .' He began ticking off the list on his left hand. 'There's Winston Chatley and B. A. King. Now, Winston is a compelling personality. I've noticed he's attractive to the ladies, despite the fact he resembles an Easter Island statue. My sense is that women trust and like him. So I suppose he's a possible. And B. A. King is a good-looking man in a going-to-seed kind of way, if otherwise repellent. She might have considered him a diamond in the rough, but it's a real stretch. Besides, I overheard her quarreling with him. Lord Easterbrook – I'm not sure . . . he's far older, but a May-December romance isn't completely out of the question. She might see forging an alliance like that as some kind of career enhancer. Then there's that reporter chap – highly unlikely, I would say, unless she thought he could come in useful to her somehow. He's near her in age, but Kimberlee was, in her way, eons older in terms of savvy. Tom Brackett? – an impossibility, on the surface, at any rate. He's well off, or so I gather, but she's well off-er, if you follow – or, she was. Also, he's married, but I see his personality as the real deterrent for a young and attractive woman like Kimberlee.

'Then, of course, there's Jay Fforde, the most likely suspect – very polished looking, very *soigné*, very much the Head Boy type. But I suppose they're all possibles, some more than others.'

'Then again, there are the men attending the conference who are staying in town rather than here at Dalmorton,' said Moor. He held up a conference brochure he'd retrieved from the dresser, using his handkerchief, and flipped it open to the center. Together, the two detectives peered at the list of authors in attendance. There were at least seventy-five masculine names.

'There's no list of attendees,' St Just pointed out. 'Just the authors. So I'm not sure what good this will do us. There are far too many people involved for us to interview them all.'

'And today was the last day of the conference, anyway,' said Moor. 'We certainly can't tell over two hundred people not to leave town. Well, we could, but most of them would never listen.'

Sergeant Kittle, emerging from Kimberlee's bathroom, where he'd been taking notes on the contents, said to the other two men, 'So this Kalder woman writes a letter. How was she going to deliver it? By mail? That makes no sense if the conference ended today.'

'My guess is – if she weren't just writing to hear herself "think" – she was planning to hand it to him clandestinely,' said St Just. 'It would add to the cloak-and-dagger drama of the whole thing. In fact, the more I think of it, that's exactly what I think she'd do.'

'Which means. . .' said Moor.

'Which means whoever it is may be at the castle.'

'Or may be at the conference, where she was going to slip him the note today.'

'Right.' St Just sighed. 'Back to square one, aren't we? Although . . . would she bother with a note today, with the conference over at noon? What would be the point of that? It seems more likely the intended recipient was here. Clandestine, romantic skulking around the castle – a candlelit castle, as it happened; she would have loved that – passing notes on a Saturday night . . . slipping a note under someone's door . . . that I can see her doing.'

'I wonder what interrupted her writing the note.'

'I wondered that, as well,' said St Just.

Inspector Moor asked, 'Had you noticed her being extra friendly with any one man at the conference?'

'She was friendly with most of them,' said St Just. 'More so than with the women, I'd say. Kimberlee liked to be admired, and she didn't shy from creating opportunities for admiring male glances.' He shook his head. 'The thing you must realize is that I know almost nothing about her – or about any of the rest of them, for that matter. In her case, it is because I didn't actively seek her out. She was very much the keenly ambitious type of female of which I, personally, am terrified. What little I do know is from her little biography in the program you're holding there.'

DCI Moor flipped to the relevant page. After a moment's reading, he summarized it for St Just.

'From near Northampton originally, read business at Cambridge – there's a surprise – wrote a weekly gossip column for a small newspaper in Sheffield. From there to London, where I gather she was a bit of a Sloane Ranger. Worked at what I'd call a rich girl's job in the fashion magazine world . . . followed by a novel, followed by riches beyond anyone's wildest dreams of avarice, I'm sure. It says here she "lives in London and New York." Either one alone would break any normal person's piggy bank.'

St Just nodded. 'I understand there's a lot of money involved. No starving artist, she. Who inherits, I wonder?'

'I'll get my team on the inheritance angle. She might have a solicitor somewhere. We might also ask, whom did she injure? To whom was she a threat?'

'What do you say we get her agent up here and see what she knows?'

Sergeant Kittle was dispatched to fetch Ninette Thomson from downstairs.

The two inspectors continued walking about the room, dangling the occasional frothy item of women's clothing at the tip of a pen or pencil. Then St Just said:

'It is rather odd, now I think of it: Kimberlee didn't give the impression of someone with heirs, but we all have heirs, don't we? Somewhere up or down the "line" there is a bloodline. In the case of Kimberlee, though, so much was manufactured, so much for show. I wonder if she had parents still living, people who will mourn her?'

'What I wonder is if the boyfriend was someone in that *Latte* book,' said Moor.

St Just shrugged. 'A possibility. What, are you saying you've read her?'

'Absorbed her, more like. Remember – four teenage daughters at home, all wanting to work in the fashion industry.

Not a doctor or lawyer or accountant in the bunch, worse luck.'

'Or policewoman. Hmm. I had heard the book was in the nature of an exposé. . .'

'No, more like a roman . . . roman. . .'

'*Roman à clef*?'

'That's it, yes. Real people disguised as fictional people.'

'That could make the wrong type of person angry, if they didn't appreciate the way they were portrayed,' said St Just.

'Very,' said Moor.

St Just noticed he was still carrying the romance novel.

'It's a low priority, I'm sure, but have someone find out if Leticia-Anne Deville is a pseudonym for one of these writers here.'

They heard muffled footsteps outside the door.

'Let's see if this agent of hers knows where at least some of the bodies are buried.'

CHAPTER 11

Practicing to Deceive

They met Ninette Thomson in the deserted hallway. St Just, who had spoken with her during the conference only briefly, took a moment now to assess the woman. Of medium height and build, she wore a leopard-skin tunic over black stretch pants, and ballet slippers. She was probably somewhere in her late forties to early fifties, but with an unnatural tautness to her skin and fullness to her lips that spoke of aggressive and frequent cosmetic intervention. As a result she looked not so much younger than her years but like a goldfish wearing hoop earrings. Her thick hair was dyed blue-black and cut in a geometric shape St Just associated with Dusty Springfield and the go-go sixties. Her heavily kohl-lined eyes harked back to a similar influence.

Not a tear or snuffle disturbed the make-up. She posited the almost obligatory question of those interviewed in connection with a murder – 'Who could have done this?' she asked in a rhetorical manner – and then seemed ready to get down to brass tacks.

'You were Kimberlee Kalder's agent, we are told,' said Moor.

Ninette nodded, setting her thick fringe in motion.

'I had the privilege, yes.'

'And for how long had you shared this relationship?'

'It was about two years ago she submitted her novel to me, asking me to represent her. There's a day I'll never forget. Let

107

me tell you straight off: Some called *Latte* a flagrant piece of mind-numbing crap. So it was – to those of a certain age. I also knew from the first moment I saw it that it would be a hit. It was a nervy book, a fast read, a fun escape: Just what the public will plunk down twenty quid for. A diversion.'

'And written by a woman with model looks thrown into the bargain,' said St Just. 'There's no question she did write her own books?'

That set the fringe swinging like a beaded curtain.

'Have you been listening to the tittle-tattle of jealous minds, or was that just a trial balloon? I know Kimberlee seemed too good to be true, somehow, but I'd stake my life the writing was hers. Oh, I had to hire a freelance editor to clean up the manuscript a bit. There was a tremendous energy to what she wrote, but she wrote quickly and she could be a bit sloppy as a result.'

'So there's no question of *Latte* being ghostwritten, anything like that? No jealous ghostwriter seething in the background, thinking he or she should have been paid more?'

'No question at all. Of course it's not unheard of for an established author at some point to let his image be used while someone else does the actual work of writing his books.'

'And in this case?' St Just prompted.

She looked him straight in the eye, a panda peering from the bamboo forest.

'In this case, no. She wasn't established, for one thing. Just trust me on this, and don't let that girly ditz-brain act of hers fool you. She liked giving the impression that deciding whether to wear strappy heels or flats was the day's biggest decision. But she has – had – a mind like a computer. She knew what she looked like; she knew what she had going for her, and she wasn't shy about using it to her advantage. So what? She wrote a book calculated to the last comma to hit its target market, and it did.'

'Which was?'

'Roughly, Sloane Rangers and those who aspire to similar status. Every girl out there who imagines she's going to dabble in PR or design leather handbags or write children's books and finally end up at the altar of St Paul's, hanging on Prince William's arm. *And* more than a few middle-aged ladies who daydream the same.'

'I see.' He stole a glance at Moor, who was nodding.

'My daughters all wanted a flat in Chelsea after reading it. *As* – as they would say – *if*.'

Ninette was nodding vigorously again.

'You see? Harmless fantasy – well, one imagines it's harmless – but it hit a real nerve. There have been imitators since, but Kimberlee Kalder got in first.'

'I do see,' said St Just. He turned to Moor as if to indicate the floor was his, but Moor, with a wave of his hand, abjured.

St Just thought a moment. 'Would you say she had rivals?' he said at last.

'I would say she had enemies.'

At St Just's encouraging look, she went on:

'Not that she went out of her way to harm people. It's just that for Kimberlee Kalder, no one existed but Kimberlee Kalder. It was a style that, shall we say, took some getting used to.'

'Really.'

'I'll tell you who loved her, though,' Ninette continued. 'Lord Easterbrook. Not in the romantic sense, of course. In the sense that she saved his bacon. I wonder what the poor man is going to do now.'

'I imagine you will miss her for much the same reasons,' put in Moor.

'Quite,' she said. 'A real money earner, she was, and now she's gone...'

St Just waited in vain for the prospect of financial loss, at least, to start the waterworks, but Ninette spoke with an ethereal detachment, as if the topic were quite remote from anything surrounding her life. Still, he knew that shock could manifest itself in exactly such a way. The reality could take days, weeks, even months to sink in.

'So,' St Just said, 'tell me about our host here, Dagger Press.'

'What about it?'

'Specifically, what can you tell me about Easterbrook, the man who brought us all here together?'

Ninette examined a cuticle before answering, then looked at the policemen in turn. The sound of Sergeant Kittle's taking advantage of the pause to flip to a new page in his notebook seemed to unsettle her.

'Well, the publishing house itself began as a rich man's hobby – eighty, ninety years ago. Possibly it was even meant to fail, as some sort of income fiddle. But Lord Easterbrook's grandfather hadn't counted on the Golden Age of mystery writing kicking in right about then. He made a ruddy fortune instead.'

'So Easterbrook inherited a going concern,' said St Just.

Ninette nodded. 'And married a wealthy woman. Never hurts to have backup insurance, does it? Anyway, fast-forward to the present day, where the market is glutted but still writers crank out novels like sausage links. An apt analogy that,' she added. 'I must remember it. Anyway, the field is lucrative for some but, frankly, it's getting crowded with too much of the same old thing. Kimberlee turned out to be the breath of fresh air the whole show needed. She was a born publicity machine and quickly established a "persona". She also had the instincts of a natural actress, where most writers are naturally shy. Wasn't it Agatha Christie who said she took up writing so she wouldn't have to speak in public? That's true of most writers.'

'But not Kimberlee,' said St Just.

'*Not* Kimberlee,' she said. 'God, no. The woman was born with a microphone in her hand. Lord Easterbrook needed a personality more than he needed another author, and with

Kimberlee he got that in spades. What can I say? Publishing is a strange business.'

'Let me share with you an observation,' said St Just. 'I can see what you mean when you indicate she was sharp, intelligent. But then she'd come out with some gushing, Valley-Girl rubbish. . .'

Again Ninette nodded.

'She was inconsistent. She wasn't pitch perfect. Would have been, given time. It was an act – somewhat O.T.T., if you know what I mean – and the cracks showed through the plaster here and there.'

'So there was a conflict with her real character or personality,' said St Just. 'I see.'

Sergeant Kittle spoke up just then.

'So who was killed, her or the "over-the-top" person she pretended to be?'

St Just thought it an excellent question, but said nothing. Ninette shrugged.

'I imagine you have contact information for her friends or family,' said Moor. 'And her solicitor. Please leave the details with Sergeant Kittle – it could save us time tracking people down. Do you have anything more to add?'

'No. Just that I don't know who her solicitor was, if she had one.'

St Just picked up a very slight hesitation.

'You're certain you've nothing to add?'

Ninette sighed and wrapped her leopard-print arms tightly around her midriff.

'I may as well tell you,' she said. 'You're bound to hear it from one of the gossipmongers down below. Kimberlee was giving every sign of leaving me. For Jay's agency. Jay Fforde.'

St Just eyed her sympathetically. 'Not a great show of gratitude there.'

'You can repeat that. After all I'd done for her.'

'There was no way to stop her? No contract tying her to you?'

'Of course there was, but surely you know how the law works, or fails to work, as well as I do – better than I do. I could have sued her and *probably* I would have won, but what would it have cost me – and not just in pounds sterling? As someone said in a different context, it would be an expense of spirit chasing after her – and very bad publicity. Kimberlee counted on me not wanting a public squabble. No. I think in the end I'd have just let her go.'

'But, obviously, you weren't happy,' put in Moor.

'I was gored, but I wouldn't kill anyone over it, if that's what you're implying. We rather quickly reached the "over my dead body" stage of negotiations, Kimberlee and I, but it was just business as usual. And a cut-throat business it is. Oh, God, she wasn't. . .?'

'Killed with a knife?' St Just shook his head.

'Thank heaven for that. I guess. Anyway, here's what you need to take away from any discussion about Kimberlee, if you want to find out who did this: In the way that a baby will think a person ceases to exist when he's no longer in the same room, so for Kimberlee most people ceased to exist when she wasn't physically with them. I found it to be . . . an eerie quality. Other people may have found her indifference harder to take. Her self-absorption was near-total.'

She paused.

'There's one other thing I suppose I should mention.'

'Yes?'

'You do realize that many of the writers Kimberlee so loved to trash were authors Jay had at some point turned down or let go.'

'How do you think she came to know so much about it?' asked Moor.

Ninette turned to him.

'That's just it. I should think pillow talk was the answer.

You only had to look at the pair of them. The body language, the way she hung on his every word. Or pretended to.'

St Just leveled an assessing gaze her way.

'Well, thank you,' he said. 'I appreciate your analysis. It might have a bearing. We'll speak again soon.'

The panda eyes grew, if possible, rounder. 'I have to get back to London. You can't keep us here forever.'

'No, but for the time being we can and we must. Now, I need everyone to continue to stay off this floor awhile longer. Be sure the others downstairs understand that as well – they are to stay put.'

The three policemen watched her go. Re-entering Kimberlee's room and closing the door, DCI Moor said: 'I've seen women have a stronger emotional attachment to their washer and drier.'

'So have I,' said St Just. 'Strange – she seems largely unaffected on both the personal and financial levels. We saw only that little spurt of annoyance over Kimberlee's defection, but that really had to have hurt – her pocketbook, if nothing else. Maybe it's just her poker face. I understand all agents have one.'

'Maybe it's Botox,' said Moor. 'She was anxious enough to bring agent Jay into the close circle of suspects, wasn't she? Well, what's next?'

Just then there was a knock on the door and a young constable entered, clutching a sheaf of papers – his notes from the interviews downstairs so far.

'There's a Tom Brackett down there raising holy hell. He says he's a diabetic and needs his medication in one hour.'

'I hope you said you'd fetch it,' said Moor.

'I wanted to clear it with you, Sir.'

Moor sighed.

'Just disturb nothing else in his room, touch nothing else. For God's sake, that's all we need is a suspect collapsing and claiming police brutality. Any other bleats of protest about the room search?' Moor asked the uniform.

'Not a one. It's different from searching someone's home, isn't it? At least, they all seem to think so.'

Moor picked Kimberlee's pink boa off the bedstead and gave it a jaunty little shake before dropping it again. 'Come along then. I think we've done all we can here. Let's have a look at the other boudoirs.'

CHAPTER 12

Search Me

The men left, locking Kimberlee's room behind them and stationing a broad-shouldered constable outside as insurance. As part of the process of elimination, they started with a search of St Just's room across the hall. He waited outside. Nothing sinister being in evidence there, the men moved on to the authors' rooms. Moor pulled from his pocket a printout sheet of room assignments which Donna Doone had earlier provided the police.

'Let's begin with Magretta Sincock's room,' he said, pointing a stubby finger at the list. 'It's right next door to Kimberlee's.'

All the rooms of the castle sported a different décor. Kimberlee's had been the George Ramsay. Magretta's, according to the plaque by the door, was the Robert the Bruce. It proved to be a high-ceilinged room decorated in blue and burgundy that also faced south to dramatic views of the castle's rolling parkland and forests.

Magretta, unlike Kimberlee, had come prepared to write, bringing with her an old-fashioned travel-writing desk made of elaborately carved wood. On closer inspection, it proved to be a reproduction of the kind of thing seen in museums, but updated for the modern writer. The lid opened down to create a slanted writing surface. Inside, it was kitted out with paper and little drawers and slots to hold pens, stamps, envelopes, and so on. St Just recognized it from the photo on the dust jacket of her book.

Perhaps she felt being photographed with this thing lent weight to her writerly persona.

Moor, looking over just then, whistled.

'That's an expensive-looking job.'

St Just nodded. 'Pretty much what royalty might use whilst perusing dispatches on safari in Kenya.'

'Quite.'

St Just stopped to look out the window, which offered a slightly different overlook of the forest from Kimberlee's – Magretta had, apparently, succeeded in getting her way over the room with a view. No mountains had materialized, however.

Moor said, from where he stood surveying the contents of the wardrobe, a touch of wonder in his voice: 'It's green. Everything. It's green.'

'Yes, I know. Well, I didn't know what she wore underneath but if one were inclined to one could make an educated guess. Wearing green was what I think they call her signature style.'

'I thought the pink was bad, but this is really bad. Like being trampled to death in an Irish parade.'

'I know.'

'Like drowning in some bilious, plague-infested—'

'Please. I know.'

St Just pulled out the notebook he'd asked Moor to retrieve from his castle bedroom, and began jotting down his impressions. Many long hours and many rooms later, he had written, in part:

'Nothing amiss or out of place in anyone's room . . . The usual travel gear . . . The usual make-up and toiletries. All authors but Kimberlee Kalder and Magretta had laptops. N.B.: Other laptops will need a looking over by IT . . . Most traveled with books, mostly their own (exception: Annabelle), some with books by the other authors. Magretta traveling with four dozen copies of her newest paperback.'

And he had underlined:

'They all had a copy of Kimberlee's book. Even those who claim not to have read it.'

St Just was mystified by Magretta's traveling with so many of her own books and made another mental note to ask Portia about it. She would certainly know the reason.

When it came time to search Portia's room, St Just hung back. Violating people's privacy was what he did for a living but he could bring himself to take only the most cursory glance at the neat, spartanly clean room. Here were none of the excess or wild abandon of Kimberlee's or Magretta's occupations, but a tacit acknowledgment that she was a guest in someone else's establishment, albeit a paying guest. He bet the maids of the castle blessed her thoughtfulness every day.

Which reminded him:

'Is anyone talking with the staff?'

'That's young Muir's job,' said Moor. 'He's getting the preliminaries. We'll have to have a word with all of them, as well, of course. It helps that the murder happened at night. That's far fewer staff to worry about as suspects.'

'Unless one of them stayed on, unnoticed, after hours.'

'There's that, I suppose. Motive would be a problem.'

And so they came to the end of a long day of sifting through closets and overturning the contents of suitcases. The sky was by now closing in on the evening. St Just leaned over the banister and by craning his neck could see some of the hotel occupants below in the lobby, waiting, quietly reading or napping. Good as children.

Minutes later, DCI Moor went downstairs to tell the group they could once again have the use of their rooms. Only Tom and Edith got up right away to leave, however. St Just imagined that, by lingering, the rest were hoping to get an update from the police.

He followed DCI Moor over the now-functioning

drawbridge to the front of the castle. He felt rather than saw that they were watched by several pairs of eyes from the sitting-room window.

'I'm headed back to headquarters for a bit, but I've left some of my top men and women on guard,' Moor told St Just. 'Best I can do for now. We should have a better idea from forensics tomorrow of where we stand. I'll go cap in hand to get them to speed things up.'

'If it's anything like Cambridge, you'll have a job talking them into it.'

'Don't I know. Well, see you then. Keep all these artistic temperaments in line for me.'

And Moor drove off. St Just went back into the well-guarded lounge, where a few more people had started to head upstairs to their rooms. He was looking for one face in particular, of course. It didn't take long to spot her. She was in the sitting room with a cup of tea and a buttered scone.

He sat down in one of the velvety chairs.

'Are you all right?' he asked.

'I think so,' she said. She put down the teacup. It made a slight rattling noise against the saucer. 'And you?'

'Business as usual. How's everyone else holding up?'

'Well, Magretta's taken it into her head that we're all going to be "knocked off", one by one. Like in *Ten Little Indians*.'

'I was afraid of that. It's going to be a long, long night at the castle.'

Portia nodded.

'She alternates between refusing to talk to any of us and interrogating each of us relentlessly, like some demented prosecutor. It's already getting tedious. There will be another murder soon if she doesn't put a sock in it.'

'I know. I mean, I know nerves must be completely raw.'

'Look,' Portia said, and paused. Her eyes held the dangerous gleam of the amateur detective on the scent. He recognized it too well: His Bethie used to get the same look.

'Is there any way I can help? Unofficially, of course. They'll talk to me, you see.'

'Absolutely not. It would place you in the most dangerous position imaginable. No.'

'But don't you see—'

'Portia . . . Ms De'Ath. Or is it Mrs?'

She shook her head. 'Never married.'

Good merciful God. 'Ms De'Ath, this is not the plot of one of your novels.'

'Of course not,' she said frostily. 'I didn't imagine for a minute that it was. It's just that—'

'You do realize there is a killer on the loose? That the danger is quite real?'

'I do of course realize that,' she said. 'Which is why I want to help. This person has to be caught, and quickly.'

'I can't possibly begin to countenance—' he began.

'There is no need to treat me like a child.' Her voice wavered on the last word.

Great. Just great. He'd come to the end of a long, exhausting, and fruitless day and to cap it off he had managed to insult her, of all people.

'Ms De'Ath,' he said, more gently. 'I would rather die myself than lose you. The answer is no.'

And he stood up – afraid to say more, afraid for himself.

She let him go.

CHAPTER 13

Outcast

St Just was the first one down to breakfast. He'd had a restless night, rehearsing in his mind the interviews and searches of the previous long day. The large brandy that he'd brought to his room, thinking it might act as a sleeping pill, had instead left him wide awake with a raging thirst at three a.m. The cast of suspects passed before him like characters in a play, taking their bows. Which of them hated or feared Kimberlee enough to kill her?

He kept circling back to the apparently unrelated image of Magretta's travel desk. In his mind's eye, she sat before it like Queen Victoria, deep in her red boxes of state papers.

When sleep did arrive it was fleet and unknowing, a sudden drop of consciousness, like a heavy stone plummeting through a black lake. He awoke in the pale light of dawn and resettled himself under the luxurious goose-down quilt, willing his mind to quiet, trying to organize his impressions. Nothing would connect. His usual ability to find the logic in chaos seemed to have deserted him. At last giving up, he rose and began to gear himself to listen to the usual recital of lies, denials, and half-truths that seemed to be a standard part of any police interrogation.

As the other castle inmates came down to their breakfasts in the Orangery, they smiled at him nervously and sat as far away as possible without actually sitting outside in the cold. Certainly no one attempted to join him at his table. He hardly expected that they would. No one is ever quite comfortable being around the police, especially when a murder investigation is on the day's agenda. When he peeked out from behind his newspaper, he saw them huddled together, whispering quietly, and sending many a furtive glance in his direction. No question about it, he was now from the dark side. No matter their state of guilt or innocence, this policeman in their midst could mean nothing but trouble.

From Portia, he expected frost. Instead, she gave him a friendly, rather shy wave as she came in. If she was aware that this show of friendliness might brand her as either a suspect or a snitch among the others, she didn't show it.

All to the good, he felt, if they thought she was a suspect. It might help keep her out of danger.

Today she had twisted her still-damp hair into a low chignon; she wore a pale yellow sweater and brown tweed slacks. Small boots of a supple brown leather peeked out from the hems. He didn't think she could look any lovelier in a ball gown. She leaned over toward him and said, 'I have got to tell you something. Something I sort of . . . forgot.' As she spoke, renewed murmurs of speculation rose from the room.

He held up a hand to forestall her.

'Interviews will take place throughout the day.' He made sure his voice carried, so as to disabuse anyone of the notion she was busy turning one of them in.

Then, lowering his voice: 'Not here. They're hanging on every word. Anyway, can I make it any clearer? There can be no impression you are helping us in any extraordinary way.'

'But I am.' It was not a question.

He sighed.

'If you know anything you have to tell me. Just . . . not now.'

She hesitated. 'You see, the thing is, I'm not sure—'

'Later today,' he interrupted. Really, he thought, he had to treat her the way he'd treat any other suspect. If only it weren't for those dark blue eyes . . . If only her skin didn't put him in mind of white rose petals . . .

'You'll have your turn,' he said, again trying to put some iron in his voice.

Noticing they did indeed have the galvanized attention of the rest of the room, he stood and, improvising, addressed them all.

'I was just saying to Ms De'Ath that in the interest of expedience, some of you might like to write down your whereabouts from the time of the dinner Saturday night until you went to bed, and/or until you heard the alarm raised. Since you all are writers, this seems the most natural outlet for your, ah—' he nearly said imaginations, '—talents.'

He did a quick survey of the room.

'Where are Tom Brackett and his wife? And Lord Easterbrook?' he asked.

They all looked at each other. There was a collective shrug.

'Not down yet,' offered Magretta.

'Very well,' said St Just. 'Inspector Moor or I will want all of you to be available for interviews. I would appreciate it if you would stay within the castle – either in your room or in one of the main sitting rooms – so we don't have to hunt for you. Please pass this information along.'

Magretta, predictably, was first to protest.

'We've already been interviewed.'

'Merely a preliminary engagement. This investigation is only just beginning.'

He left to pre-empt further argument. The chatter level rose to a hectoring roar at his back.

But moments later: 'Inspector!'

He was halfway down the hallway. He turned.

'Don't worry,' said Portia. She offered him a small, disarming smile. 'I won't do anything foolish – not to the point where I'd need police protection, at any rate.'

'I would be first to volunteer if you did.'

She seemed to ignore that. *Quite right,* he thought. *Prat.*

'It's just that they do seem to think I've an inside track with you. It started yesterday. There's a lot of morbid curiosity about the condition of . . . the body, for example. Anyway, for today, I'll either be in my room or at the spa – keeping my ears open, that's all – if you need me. Let me know how I can help. Oh – and what I wanted to tell you: Winston insists he saw Kimberlee on the stairs, just after the lights went out – that would be about a quarter to eleven. I thought I saw something, too. I guess I decided it was Kimberlee because Winston thought it was. But neither of us is sure now. It was all a bit . . . hazy.'

And she lit off toward the stairs. She had an attractive back – lean and supple.

How she can help. Where to begin.

CHAPTER 14

In the Library

Upstairs, DCI Moor and Sergeant Kittle had already reported for duty. A tech crew, having finished with the bottle dungeon – into which they had been lowered by cable as if from a rescue helicopter – was working on Kimberlee's room, which seemed to float above a low silver cloud of magnetic fingerprint powder. St Just, stifling the urge to sneeze, asked one of the technicians dusting for prints if he could take a copy of Kimberlee's book from her dresser.

The taciturn-looking man glanced over to the photographer, who nodded.

'Sure, done with that.'

Moor said to St Just, 'Let me show you the incident room they've set up.'

He led the way down several twisting, dark corridors that seemed to lead nowhere but eventually deposited them in a room tucked into another of the small turrets of the castle. Computers, fax machines, and phone lines sprouted on the antique tables and dressers.

'We're going through the suspects' rooms again in case we missed anything yesterday,' Moor said. 'Or in case, their guard down now that they think the search is over, they've left something of interest overnight. So, who's on your list today for a cozy chat?'

St Just, who had been skimming some of yesterday's preliminary reports, looked over to his colleague. Moor didn't quite seem to have tamed the cowlicks that sprouted from the top of his head, and the handlebars of his white mustaches drooped asymmetrically, like a plane banking after takeoff. Probably he'd lost the latest skirmish for the bathroom in the Moor household.

'Anything of interest in here?' St Just indicated the stack of reports.

'Not really. They're all singing from the same hymn sheet,' said Moor.

'"I Wandered in the Shades of Night?"'

'"Let All Mortal Flesh Keep Silence", more like. They're all as innocent as newborn lambs, to hear them tell it,' said Moor. 'Either surrounded by Archbishop-caliber witnesses or tucked up sound asleep while bloody mayhem broke out elsewhere in the castle.'

St Just murmured, not expecting to be overheard, 'An omerta?'

'What's that?'

'Oh, nothing. Just . . . seeing as how they're crime writers, maybe there's some unwritten code that prohibits them cooperating with police.'

'Ah. Well, Cambridge, we now know the time of death was no earlier than nine-thirty. Our pathologist won't be pinned down yet to an official time range, but from the stomach contents and so on, he says the body had been there "maybe" two hours when it was found at midnight. Samples taken from the body and underneath her nails show nothing so far – no samples from her attacker.'

'She was seen alive just after nine,' said St Just. 'By several people, I should think – including me. And Winston Chatley, according to Portia De'Ath, *thinks* – but is uncertain now – that he saw Kimberlee just after the lights went out. That was around ten forty-five. I wish these examiners weren't always quite so elastic about the time of death.'

'I'm just the messenger,' said Moor.

'Anything on her mobile?'

'Nothing of interest. We're going through her list of contacts, of course. And she'd received a message from someone named Desmond at ten the night she died – just wishing her good luck at the conference.'

St Just pulled at his chin in a gesture of frustration. 'As I've said, someone really determined could circle around through the woods or even paddle downriver, swim across the moat, and slip in somehow, but what are the chances? You'll need to eliminate that possibility, obviously. But I think we're dealing with one of the castle guests. Which means we're almost certainly dealing with someone connected with the conference. Possibly a mystery writer. Bugger it.'

'How so?'

'Just what we need is some clever-dick crime writer, or someone steeped in crime novels, trying to outwit the police. Even if and when we catch him or her, the red herrings may be so numerous we'll never be able to explain the case properly to a jury.'

Moor mused on this a moment and said:

'It could work to our advantage, though, don't you think?'

'How so?' asked St Just in his turn.

'If some kind of revenge or envy or spite is the motive, we just look for the writer with the biggest ego.'

St Just bared his teeth in a bleak smile.

'You really don't know this lot yet, do you? They're all quite, quite taken with themselves, in one way or the other.' He thought of clear-eyed Portia, long-necked Portia, Portia of the silken skin. He amended: 'Nearly all.'

Moor grunted. 'I'm sure you're right. I'd put nothing past them. Any of them. One oddity, I guess you could call it. They found a well-thumbed paperback copy of *Persuasion* in Kimberlee's purse. Stuffed way at the bottom of her purse. Hidden, like.'

'Hmm. Not exactly a book on nuclear physics, but not quite what I'd expect, either, would you? Well, well. Together with the Cambridge degree, and what her agent has told us, I'd say we're starting to see a pattern. What you saw with Kimberlee was not necessarily what you got.'

St Just paused, then answered Moor's original question:

'What do you say we have our cozy chat with Easterbrook? He's the catalyst – the reason for all of them being here. So let's start unpicking the thread at the beginning.'

There was some ado when it came to actually locating Lord Easterbrook, as it turned out. He was not in his room, reported Sergeant Kittle.

'He wasn't at breakfast, either,' said St Just. 'I assumed he was having food sent up.'

'He's probably walking the grounds,' said Moor. 'I'll send a uniform to fetch him.'

Waiting for Easterbrook to appear, St Just began flipping again through Kimberlee's book. It was the literary equivalent of the type of girl movie to which he could never be dragged. Why did women think men were so complicated, he wondered?

Moor's 'uniform' came back into the room.

'He's in the library,' he reported. 'He said he'd be straight up once he finished his coffee.'

'Bollocks to that,' said Moor. 'You go tell that toffee-nosed—'

'Never mind, Moor.' St Just put down the book, which, with its pink cover, seemed to glow like an object undergoing radioactive decay. He was used to the aristocracy trying this on. 'I'll go and have a look for the panjandrum of publishing. Do you want to come with me?'

It was a somewhat chastened Julius Easterbrook who could be found talking with the three policemen half an hour later, Moor having explained to him at great length that murder took priority over coffee. Sergeant Kittle sat quietly in a nearby corner with his policeman's notebook. A wood fire crackled in the fireplace, dispelling the morning chill of the room.

'Poor Kimberlee,' said Easterbrook. He stood before the hearth, wringing his age-mottled hands. 'She didn't deserve this.'

Clearly, the man was worried, thought St Just. The patrician sheen of Saturday night had given way to a somewhat seedy and unkempt air, like a stately home in need of renovation. He looked in any event to St Just the sort of man more at home in a showerproof jacket and green wellies, dog at his side, than in a dinner jacket.

St Just invited the older man to sit in one of the leather chairs. He imagined at least part of Easterbrook's worry was over how to replace a best-selling author. Or did the anxiety run deeper? His standard expression of mourning had a sincere ring.

'When did you last see her alive?' asked St Just.

'I didn't see her at all after the dinner,' Easterbrook replied, his voice an aristocratic honk. What made elderly aristocrats talk like that, wondered St Just. Some kind of old-school cricket injury?

'I went to my room – correspondence to catch up on, you know,' continued Easterbrook. 'Then, of course, the lights went out.'

'And where were you—' began Moor.

'When the lights went out?' Easterbrook's voice made it clear he expected the police to take his version of events without question. He was civil but icily so. 'Wasn't there a rather dreadful American movie by that name? I think I've just answered that question, Inspector. I was writing a letter. The lights went out, so I stopped writing a letter. I said, "Bother" and went straight to bed.'

'I see,' said St Just. He glanced over at Kittle, who was idly drawing what looked like a hangman's noose in his notebook.

'What exactly happened to her, do you know yet?' asked the publisher.

St Just shook his head.

'Early days yet.'

'I hope you don't mean that literally. We can't all be kept here indefinitely while you try to sort this out. Oh, dear,' he said, and began to wring his hands again, emitting well-bred little brays of concern. 'I do hope our PR department can make the best of this.'

'I somehow doubt it.'

'You've not met my PR department. But even without them there is bound to be a spike in sales of Kimberlee's book. Not to mention, avid interest in the next book.'

'I wonder if they could be induced to stay off the topic of exactly how and where she was found,' said Moor. 'Your PR department, I mean.'

'Whatever for?' Lord Easterbrook looked genuinely puzzled.

'It's morbid?' suggested Moor. 'Ghoulish? In poor taste?'

'Oh. Yes, quite. Quite. But later, surely . . .' said Easterbrook. It was no doubt the same tone of voice he used to wheedle an invitation to a shooting party at Sandringham. He drew back his mouth in a propitiatory smile, revealing a suspiciously even row of large teeth.

St Just decided it was time to steer him to a new topic.

'Her agent Ninette Thomson tells us Kimberlee's book needed a bit of a cleanup when she first saw it, but that it was a remarkably fresh piece of work. Would you agree with that assessment?'

'Good Lord, man. You don't think I read the thing all the way through, do you? Merciful heavens, no. *No.* (*Honk.*) All it took was one look at Kimberlee, and a synopsis from the agent, for me to know we had a winning package. We happened to have a stable of rather predictable writers at the time – writing to formula, riding the coat-tails of past successes.

Still do, in fact. Then here was Kimberlee – glamorous, born talking into a microphone, completely savvy about the business. Most of them have stars in their eyes these days, you know – the young authors, especially. Hope springing eternal. Don't want to hear it's a business, and a hard business. Kimberlee understood. I didn't have to teach her a thing.'

'What can you tell me about her background?' asked St Just. 'Something beyond the little biography on her book jacket.'

Lord Easterbrook, having produced a linen handkerchief the size of a small tablecloth, blew into it thunderously before fussily folding and replacing it in his pocket. Eventually he replied, 'Not much. It's difficult to say. I met her two years ago, and even though I've dealt with her frequently since then . . . it's difficult to describe. She was businesslike, as I say, but she often cloaked that in a little-me silliness that was wholly deceptive – something she'd begun doing more and more in recent days, by the way. But, for example, her agent had negotiated with us a perfectly reasonable contract – if I may say so, an exceptional contract – for what was effectively an untested author. Kimberlee Kalder came to my office herself to demand a larger advance.'

'Which she got?'

'Not right away. That's just not on, you know – we deal with the agents, not the authors. But, next, she threatened to walk.'

'Confidence bordering on arrogance, then?'

'Quite. Not even *stealing* across the border, but marching brazenly across. Normally I would say don't let the door slam on your way out. But one of the editors talked me into keeping her. And frankly, it didn't take a lot of persuasion. I sensed she would be the injection of life – and cash – the business needed. I've been batting on rather a sticky wicket, you see. Publishing in these days is not for the faint of heart. The whole thing is positively going to hell on a sled.'

'So, Kimberlee's silly-me act—'

'Wholly an act. And as I say, she became more silly in recent months. Superficial. Always talking about hair extensions and things. I guess she figured out that it helped sell books. I only know it was an act because generally, if we weren't in public, she'd revert to the real Kimberlee. Her vocabulary would go up several levels, for example, and every other sentence wouldn't be peppered with "like" or "radical". My sense was that she was finding it harder to do, though – to lose the act.'

'So, where the real person began and ended it was hard to say?' asked St Just.

'Quite.'

'And no one guessed?'

'No one cared enough to guess, I would imagine. No one among the reading public. And as far as Kimberlee was concerned, her performance sold books. She probably saw the whole thing as a lark. You know, I say. . .' Lord Easterbrook, who had been studying St Just closely, now peered at him over the tops of his glasses. 'Wasn't there a St Just who married Bloreheather some years ago?'

'My sister,' said St Just.

Easterbrook raised his eyebrows, digesting the news. No doubt he was wondering how Lord Bloreheather liked having a black sheep of a policeman in the family. St Just spared a fleeting thought for his elder sister, sitting in her handsome stone mansion sheltered by beeches and oaks, no doubt awaiting the late-March start of the London season. She would get on like a house on fire with Easterbrook.

'Is it possible. . .' St Just paused to find the words for a rather far-fetched theory that was beginning to crystallize in his mind. 'Is it possible this attack on Kimberlee was actually an attack on the publishing house? On you, indirectly?'

Easterbrook seemed to take his meaning immediately. He nodded. 'I've considered that. Sometimes, umbrage is taken by various people with whom one comes in contact. One is, after all, in the business of criticizing the contents of another's brain. Which can be just as frightening as it sounds. This is why I have assistants, you know, to read through what we call the slush pile. So, yes, I suppose some disgruntled writer could seek to bring the house down by killing Kimberlee, its chief moneymaker. Far-fetched, but then, you should see some of the manuscripts we receive. As I say, the contents of people's brains. Terrifying.'

'Does anyone in particular come to mind?'

'Unfortunately, no. I could have my office send you some of the choicer letters we've received. We do save some of them, in a file labeled Broadmoor.' Easterbrook paused, considering. When he spoke, his own mind had taken a new tack.

'I say, I wonder just how far along Kimberlee was on the new book. She was a bit cagey with me about that. Perhaps we could pretend she left behind a completed manuscript? That is to say, really completed, the way Christie wrote the concluding novel to her Miss Marple series far in advance.'

'And have someone ghostwrite the rest, you mean? I suppose you could,' said St Just with a shrug. The honesty or otherwise of the plan was not for him to say. 'But, Lord Easterbrook, I would tread carefully if I were you. Murder has a way of forcing out the truth, on matters great and small.'

CHAPTER 15

In the Garden

They left Lord Easterbrook still surveying the shell of his publishing empire, hoping something could be rebuilt from the ruins.

Outside the rain had stopped, and a hesitant sun peered over clouds shot through with quicksilver. St Just announced he was going for a walk, to catch the freshened air.

'I've seen enough plaid to last me a few days,' he said.

'Where are you going?' Moor asked, as he and Kittle headed back up to the incident room. 'Thailand?'

St Just first bundled against the weather in an overcoat, a somewhat crumpled Borsalino hat, and a blue and white Peterhouse scarf, among the most ancient items in his ancient wardrobe. His clothing had been chosen, in fact, almost entirely by the females in his life: mother, then sister, then wife. As all but his sister were now deceased, he found it impossible to throw or give away the gifts that had been chosen for him with such care.

Besides which, he had the male's instinctive fear and dread of department stores. He'd probably be buried in these clothes, he reflected.

The wind of the previous night had vacuumed the cold air clean, but the rain had released a lingering odor of decaying leaves and undergrowth, mingled with the muddy scent of the disturbed riverbed. Twigs and fallen branches littered the ground. St Just was wandering the denuded gardens at the back of the castle when he spotted Winston Chatley, defying St Just's earlier request that everyone stay indoors, sitting swathed in Gore-Tex on a stone bench by the kitchen garden wall. He held a small notebook balanced on one knee and was scribbling so furiously he didn't at first notice the policeman's approach. St Just was loathe to interrupt such a show of industry, but reminded himself this was a murder investigation, not a writers' retreat.

He watched Chatley surreptitiously for a moment. As a suspect, he had a lot to recommend him, St Just felt, if only going by appearances. Winston was probably a bit over six feet tall, but his stork-like limbs sprouting from a smallish, narrow torso were what gave the impression of vast height. His features could be kindly described as craggy, his face carved into great hillocks and valleys, with a large overhanging brow. It was a face crowded with bones, reminding one of the skull beneath. As St Just drew closer, he could see deep lines etched into the man's forehead. He looked like a crime writer of a particularly sinister sort.

Then Winston spotted St Just and smiled. The illusion of menace disappeared. The man looked as approachable as a puppy.

Or was that the illusion?

'I say,' said St Just. 'Terribly sorry to interrupt you, but needs must.'

Winston carefully closed his notebook and tucked his pen in the inside pocket of his jacket. St Just noticed the worn lining of the garment as he did so.

'Not at all, Inspector. I realize you have a job to do. And the sooner you do it, the sooner we all can leave.'

'A man after my own heart,' said St Just. 'Would that all suspects so easily made that connection.'

St Just sat beside him.

'I think it won't be much longer,' he said. He had no idea if that were true but it sounded reassuring and competent.

St Just had a vast fund of platitudes to help put suspects at ease. And Winston, he had to remind himself, was a suspect. Kimberlee Kalder's success had put all the other, more established, writers' noses out of joint. He'd seen dafter motives for murder.

'You told one of the policemen yesterday that a group of you staying here at the castle broke off from the rest for a tête-à-tête, so to speak, on the night of Kimberlee's murder.'

'That's right. It wasn't exactly by prearrangement or anything. It was that the noise level in the library was bound to get a little louder with each round. I speak from long professional experience of crime writers gathered *en masse*. Football hooligans tearing apart a stadium are far quieter and generally better behaved. So we four decided to escape to the oasis of the sitting room. You know, that little area at the front of the castle where they serve afternoon tea.'

'And you four were . . . remind me . . .'

'Tom and his wife Edith. B. A. King, the agent or publicist or whatever he is, decided to join in – uninvited. Odious little toad. Quentin Swope flitted in and out – mostly in. Looking for something scurrilous to write about, I imagine. He was in fact just packing up to leave for the night when we lost the lights.'

'So except for Quentin, you all can alibi each other?'

Winston shifted slightly, turning to face him.

'Oh, I say. This is a first. I've been writing about alibis for years and now I'm expected to provide one myself. That's jolly goo – oh, sorry. I do realize the matter is serious. Well, the answer to your question is essentially yes, sort of. But to be truthful, they weren't all there all the time. People drifted in and out, to the powder room and so on. There was a lot of traipsing back and forth for drinks, since the bar, as you know, is in the library.'

'And what did you talk about?'

'What writers always talk about if left unattended for

two seconds. Money. Royalties. Foreign rights – the sweetest words in the English language, those. Amazon.com rankings. Barnes and Noble rankings. Bookscan. Agents. Editors. The Imminent Death of Publishing as We Know It.'

'And you talked for how long?'

Winston considered. 'I'm not entirely sure. The conversation eventually moved on to a rather remorseless narrative from Tom of his literary achievements. That seemed to go on for hours – simply *hours*. The storm reached a high pitch while we were there. You'll recall, of course, that it was an absolute corker of a storm. Gale-force or worse. I enjoyed it immensely, I must say – the sensation of being snug inside whilst nature beat itself senseless against the thick stone walls. Anyway, we'd all had a lot to drink so anything like an exact accounting is nigh impossible. We were all blowing off steam after the build-up of the past few days.'

'There was a lot of tension?' St Just prompted.

'I should jolly well say there was a lot of tension. What was Easterbrook thinking, bringing his authors together only to treat one like the golden-haired child and the rest of us like darkling orphans? That bonus cheque – a monstrously bad idea. I shouldn't be surprised if some of his authors defected.'

'So Kimberlee was unpopular with the others?'

'Yes. Stupendously so. Not entirely her fault, as I've said. It was Easterbrook who put the match to the tinder, deliberately or otherwise.'

'I see,' said St Just. His guess, from the little he knew of Easterbrook, was that a sense of *noblesse oblige* did not constitute a large part of his make-up. He might never stop to consider how others might take his actions. He just acted. 'So, what else did you talk about?'

'Really, just books. Publishing. The American market. I thought I might pick up some tips or contacts from Tom, expand my sales-and-marketing horizons.'

'And did you?'

'Not really. Tom labors in a different field altogether from mine – the spy thriller. And even if we were in the same field, I doubt he'd go out of his way to help a competitor.'

That had the ring of truth, certainly, from St Just's observations of the man. 'So, can you remember anything else you talked about?'

'Not about Kimberlee. Not how she had to be done in or got out of the way or anything like that. I don't think her name came up apart from a few snippy remarks early on about the bonus cheque Easterbrook gave her.'

'You say there was a lot of to and fro for drinks and so on. I'll ask again: Can you be at all more specific as to times?'

Winston paused, cradling his chin in one large hand as he canvassed the previous night's events.

'B. A. King and I were in the library for about the first half an hour. Maybe more. Then we both fetched new drinks and trotted over to the sitting room. Tom, Edith, and Quentin were already there. We talked awhile, then I volunteered to fetch a round for all of us – as I say, we all needed a refill fairly quickly. So, add another half hour? Tom and B. A. – whatever does that stand for? – went to the gent's, separately, and Edith went to powder her nose. But it's not exactly the kind of occasion that makes one whip out one's notebook and jot down the time. I'm afraid you'll have to ask them what they remember. I left them to it some time before eleven and as I was headed upstairs, we lost the lights. I went to find candles – well, you know all this. I left Portia as she was going downstairs to fetch a book. The darkness and the drink were making me drowsy – I thought I saw Kimberlee on the stairs, you know, but now I doubt the evidence of my own eyes; it was more an impression, really. In the dark . . . now I'm not so sure. I can only say I saw a whitish form – that blonde hair, and the white dress. Anyway, when I called to her she didn't reply.'

'Go on.'

'Then Magretta sounded the alarm – this had to have been close to or spot on midnight – and we all scurried out to see what was the matter. Everyone seemed to come from all directions then. It's impossible to be clear about everyone's locations at that point.'

St Just sat absorbing this narrative, wondering how much of it could be corroborated. He was going to have the devil's own time sorting out everyone's whereabouts the night of the murder.

'I gather from the tenor of your questions,' Winston added, 'that we are indeed suspects? You've ruled out anyone on the staff, for example? Or an interloper?'

'We've ruled out nothing,' said St Just. 'But of course if you were in the castle that night, you're a suspect.'

'Only if I could walk through walls, Inspector.'

Nonsense, thought St Just. The bottle dungeon was less than thirty seconds away from the sitting room – a sprint down the hall and across the lobby. Any of them could have killed Kimberlee under the pretext of nose powdering. The lobby was vast and sparsely furnished, so there was a real risk of being seen, but still. . .

'You were in your room until the body was found?' he asked.

'Yes. Funny thing, that. . .'

'How so?'

'It was all just so – I don't know . . . dramatic. The lights, the scream at midnight. It was like being in a movie.'

St Just looked down at the closed notebook Winston held in his hand.

'Notes for a future book?' he asked.

'I'm afraid so.' Winston grimaced apologetically. 'Actually, I was thinking in terms of a screenplay. It's the writer's curse to take absolutely anything that happens and turn it into grist for the mill. Being involved in an actual murder investigation is too good an opportunity to pass up. Sorry – what an awful way to phrase that, but I'm sure you must know what I mean. I'm also working on the timeline you asked us for but it's going to be damn-all use, I'm afraid – as you've just seen.'

'How is it you started to write mysteries for a living, Mr Chatley?' St Just asked. 'What did you do *before* you became a writer?'

'Winston, please. I was always a writer, I just wasn't paid for it the first fifteen years or so. Being a bartender was my day job. Or my night job, as it were. At a place in London called the Serengeti.'

'It took fifteen years for you to sell a book?'

Winston shook his head bleakly. 'Well, it took fifteen years for me to make enough money from my writing to keep a cat alive. The writing bug – it's a virus. There is no cure. And sometimes you write whatever anyone will pay you for.'

'I gather you've done fairly well in recent years.'

Winston flapped his hand in a see-saw motion, noncommittally. This time, something like a smile lit up his sober countenance. In his Eeyoreish way, Winston was an appealing character.

'I'm not rich or even comfortably off, but I was able to quit the day/night job, and that was always the goal. I have a parent who needs my attention, you see. In that regard, it's worked out well. There is no other job that offers the freedom and mobility of writing. And, as I say, any other job is unthinkable once you've been bitten.'

'Hmm.' St Just felt he'd heard mania described in much the same way. And here he was with a whole castle of these Type-A, driven personalities.

'One further question,' he said. 'Did you have any impression Kimberlee had paired up with someone on this trip?'

A shake of the head. 'Some kind of fling, you mean? It wouldn't be uncommon on this kind of jaunt, but no, I hadn't noticed in particular. She seemed to spend a lot of time with Jay, but I rather thought she was just buttering him up, for whatever purposes of her own. I assumed those purposes were professional rather than personal. But the fact is, I avoided her where I could. I know she was charming, but it was lost on me, I'm afraid.'

St Just couldn't but agree. But was Winston telling the truth there – or did he realize it was safer for the police to believe in his indifference?

Not long afterward, St Just bade farewell and left Winston in the garden, his unhandsome head again bent to the notebook open on his knees.

CHAPTER 16

In the Presence

'I don't think Tom is available to see you right now.'

The woman standing at the open door to the Tartan Suite was by far the dreariest thing in the hectic room. Her hair was of an indeterminate color that could best be described as taupe, and she had pale eyes to match. St Just was strongly reminded of a Weimaraner. Her lumpy skirt and twinset might have been woven from pottery shards and twine. St Just had once owned a rucksack that looked like Edith Brackett.

The thought triggered a niggling memory – something he'd seen in recent days, surely – or was it? The memory eluding him, he reluctantly let it float free. Maybe if he didn't worry at it. . .

It was a shame, really, he thought now. The woman had classic, even features and, from what he could tell, a neat, trim figure. But she looked the type of woman who was allergic to everything and existed mainly on tofu. With a little embellishment and the application of some of Kimberlee's powders and potions, he thought she could approach eye-catching.

'Mrs Brackett,' he said. 'This is a police investigation.' (Was he condemned to spend his life reminding people of that fact? He imagined he was.) 'Your husband, ready or not, will have to see me. Would you go and fetch him here, please?'

She indicated the closed door to her left. 'He's asleep. I think.'

Oh, well. There's an end on it – poor bloke's asleep. I'll just take my tiresome little investigation and go away.

Feeling the lack of sleep himself, St Just repeated, smiling, but with a hint of sternness in the smile: 'Fetch him now, please.'

A look of something like fear darted across her features – a mad thing that appeared and vanished so quickly St Just wasn't sure he'd seen it. Was the woman *afraid* of disturbing her husband?

'I'll awaken him, if you prefer,' he said.

A kaleidoscope of emotion at that: relief, gratitude, embarrassment.

'If you wish,' she said, an attempt at indifference that didn't play well. She *was* afraid.

St Just made a mental note to get her alone and suss out what that was all about. Even better, perhaps Moor had a WPC who could be co-opted for the job. For now, he rapped sharply on the door between the suite's sitting area and bedroom – more sharply than he'd intended. He had a particular and unapologetic hatred for bullies.

A huge bellow leaked like smoke from around the sides of the closed door.

'Goddammit, Edith. I told you—'

The door was flung open. Tom Brackett stood wrapped in one of the hotel's voluminous white terrycloth robes. A rotund Banquo's ghost, thought St Just, but with a face brick-red with anger. St Just felt he had seen worse sights than Tom Brackett's hairy legs emerging from the robe, but thankfully, not often.

'Terribly sorry to disturb you, Sir. I just need to ask you and your wife a few questions.'

Brackett jutted his chin aggressively in Edith's direction.

'You really never learn, do you—'

'Actually, Mrs Brackett tried to stop me, Sir. I insisted that you wouldn't both want to be charged with obstructing a police inquiry. Now, would you like to get dressed before we continue? If you'd prefer, we can have our chat at the police station.'

Brackett glared. He had tried to tame his thick eyebrows with clipping and gel, a toilette that somehow irresist-ibly recalled Joan Crawford, but he otherwise resembled a bad-tempered sea lion with a day-old growth of dark hair surrounding his Van Dyke beard.

'Continue what? That little tart's getting herself knocked off is nothing to do with me. And if you think she—' here a jerk of the head in Edith's direction – 'had anything to do with it, you've only to take a look at her. She wouldn't have the guts to say boo to a ghost.'

St Just, realizing the man was perfectly capable of carrying on an hours-long conversation while treating his wife as if she weren't even in the room, deliberately turned to Edith.

'I've been wondering, Mrs Brackett, at your middle name – your maiden name, I assume? Edith Bean Brackett. It sounds awfully familiar to me and I can't think why.'

'Tilly Toggle,' she said shyly. Her cheeks flushed a bright pink and her eyes suddenly shone. He had confirmation that Edith, in the right circumstances – mainly, out from under her husband's thumb – was beautiful.

Tilly. He barely managed to avoid saying, 'Huh?' when the penny dropped. He'd bought those books, a boxed set of five of them, as he recalled, for his sergeant's daughter Emma. Emma wasn't reading yet but, as she could practically program a com-puter, St Just had opted to anticipate the day.

'Of course,' he said. 'I should have realized. Edith Bean. Author of the Tilly books. You must be proud – I see those books everywhere I—'

'Are you here to discuss murder or are you here to dis-cuss books a twelve-year-old could write?' demanded Tom Brackett. 'Attack' seemed to be the man's default mode. He sat down heavily in one of the room's two upholstered armchairs, unlovely knees apart, dark brows clouding beneath the sky of his bald pink head. The mustache above his goatee quivered with annoyance.

This was not, thought St Just, a man who could stand to have the attention removed from himself for one second.

And: He's jealous as hell of his wife's success. Good. *Good.*

St Just, motioning Edith to the other armchair, remained standing. He toyed with the idea of interviewing them separately, which would have been truer to established procedure in any case, but he thought more might be learned from the apparently complicated relationship between this pair by keeping them together.

'I gather,' said St Just, 'that, on the night of the murder, several of you separated from the main group. I would appreciate it if you would tell me who was with you and what you talked about.'

'We've already told—' began Tom.

'I was actually speaking to your wife. Sir.'

'That's right,' said Edith, earning herself a *Why don't you shut up for once?* glower from her husband. 'We started to watch a television show in the sitting room. Winston Chatley and B. A. King joined us. That reporter Quentin was there some of the time.'

'What show was that?' asked St Just.

'One of the *Midsomer Murders*,' answered Tom. His fingers drummed against the arms of his chair. 'Not my onion, of course, but Edith and the others liked it.'

St Just was left to wonder since when Tom cared what others liked. He had recently emerged from an investigation into the death of a mystery writer of supreme awfulness – the writer's persona being awful, not his books – and had imagined he'd never come across his like again. After a few minutes in the company of Tom Brackett, St Just was drastically revising his opinion.

'After the show, we watched news on the telly,' Tom

volunteered. 'There was some story about one of the lesser royals found in a gutter in Majorca, clutching a bottle of rum. The pundits weighed in with a debate over whether Great Britain really needs a monarchy in the twenty-first century, the commentary voiced over the usual film of Prince Charles talking to his organic peas. You know the kind of thing.'

The police could of course check his statement against the broadcaster's tapes. But then, was it really recall, or had he teamed up with his wife to compare notes for the times he was actually not in the room? Could Edith be the *apparatchik* chosen to provide Tom an alibi?

'What did you talk about?' Again, St Just aimed the question at Edith, who was blooming nicely under the attention.

'The men talked about the book business,' she said, smiling, eager to help. 'Mostly, I listened.'

'Everyone remained in the room the whole time, did they?'

'I think I did,' said Tom. He seemed to be studying the air behind St Just, not meeting his eyes.

'No, dear, you went to the men's room, don't you remember?'

Tom's wandering focus honed in on his wife. He shot her an expression of outraged disbelief.

That little defection may cost her, thought St Just.

But Edith went on. 'There was only the one bartender on duty so anything we wanted in the sitting room we had to fetch ourselves,' she explained. 'Winston Chatley went to the gents maybe twice. B. A. King went to his room to get some special Scotch whiskey he wanted the men to try. I think he also went to the gents at some later point. I went for drinks once or twice. Twice, that's right.'

'How long was everyone gone on these various errands?'

She looked to her husband.

'I really don't recall. Do you, Tom?'

'It's not as if we knew someone was going to get bumped off, is it?' said Tom with his usual delicacy. 'If we'd known we might all have paid more attention. Everyone went for a reload, is all I recall.'

'Let me ask this way,' said St Just. 'Who was gone from the room the longest?'

'Winston, I think,' said Edith.

'B. A. King, I think,' said Tom simultaneously.

'What, by the way, does B. A. stand for?' asked Edith of St Just.

'We really don't know yet.'

'Depends who you ask,' said Tom. 'Bullshit Artist is the hands-down favorite, followed by Benedict Arnold.'

'What did you do while waiting for his return?'

'We talked about the conference, the people there,' said Edith.

'And B. A. was gone how long? Ten minutes? Fifteen minutes?'

'No, longer,' said Tom. 'But then, time became rather elastic. We'd all been drinking, talking, watching people on *Midsomer* be impaled on pitchforks and run over by threshing machines and whatnot. It's impossible to say for certain.'

'Except me,' said Edith. 'I don't drink. I don't think he was gone more than fifteen minutes, Tom.'

Which sobriety probably made her the more reliable witness of the pair, thought St Just. Her words earned her another glare from Tom. *I'll have to offer her police protection if she keeps contradicting her oaf of a husband.*

Which of them was telling the truth? St Just would put his money on Edith. Tom's focus seemed to be on getting everyone but himself in trouble.

'Mrs Brackett, how often did you say you went to get drinks from the bar?

'Twice.'

'How long did it take each time?'

'Maybe ten minutes – it took longer the second trip because the bartender was busier then. The people in the library were all pretty much, how do you say? – three sheets to the wind? Also, I stopped to talk with Annabelle Pace – just mentioning the storm in passing, you know. It was starting to gale by then. It added to the . . . disorientation I think we all felt. Everything, time, seemed 'out of joint' – you know the feeling?'

'So you don't remember with any certainty when you left and came back?'

'She's already answered that,' snarled Tom.

Still Edith soldiered bravely on. She seemed to be one of those witnesses who love helping the police – not always the most helpful type, in St Just's experience. Some tended to embroider or invent where they couldn't remember.

'Not really,' she said. 'I went for the first round shortly after we'd collected in the sitting room. That was soon after dinner, of course. The second time was maybe forty-five minutes later.' As often before, her voice rose at the end of the sentence, forming a question. 'It was just before the television show started, I do recall that.'

St Just made a mental note to check the telly schedule for that night.

'We were watching the news when we lost the power,' said Edith. 'You have to remember all these times are rough guesses at best.'

'And what did you do then?'

'We went to bed,' they answered together.

Tom added, 'We sat around a bit to see if it was a temporary situation. When it became evident it was not, we went to bed.'

'Had either of you met Kimberlee before?' asked St Just.

They both shook their heads.

'How about the others? Had you met your fellow Americans, for example?'

'We might have run across some of them at the occasional New York conference. I really don't recall,' said Tom. His voice was harsh and phlegmy, like a clarinet played under water. Again, he spoke over Edith, drowning out her soft voice.

'Tell me how you came to be here.' St Just, leaning against a low cabinet, directed the question to Tom this time. Not that it mattered whom he addressed. The man would prevent his wife speaking wherever he could, probably just from force of habit.

'We'd had a good year, financially speaking. Easterbrook invited us and there seemed no reason to decline. Right about then I saw an ad for airfare to Scotland that was too good to pass up, even allowing for the absolute drubbing the US dollar has been taking lately.'

'This is unusual – Easterbrook picking up the hotel tab?'

'I should say it is. Usually, only agents and editors get compensated at these conference affairs. Then they spend all their time actively avoiding anyone who looks like he might be harboring a manuscript about his or her person. The attendees believe the agents and editors are here as talent scouts – can you believe it? Quite the opposite, of course. They're here to see, in this case, Edinburgh, and to stay in a castle or hotel with room service. Full stop.'

'A boondoggle, then?'

'Quite. One of the perks of the job, you see.'

'A bit misleading to the attendees, perhaps? The aspiring authors?'

Brackett shrugged. 'That's their lookout.'

St Just wondered how much of Tom's good year had to do with Edith's book sales rather than his own. St Just struggled to keep his usual easy-going expression pasted on his face: The man seemed to roil with an undercurrent of rage and contempt for the world at large. If that rage found a target in anyone who thwarted him, how dangerous could Tom Brackett be?

'Inspector,' said Edith. He turned to her. 'If you have no

further questions of me I would like to lie down. It has been a trying day.'

The request surprised him but he could see no reason to detain her. Later, he would see her downstairs – not resting, but sketching in a notebook. There was apparently another door into the hallway from their bedroom. He wondered then if her withdrawal was diplomatic – if she suspected he might get further with Tom without her there.

When the door closed behind her, St Just turned to the man and said, 'Let's go through this one more time.'

'Why?'

'Because Edith is too close to you' – *too afraid of you* – 'for me to bank on her neutrality as a witness. Besides, you were there most of the time. It's the others who need you to vouch for them.'

To this there was no reply. Brackett looked away, but his cross expression plainly said keeping the others out of trouble was a very low priority with him.

'Can you verify what Edith said about her own movements?'

Tom lit a cigarette in the nonsmoking room, taking his time about it, the rasp of the strike wheel of his disposable lighter puncturing the quiet. Finally, he said, 'Edith fetched drinks, maybe twice, maybe three times.'

'Three? That's not what was said earlier.'

A shrug. 'I don't remember, I told you. I'd had a few drinks. I wasn't watching the clock.'

'And the men?'

'Winston went to the john a couple times. Or at least he *said* that's where he was going. That King jackass went to his room and to the john. I'm not sure about Quentin.'

'When did you first meet Kimberlee?'

'We've been over this. I didn't know the woman.'

'You lived in London at one point in your life, did you not?'

Finally. Brackett's consternation at St Just's easy knowledge of his past had at last wiped the irritable expression from his face, replacing it with a look of wariness. *What else might the police know?*

'When was this?' St Just pressed home the advantage.

'You tell me,' said Brackett. 'You know everything.'

St Just lost his temper, a luxury he rarely allowed himself with a suspect. He moved a menacing step closer to Brackett's chair. As usual with bullies, Tom, surprised, simmered down immediately.

'This is how it works. I ask the questions. You answer them. When did you live in London?'

'In the late eighties.'

'Why?'

'I worked for the CIA in those days. And our pals at MI6.'

'Where did you live?'

'I had a flat just off Sloane Square.'

'Nice. I didn't know government work paid that well.'

'I was high up the ladder.' Another shrug, elaborately casual this time. His eyes held a glint of triumph, and of warning, as if to imply there were still strings he might pull from those days, if he chose. 'Also, I had started writing by then. The job bored me. For something to do I began writing. The advance on my first novel helped pay the rent.'

'Were you published by Deadly Dagger Press then?'

'No. Dagger acquired my house in a merger. They kept me on, naturally.'

'You always wrote thrillers?'

'Yes. "Write what you know" is the accepted wisdom. What I knew about was spies. So I did – write about them.'

'What did you do before and after you lived in London?'

'A lot of that is classified, but it's nothing to do with this situation, anyway.'

St Just's fists came crashing down on both arms of Tom's chair, effectively pinning him in. He bent down until his face was just inches away. 'Quit screwing with me. I'll find out eventually but it would be better to hear it from you.'

Tom turned his head, sparing St Just the strong smell of cigarette fumes. An exaggerated sigh, now – the sigh of an adult indulging a particularly fractious child.

'From London I went to Russia,' Tom muttered. 'From Russia I went to the US. I met Edith. I worked. I retired.'

St Just stepped back, releasing him.

'That's much more the kind of cooperative spirit I was hoping for,' he said. 'Now, do you have much contact with other writers?'

'Not if I can help it. The usual tours and signings. I go out to meet my fans, not other authors. What would the point be of that?'

'So you don't normally come to conferences. Why come to this one?'

Brackett seemed to realize the contradiction. He paused to blow a smoke ring, looking like a man trying to remember where he'd mislaid his keys.

'It's lonely work, writing. Besides, I told you, Easterbrook was paying.'

'How often did you speak with Kimberlee here at the castle?'

Another pull on the cigarette.

'That first night at dinner. Maybe I congratulated her on her upcoming award.'

St Just talked with the man a further twenty minutes, and managed to wrench no more from him than a reiteration of how the murder had nothing to do with him. St Just, fuming, went downstairs, which was where he found Edith busy with her sketching. She seemed to be an exceptional artist in addition to her other gifts; he hadn't realized that she probably illustrated her own books. He watched as a gentle, comic illustration of field mice emerged from her pencil, and felt a small twinge of envy. He had enough experience of the difficulty of drawing well to know talent when he saw it. He told her this, and once again watched the flush of pleasure beautify her transparent skin like a sunrise.

'It's safe to go back up,' he told her. 'I think. Mrs Brackett – Edith – if there is anything you feel you need to tell me, or if the police can help you in any way—'

But she cut him off. 'He'll be needing me. I have to get back to him,' she said, quickly gathering her things. Worried, he followed her back up slowly, heading for the incident room. He passed the Bracketts' door again on the way.

'And just what the fuck did you think you were doing?' he heard Tom say, before she could safely shut the door.

Now there, thought St Just, was a man who lived in a world of paranoia and distrust. Did belonging to the CIA do that to one, St Just wondered? Or were you paranoid to start with, to want to join?

He sat in the currently empty incident room, rifled through some of the new reports that had come in, and fought down his frustration. He was operating at a disadvantage. These people were separated from their homes and daily lives, thrust against the foreign, outlandish backdrop of a Scottish castle. Thrust into a *murder* investigation in a Scottish castle.

The clothes on their backs and in their suitcases, and the few personal items they had brought with them, were all he had to go on for clues to their personalities. That, and the potted biographies on their book jackets.

How much truth, and how much advertising, might have gone into those? They might be the fabricated product of some fevered brain in the publisher's marketing department, for all he knew.

And he was working at another disadvantage: His instinctive avoidance of Kimberlee Kalder meant he had to rely largely on second-hand accounts of her from people he barely knew.

He reached across the desk for a phone. His first call was to Sergeant Fear, his usual *aide de camp* in Cambridge. Fear had embarked on a three-day course of thatching in Shropshire, of all things, bringing his small family in tow. St Just gathered that Fear regarded a part-time job as a thatcher as a hedge against future inflation. St Just managed to reach him on a mobile with an appalling connection.

'How are you, Sergeant?'

'Nothing a bit of sleep wouldn't cure, Sir.'

'Devin? How old is he now? Nine weeks?'

'Nearly ten, Sir.'

'He won't sleep?'

'No, Sir.'

'Have you tried – ?'

'Yes,' said Fear, a bit more curtly than his usual respect for his superior would dictate. After a pause: 'Yes, Sir. We have tried feeding him before bed, not feeding him before bed, giving him warm baths, massages, driving him around in the car – my God, I've seen more of the back roads of England in the last few weeks than ever before in my life. Do you know when the bakeries deliver to the restaurants? I do. They—'

'Have you tried placing him on top of the drier?'

'The what?'

'The clothes drier. They like the permanent press cycle best, not too warm. Now, why I was calling. . .'

He rang off after a few minutes, leaving Fear still wondering how St Just had become an expert on every subject, however obscure.

Next, St Just put in a call to a friend of his at Scotland Yard. It was time to sketch in a little more background on the American contingent.

CHAPTER 17

Just the Facts

Having finished his calls, St Just headed downstairs, in search of a life-restoring cup of tea. He needed to learn what forensics had come up with, but first, according to his stomach, he needed some sustenance.

He used the back stairs of the castle, which led directly past the spa. Coming out of the main spa door, wrapped in one of the ubiquitous hotel robes, and with a towel over one arm, was Portia, her face painted with what looked like blue plaster of Paris.

They both leapt back, emitting small yips of surprise.

'Good God. Are the Picts invading?' he asked her.

From between stiffened lips, she muttered, 'It's a facial, of course.' She wiped off some of the mask with the towel before spearing him with her characteristically direct gaze.

'Most of the women are taking advantage of the "lull" to visit the spa,' she told him. 'Even Edith Brackett managed to escape Tom's clutches for a bit. You should see her – she's starting to look fabulous. Anyway, I've been in there all day, being steamed like an oyster – I was just nipping up to my room for a book, hoping not to run into anyone.' She gave him an ironic scowl. Only Portia, he felt, could retain her composure with a face covered in blue goo. It was the kind of instinctive poise that could not be taught or learned. She would look dignified in a clown's suit.

'Anyway,' she went on, 'I've been buffed and polished

and sprayed to within an inch of my life' – and here she lowered her voice – 'eavesdropping all the while. I'll tell you all about it later. It's hard to talk with my face glued like this. But you should know this before I forget: Kimberlee lost her key at some point. I saw her rootling around in her purse after the dinner, and she said something like, "Drat, I'll have to get another one from reception." I assume she meant key.'

'Yes, one of Moor's men learned she'd asked for a replacement key,' he said. He stood quietly a moment, weighing how the missing key could fit in. It might be important, but he wasn't sure just how.

'Well,' he said, 'at least you have the perfect disguise for undercover work.' He looked her up and down, and smiled. 'Your own mother wouldn't recognize you.'

'Ha. Ha. You can thank me when I've helped you solve this case. We exercise zee leetle gray cells, *non*?'

'*Non*. I would much prefer you went back to your room and stayed there. Don't let anyone in who isn't a policeman, either. Don't you have a novel you're supposed to be writing?'

'With all of this going on? Are you joking? If this isn't the perfect excuse for procrastination, I don't know what is.' She turned to go. 'See you later.'

He gently took hold of her arm.

'Is there any point in warning you to be careful?' he hissed quietly.

She shook her head.

'None. You know as well as I do – they'll say things to me they'd never say to you. Most of them admit to a dislike of the victim. An active dislike, in fact.'

'A festering dislike, if you prefer. It gets us no closer.'

'Count your blessings that I'm around,' said Portia. 'It's you who should be careful. Remember, these people lie for a living: They write novels.'

She smiled, a somewhat stiff and lopsided but endearing

smile because of the hardening mask, like a dentist's victim before the Novocain has worn off.

'Keep in mind,' she said, here holding up a forefinger as if lecturing a roomful of pillocky undergraduates, 'that writers are determined, motivated, often highly organized – belying the notion of the scatterbrained creative artist. One has to be organized to withstand the long haul of a novel. They're also driven, persevering, resilient, and – mostly – able to withstand a lot of setbacks, criticism, and rejection. Apart from the criticism and rejection part, I can't think of a better definition for a methodical killer, can you?'

The admonishing hand fell to her side. She added quietly, her words slowing, her face struggling against the mask to crease with a frown of concentration. 'I realize now I've been writing of murder as if it were an academic exercise, all this time. But now I'm faced with the real horror of it.' The fathomless eyes pinned his gaze. 'They say people read crime novels because of a human need to see the world set right after any kind of disturbance. What happened to Kimberlee was a desecration. The world has to be righted.'

'Not your job. . .' he began.

'It's everybody's job, in a way – if only from a practical standpoint. We're trapped here with a murderer. A sense of self-preservation demands that the killer be caught. And soon.'

She turned from him and glided away down the corridor. He continued to watch her disappear up the stairs, thinking how different their time together here might have been. If only.

Tea had been set out in the sitting room in a serve-yourself fashion, attracting several of the castle's inhabitants.

As Portia had indicated, most of the ladies were missing, presumably being roasted or pummeled in the spa. Jay Fforde sat apart from the rest, draped across the window seat, a book open on his lap. Winston Chatley and Julius Easterbrook held down opposite ends of the silk-covered sofa. Annabelle Pace sat slumped in one of the plush chairs. The room was bathed in an ocher light from the table lamps. They might have been posing, carefree guests, for a castle brochure.

Annabelle looked up from the *Tatler* magazine she'd been flipping through in an aimless way, as if she'd read the issue several times already. Today she wore a loose smock and trousers the color of London smog. She looked less as if she had dressed herself than as if someone had thrown clothes at her until they stuck. She had made an unwise attempt to enliven this subfusc costume with a polyester scarf of a malignant shade of yellow, the effect of which was to further deplete her bloodless, sallow complexion.

The papers were spread out everywhere on the tables that dotted the room. Much like a gentleman's club, Dalmorton provided its guests with all the popular and serious daily newspapers, from the tabloid red tops like the *Mirror* to the broadsheet *Telegraph*. St Just winced at one of the headlines: 'Chick Lit Author: Victim of Fowl Play?' Another shouted, 'Chick Author Slaughtered.' He thought of the editorial meetings that had resulted in that headline, where no doubt 'Fricasseed' had also been given serious consideration.

He considered, not for the first time, that Winston was right: There was something dramatic, something theatrical, about the way Kimberlee was killed. After all, there were a thousand places to kill her in the castle. Why kill her and then throw her into a bottle dungeon? *Why?* He wasn't sure the papers had gotten hold of that bit of information yet, but when they did . . . It was as if the dark arts of public relations that Kimberlee practiced during her short life had lived on after her in death.

'So, Inspector,' said Annabelle, throwing the magazine onto the low table before her. She leaned back, heaving her heavy, maternal bosom, and said, 'How's the investigation going? We can't all stop here much longer.'

'Indeed,' said Easterbrook. One foot crossed over his knee, he impatiently jiggled one polished shoe. St Just was reminded that in his youth, Easterbrook would probably have been most at home scaling the north face of the Eiger or hunting tigers on safari. Imposed inaction would quickly wear him thin. 'You've had plenty of time, man. Don't tell me you can't resolve this.'

Annabelle said, 'As for me, I was with either Mrs Elksworthy or your friend Portia the whole time. Just ask them. So you see, there's no earthly reason to detain me here longer.'

'The police will be cross-checking everyone's statements,' said St Just, hoping against hope that her casually tossed phrase, 'your friend,' was not making him blush to the roots of his hair. He'd fondly hoped he'd kept his interest in Portia rather well hidden.

He sat in one of the chairs across from the sofa, addressing Easterbrook.

'It's not like one of the mysteries you publish, you know, where everything is neatly wrapped up in the course of a few hours, or pages.'

'I've been interviewed by a veritable platoon of your Scottish colleagues,' said Easterbrook peevishly. 'And by you, as well. I repeat, I don't see what earthly use there is keeping those of us who have been thoroughly interviewed hanging about, wasting our valuable time. I've been on to my solicitor, of course. Annabelle is quite right. You can't hold us here indefinitely.'

St Just thought, *You're right. Not without evidence, which I shall have.*

He said nothing. Let Easterbrook get his solicitor up here, then. The wait would buy the investigation some time, anyway – time he felt they might sorely need.

'Once all the interviews are complete, we may need to cross-check what we've learned,' St Just repeated equably, but his tone left no room for argument. Easterbrook, seeming to weigh the odds against winning the toss, subsided into a grumbling acquiescence.

Annabelle dipped her head once more into her magazine, ignoring them. She looked strangely disheveled, even given her usual standard. The glasses on top of her head acted as a head-band, pinning back her hair, which otherwise fell in stringy waves to her shoulders. Of all the women at the castle, thought St Just, she might have benefited most from a bit of spa pampering. Instead, Portia was busy gilding the lily, while Annabelle. . .

Easterbrook, who had been looking on darkly over his reading glasses as if to emphasize nothing thus far in the proceedings met with his favor, spluttered again into life. 'All these questions about where we were, and when. How can we possibly know? Do you have any idea the amount of drinking that went on last night?'

Jay Fforde, who seemed to have adopted a Lord Peter Wimsey demeanor for the occasion, looked over and said, 'Quite.'

'There were far too many of us for any one to really be accounted for,' continued Easterbrook. Winston nodded agreement.

'Quite,' said Jay again. 'Everyone came and went.'

'I didn't,' said Annabelle flatly, from behind the magazine. 'Like I said, I was with Mrs E – oh, and then I was trapped by that ghastly little creep B. A. King for simply hours. He'll tell you.'

'You'll have a chance to tell me yourself later on,' said St Just.

St Just, carrying a mug of strong black tea, found the Inspector and Sergeant Kittle in Kimberlee's room.

'The press are onto us,' he informed them.

'I know,' said Inspector Moor. He leaned over and switched on a television set in the corner of the room. An excited young BBC announcer, clearly struggling to wipe the ecstatic smile off her face, was offering a breathless recap of Kimberlee's short career as Kimberlee herself smiled in frozen perpetuity from the upper left corner of the screen. As the policemen watched, the screen faded to black, to be replaced by an aerial shot of Dalmorton Castle. Moor leaned over again and switched off. 'We've got guarded barriers keeping their vehicles out. Keeping the photographers themselves from skulking around the grounds on foot is going to be more difficult. That's stock footage they've got from somewhere but it's probably just a matter of time before we have helicopters whirring overhead.' The torque of his Scottish accent managed to find at least four extra 'r's' in 'whirring.'

St Just nodded. 'So, what's the status?'

'We've only got the preliminary results from the body,' Moor replied, 'But I don't think there will be any big surprises. She was struck a blow to the head which almost certainly would have killed her eventually, but being thrown into the dungeon killed her first.'

'Any sign of a weapon?'

Moor shook his head.

'It could have been anything, really. But there was nothing kept down there that would serve as a handy weapon – fire extinguisher or suchlike. Whoever it was, brought the thing with him. Or her. And carried it away with them.'

'Premeditated, then,' said St Just.

'Almost certainly. Especially given that she must have been keeping some kind of pre-arranged rendezvous – it's unlikely she just took it into her head to pop into the dungeon that time of night.'

'And the lights went out, don't forget. In which case. . .'

'Where's the candle?' Moor finished for him. 'It helps us pinpoint the time a bit more, doesn't it?'

'Unless the murderer had the wit to take the candle away with him or her.'

'Hmm,' grunted Moor. 'Anyway, the way we see it is, some-one hid beneath the spiral stairs leading down to the dungeon room. There's just enough space. It was dark, or darkish. The person leapt out. Struck her from behind. Tipped her over into the dungeon proper. The element of surprise had to have helped, which is why a female assailant is every bit as likely as a male – she was a wee thing, so leveraging her over the rail wouldn't be all that difficult.'

'Still, it's hard to picture Mrs Elksworthy, for example, in that kind of weight-lifting role. What have you got over there?' He indicated an evidence bag.

'It's the contents of Kimberlee's purse.'

St Just walked over and picked it up. Lipstick, compact, all the usual. 'This is from the purse we found here in her room?'

'Yes.'

'There's no key in here.'

Moor took the evidence bag and held it to the light.

'So there isn't. Which means—'

'I'm not sure I know what it means. Someone stole her key?'

'I don't understand,' said Moor. 'We know she got a replace-ment key from reception. She told them she'd lost hers.'

'It only makes sense if . . . Hmm. Let me chew on this a bit. What else do you have?'

'Lots,' said Moor, waving a few faxed pages in St Just's direction. 'First, that snarky little Quentin character – the reporter with the hair – he used to work at the same news-paper as Kimberlee, a few years back.'

'At the same time?'

Moor nodded. 'Something he didn't think to mention when my men talked with him.'

'I can certainly correct the oversight later today, if you like,' said St Just. 'What else? I don't suppose her watch stopped when she fell, or anything helpful like that, pinpointing the time?'

'Doesn't appear so. But that's not the big news,' said Moor. 'I've saved that for last.' The man grinned from ear to ear. 'The big news is – wait for it – our Kimberlee was pregnant.'

CHAPTER 18

Femme Fatale

'Well, if it was Jay,' St Just was saying, 'that was fast work.'

The three men stood by the window overlooking the castle grounds – a vista Kimberlee Kalder, tucked on a cold morgue slab, would never again enjoy.

Moor said, 'He gave us a statement saying he and Kimberlee were star-crossed right until the end – there was interest on both sides, but the union was not consummated.' He pulled absently on his mustache, adding, 'She was only four weeks along, but that's not to say she and Jay didn't meet up in London or somewhere four weeks ago.'

'Right. I assume you've got men on it?' asked St Just.

'Men and women. Yes.'

'This whole business with room service might need looking into,' said St Just. 'I'll have a word with whoever it was brought that tray to her room next, I think. Quentin can wait. Let him think he's gotten away with something.'

'That would be Florie Macintosh you want – the one who brought the tray,' said Moor. 'I saw her just now, talking with that Donna Doone woman, in her office. The prehistoric historic writer one. Oh, by the way, some of them have presented us with written accounts of their whereabouts.' Moor handed St Just a sheaf of pages. 'That really was rather naughty of you, Inspector.'

St Just grinned back at him. 'Are they dreadful?'

'Some are not bad: quite straightforward, bare-bones

163

timetables or accounts of where they "think" they were, and when. Followed by a rash of question marks, of course, in case we try to pin them down. Possibly they are even truthful accounts – there is no telling. Could come in useful for cross-checking their statements. Magretta Sincock, however – but there, I wouldn't want to spoil it for you. You'll just have to read it yourself.'

St Just pocketed the pages Moor handed him and again headed downstairs, this time taking the grand staircase that would deposit him near both the bottle dungeon and the hotel's reception area. All was preternaturally quiet, but he sensed the presence of his suspects, like mice behind the walls.

The young receptionist pointed him to the hallway leading to the business offices. Her eyes and nose were reddened, as if she had been crying. The investigation had to be taking a toll on the staff, he reflected. He smiled with more assurance then he felt, and she seemed to perk up a fraction.

Navigating the narrow hallway, he heard a voice coming from a partially opened door to his right. He thought he recognized the strong Scottish burr as belonging to the woman who'd brought his brandy the night before.

He soon saw he was right. A small, brindle-haired terrier of a woman in her middle years stood in the center of the room with her short legs braced and fists dug into her wide, sturdy hips. She was also the same woman he'd seen outside the bottle dungeon, tut-tutting over the lazy workmen.

'So I told Frank,' she was saying, 'about this old Australian chap. He was such a scamp; he kept saying he wanted to run off with me. He was joking like, of course, but didn't he just make me laugh. So I told Frank and what do you think he said? He said, "Pack your bags. I'll drive you to the airport."'

She cackled at that, slapping her hands against her thighs and ending on a whoop of laughter. Donna Doone, seated at her desk, smiled back distractedly, arrested in the act of sorting papers into a pink foolscap folder.

'Sorry to interrupt, ladies,' he said, pushing the door wider and walking into the room. It was furnished in a utilitarian style, lacking the plushy comforts of the public rooms. Steel file cabinets lined the stone walls, and a stack of cartons of brochures, hotel stationery, and assorted corporate advertising filled one corner. A serviceable glazed teapot with matching cups and saucers sat on a tray at one corner of the desk.

'Do you know anything about who did it yet?' Donna Doone asked him. 'The staff are half scared out of their wits. I think more than a few may give notice.'

'Ruddy cowards,' said Florie Macintosh.

St Just shook his head.

'I realize this is upsetting,' he told Donna. With a nod to Florie, he added, 'For most of you, anyway. We're doing all we can.'

'I don't find it upsetting, not at all,' confirmed Florie. 'Makes a break from routine. I didn't even mind stopping here all night. It was my usual night, anyway – but this is my day off now. That policeman asked would I stay around a bit. "To help with inquires," he says. Ha! I know what that means. I don't reckon I'll be paid extra for helping anyone with their inquiries. But what I really want to know about is that nasty dust you lot have spread on everything, like they do on the telly.' Here outrage deepened her already thick brogue: 'Who's gang to clean that oop?' she demanded.

'The fingerprint dust? I'm afraid the hotel will be responsible for that.'

'Och! It wasn't me who made the mess, now was it?'

'I know it seems unfair, but you wouldn't really expect the police to expend their resources cleaning up crime scenes, now would you?'

'I'm saying that's exactly what I would expect. You can't—'

'I'm certain what the hotel will do is hire a professional crime-scene cleaning company. There are specialists who handle that sort of thing. Now, tell me, Ms Macintosh, how long have you worked here?'

'They'd better. To answer your question: twenty year. And it's Mrs Macintosh. Last time I looked, himself was still parked in front of the telly at home, sound asleep. Anyway, I worked for the Dalmorton family before they sold the pile to the hotel chain. But this is my first murder.'

St Just grinned. 'I am relieved to hear it. Now, did either of you talk much with Kimberlee Kalder during her stay?'

Donna Doone shook her head vigorously. Her tightly wound curls stood momentarily out from her head before snapping back into formation.

'No,' she said. She stood abruptly and began trying to pour herself a cup of tea. How long before she realized she'd already emptied the teapot, he wondered? Her hands shook, making the lid rattle. She was nervous and distracted, no question. But it was difficult for him to think of Donna as truly unbalanced or the type easily driven to kill, despite the peculiar judgment betrayed by her strange little novel. Misguided was surely a better word. As to motive – what possible motive could there be except an explosive jealousy over Kimberlee Kalder's easy success? He'd seen weaker motives, but still . . .

If only the murderer had thrown a latte on her or knocked her out with a handbag, we'd have a better handle on the professional jealousy angle, he thought.

Florie was saying, her face a mask of pinched disapproval, 'I talked with her as little as possible. She were a right young miss and no mistake. Didn't half think the sun shown out of her arse.'

'Florie!' admonished Donna. For a largish woman her voice was surprisingly high, with a yippy undertone. He imagined one of the Queen's corgis would sound like that if it could talk. It was in complete contrast with that of her small co-worker, who he felt could hold her own against an opera singer. 'Ill of the dead, and all.' Giving up at last on the tea, Donna began nervously smoothing her tight-fitting skirt against her thighs.

'Their being dead doesn't make them better folk than they were alive,' Florie countered. 'Only quieter.'

St Just interrupted, clearing his throat. He felt that, left to her own devices, Florie would burble along endlessly, her conversation ranging widely over everything but the murder itself. Sometimes that kind of interviewee was helpful: You could just wind them up and off they'd go. How much useful information could be forked out of the detritus was anyone's guess. Directing his question at Donna, he said, 'Tell me about that drawbridge.'

She knew immediately what he meant.

'I raised it just before the dinner. There were no guests scheduled to arrive, you see, and we needed all hands on deck to handle the meal. We've a small staff and we run the place more like a private club, really, than a hotel. Anyway, when Rachel Twalley and the other people from Edinburgh wanted to leave, I let them out and closed it behind them.'

'That was at what time?'

She wrung her hands.

'I've been trying to remember and I can't. About nine forty-five at a guess. Earlier than the normal.'

'I think I heard the clanking and groaning when it went up. It doesn't half make a racket, doesn't it?'

'That it does,' she agreed. 'By the way, the press have started calling.' She looked aggrieved: *This is all your fault.*

'You've not talked to them, but passed them along to the communications officer, as we asked?'

'Yes, yes, of course. But to tell you the truth, I've started letting the answerphone deal with it.'

'Even better.'

He turned back to Florie, who had taken advantage of the lull to begin attacking the pile of cartons with a dust rag.

'Now, Mrs Macintosh, you told the other policemen you'd delivered a tray to Kimberlee the night she died,' he said.

'I did that,' she said, stowing the rag in her apron. 'I was the last to know of her alive, I suppose, excepting her killer, of course.'

'Of course. Now, tell me, what time was this?'

'Near enough ten as makes no difference. Maybe a quarter after. I still had to do the castle recce, which I do last thing at night.'

'What time did she place the order? And what did she order?'

'Say nine-thirty or nine-forty. There's a record kept of room service orders. You can check that. I took up wine and some cheese and cream crackers, things like that.'

'For two?'

'For two. Two glasses. While I was on my way, I delivered a hottie to the room next door to the Kalder woman's.'

'I see. You delivered this hot water bottle to Magretta Sincock's room?'

'If she be the daft one the staff've taken to calling Greensleeves, aye. She'd let it be known this was a standing request for each night.'

Something Florie had said just registered with him. 'You say you were the last to "know of" Kimberlee alive. Did you actually *see* Kimberlee?'

She shot him an appreciative glance: No dust on *this* fellow. 'She didn't answer her door. Just shouted for me to leave it outside. Folk do that sometime – they want to get out of tipping, the cheap bastards.'

'Florie!' This again from Donna, who seemed to regard Florie as a fractious child making a bad impression on the nice visitor.

'Now, both of you: In the time Kimberlee was here, did you notice anything in particular about her demeanor or behavior? Did she seem worried or anxious about anything?'

They shook their heads simultaneously.

'She seemed happy enough to me,' said Donna. 'She flirted with most of the men, I can tell you. That good-looking agent especially set her preening. If anything she seemed to be in great high spirits. But it was harmless larking about, just general silliness.'

'You think so, do you?' asked Florie Macintosh. 'Since when has that kind of thing not harmed *some*one? And are you forgetting how she laughed at that book you're working on?'

'Did she?' St Just asked Donna, who, averting her eyes, looked as if she were praying for the earth to open and swallow her.

'I asked Kimberlee for her opinion on a few pages of *Caveman Death*,' Donna said at last. 'I thought – I actually thought if she liked it, my book, she might help me get an agent. Then I found her reading it aloud to Ninette Thomson. Laughing, as Florie said. She didn't have to be so . . . mean.'

'No,' he said gently. 'Try not to let it bother you. Kimberlee did have a mean streak.'

'You can say that again,' said Florie. 'She was a bleedin' barracuda, that one.'

'But do you know' – and here Donna brightened and raised her head, the look in her eyes both defiant and defenseless – 'Ninette told me later she thought she could sell *Caveman Death*. Told me to send the manuscript to her when I finished it.'

'That's wonderful,' St Just said, struggling to hide his amazement. 'I'm sure her advice will be good; Ninette seems to know exactly what she's doing.' He stood to take his leave of them. 'Now, I want you both to think back. You have wider access to the hotel than the visitors. Maybe you saw something you didn't realize was significant.'

The two women looked at each other, shrugged, and turned bemused looks to him.

'And you, Mrs Macintosh, I want you to think very hard about this.'

She frowned, preparatory to thinking.

'The voice you heard telling you to leave the tray outside the door. Are you certain it was Kimberlee Kalder's?'

She gazed at him, her face tense with concentration.

'Now you mention it, no. No, I'm not.'

CHAPTER 19

Fit for a King

St Just walked away from Donna Doone's office, lost in thought. He had to take Florie's statement on faith, since only she could verify her experience. And he tended to think her an honest and down-to-earth personality. Would she lie? Alter the room service record? *Why* would she?

But the fact was, she'd been on the scene, trapped by the power failure like the rest of them. For that matter, any of the day staff could have stayed behind, hidden somewhere in the castle, despite claims of having gotten out before they lost the electricity. An exception was the bartender: The police had learned that, because he generally kept such late hours, he had been given his own room at the bottom of the castle, where he routinely slept, like a sailor in the belly of a luxury cruise ship.

What on earth the motive for any of the staff could be, St Just couldn't imagine. Even Kimberlee, self-centered as she was, couldn't inspire the kind of instantaneous hatred that would lead an apparent stranger to kill her.

St Just had always maintained that gossip was the policeman's friend, and gossip about all these writers was what was needed now. Stopping at the reception desk, he asked the red-nosed girl, whose nametag identified her as Mary, to ring the room of B. A. King. It was time to round out his interviews with the Fab Four who had been in the sitting room. Fab Four plus One, he reminded himself, as Quentin had remained with them at least part of the time.

171

'You're looking for that oily bloke?' she asked, then, seeming to realize she was talking about a hotel guest, tried valiantly for a recovery. She couldn't have been more than a day over eighteen. 'I mean—'

'It's a perfect description. Why, you've seen him?'

'He's in the library, drunk as a laird. We asked the bartender to keep him in there so's we'd all see a bit less of him.'

'Flirting with you, has he been?'

She wrinkled up her nose. 'A bit more and less than that, really. Just general goatishness. Given to ambushing the maids in the hallways, that sort of thing. I don't like the way he looks at me, is all. Staring, and winking. Telling me how his Gran was Scottish, as if I cared. The girls are that sick of him.'

'I can well imagine. I'll have a word with him.' Off her look, he added, 'Don't worry. He won't know I heard it from you.'

He found B. A. King as promised, parked, or rather deposited in a heap, on one of the room's leather sofas. Perhaps interviewing him now wasn't such a good idea, after all, St Just thought. But *in vino veritas*. Or in this case, in Laphroaig. The man smelt as if he'd poured it over himself and then jumped in a peat bog.

King was a big man with the pink complexion of the committed, lifelong drinker. Much the same height and weight as the detective, he was somehow, well, *fleshier*, his weight oddly distributed like a tyre around his middle. As Mary had said, he was oily, like undercooked salmon. He was attached to a dark hairpiece that sat at a jaunty angle, slicked back from his forehead. The cloth of his gray suit put St Just in mind of sharkskin. The unfocused eyes were sharklike, as well: dark and flat, seeming not to reflect light.

St Just smiled, realizing where his train of thought had led him. There was no doubt about it: The man was fishy.

'I need a few words with you, Mr King.'

King nodded in hazy recognition.

'I gather you knew Kimberlee Kalder quite well,' said St Just.

'I did not. Who says so?'

No one, in fact, thought St Just. But angry denials were often a good starting point. The police could teach the press a thing or two about interrogation techniques. At least he'd gotten the man's attention.

'Why talk to me?' King demanded. He looked at St Just with a fierce, drunken concentration. 'I never represented Kimberlee Kalder. Hardly knew the freakin' bimbo.'

King drained his glass and reached for a refill from the half-empty bottle on the table. St Just was half tempted to join him. Since breakfast he'd had only a crumpet and half a sandwich he'd found in the incident room. The sandwich had been water-cress and a thin smear of butter. As good as a drink sounded to him, a steak to go with it sounded better.

'You were pointed out to me as someone who knew the business, who knew a lot of crime writers.'

'By who? Whom?' said B. A. King belligerently, peering at him over his glass. His voice was a deep, tuba-like rumble. In other circumstances, St Just thought he might find it oddly soothing.

He sat down opposite the man, leaned back, and folded his arms.

'Here's the way this works, Mr King,' he said. 'I ask the questions. You answer the questions. You answer them com-pletely and honestly. Then I leave you to go back to your whiskey.'

B. A. King started to interrupt and St Just held up a hand to ward him off. He had come to recognize two basic types of American visitor to Great Britain: the type that would do whatever you asked because they liked your accent, and the type that viewed British reticence and politeness as weaknesses ripe for exploitation. He suspected King fell into the latter category. St Just pierced him with a look that his sergeant would have read as an unambiguous storm warning. King, however, being less attuned than Sergeant Fear, looked back with the same devil-may-care swagger as before.

'If you don't, you'll not see your passport again for a long time. A *very* long time. Not until the photo resembles you even less than the usual passport photo, because so much time has passed. Not until we say we're through with you, in fact. Push it too far, and you may not see the outside of the local nick for awhile, either, while we discuss your problem with the people at your embassy. Am I making myself clear?'

'Look here, you. I know my rights.'

'Good. Then you know I'm within mine to detain you if you obstruct this investigation.'

Just then, the bartender – whose name, St Just recalled, was Randolph – returned from some errand or another. St Just signaled him for two coffees.

'I don't want coffee.' King adjusted his improbable hair, making matters somewhat worse.

'Make that extra dark, please,' St Just said to the back of the retreating young man.

'All right, then,' grumbled King. 'What is it you want to know?'

'How well did you know Kimberlee?'

'I didn't. I only knew the Americans, really. She was British. Well, part British. London was where she mostly lived.'

'How do you know that?'

King exploded. 'I talked with her – briefly – during the conference. *That's* how. Idle chitchat. Nothing more.'

'I overheard that idle chitchat. She "idly" accused you of stealing from her.'

'Nah, she . . . You see, I had borrowed her pen at the conference and lost it somewhere. She wanted me to replace it and I promised to. No big deal. Once I lost the pen Magretta used to pen the immortal *Death Be Not Cowed*. Or was it *Dead Ducky*? Anyway, now, *there* was a fuss. But Kimberlee? Not a big deal, I tell you.'

St Just doubted this story in the extreme, but to keep the conversation from devolving into a Did Too/Did Not contest, he decided to let it go for the moment.

'All right. What about the writers from your own side of the pond? What can you tell me about them? Start with the Bracketts.'

'Tom Brackett? He's a jerk. Used to sell at a good clip. Still sells, just not like before. Then everyone started to notice the Berlin Wall had come down, we were all in the Middle East now, but Tom Brackett was still writing the same Cold War spy novel that had made him famous decades ago. It won't do. You have to be flexible in this business, keep up with things.'

'Yes, wars do have a way of switching locations, don't they? Shifting around? One has to pay close attention.' St Just thought it interesting how often he'd heard all the writers defined less in terms of personality than in the volume of books they sold. He was almost getting used to it.

King nodded. 'You betcha. Fewer people are reading Tom's particular brand of spy crap, anyway. It's all psychic paranormal stuff at the moment. Who knew that shit would catch on?'

'The psychics knew, presumably,' St Just said mildly. 'I meant, what about Brackett's background?'

King shrugged. 'Only know what I read on his book jackets, really. Or, used to read.'

'But you do know both of them. Him and his wife.'

'Known them both for years, in that way you know people you see at some conference or other. She was always there, pretty much as bag carrier.'

'How often would that be?'

B. A. King stopped to scratch his armpit. 'Once, twice a year. Maybe more.'

So Tom had perhaps been less than truthful about how often he went to conferences, thought St Just – which would increase the chances Brackett knew more about the others than he claimed. Because he was guilty? Or because he was naturally contrary whenever the occasion arose?

'Anyway,' B. A. King was saying, 'that wife of his took us all by surprise with those children's books.'

'Was Tom happy about that?'

'What do you think? There is only room for one genius in that household. I don't think Edith enjoys much of a life. She should leave him now she's got the money. He's probably threatened to stick her with huge alimony payments if she does.'

'Perhaps she will. Leave him, I mean.'

King shook his head. 'Nah. That type – it's like the Stockholm syndrome. They never leave.' A harsh laugh. 'Even if you beg them.'

'You don't represent Tom? Or Edith?'

'Nah. My only client here is that cow, Annabelle.'

'Since she's a client you know her well, I would imagine.'

'You could say I *knew* her.' Here a wolfish waggle of the eyebrows, apparently a key component of his trademark leer. The coffee arrived. St Just resisted the urge to grab the pot and force some of the liquid down King's throat. Instead, he poured out two cups, as demure as a vicar's wife. As expected, King ignored his. St Just let it go – an ocean of coffee wouldn't begin to penetrate.

'What exactly do you know about Annabelle?'

'Not a lot. It wasn't the bitch's pedigree that interested me.'

'Try.'

A sigh, another scratch of the armpit.

'She's from Birmingham. I think. Nottingham? One of the 'hams, anyway. Married an American and divorced him toot doo sweet. Took up writing as a lark, or so she likes to pretend. I think she needed the money just like the rest of us mortals. More.'

'How so?'

King paused for a little sip, his dark eyes impenetrable. He put down his glass, nearly missing the table. 'Needing the money, you mean? Well . . . I did have the idea her husband ran through what little she had. Or tried to. She odd-jobbed awhile. Worked as a typist, a photographer's assistant, a waitress – stuff like that. She got rid of the husband in short order, anyway – they were married maybe two years, I think she said. You ask me, just long enough to get citizenship papers. But I didn't pay particular attention, I tell you.'

'What's your take on her personality?' Not that he held any great store by King's powers of observation, let alone his opinion, but the least likely people could prove perceptive.

Not this time.

'Oh, I don't know,' said King. 'I wasn't interested in her personality either, was I?'

It was hard to imagine what a man like King did find interesting about a woman like Annabelle, but St Just realized such odd biological imperatives were likely irrelevant to Kimberlee's death. His mind instead ran down the list of writers staying at the castle. Something made him think of Mrs Elksworthy, whom he hadn't seen for awhile. He asked about her.

'Mrs E? Joan Elksworthy? Nice enough woman. Not my type, of course. Old. She's not on my client list, so I don't think I've ever read her, but I've heard she's a competent writer for the tea-and-crumpets crowd. Sells at a small, steady clip.'

'Who else staying here at the castle do you know, or know of?'

'Well, I know of all of them, of course. It's my job. I think the only other one I've met before is Magretta Sincock.'

'You *think*?'

'You're right, you'd hardly forget her, would you? But as to the rest – I meet a ton of people in my line of work. You can't expect me to remember them all.'

Not when you're half in the bag all the time. No, one couldn't hope for that.

'So, what do you remember about Magretta?'

'Really, Inspector. Why don't you just read all their bios? It'll give you the basics.'

'Thanks for the tip. I know the basics. What I need is what's not in the standard-issue PR information.'

'Well, with Magretta it really is a case of what you see is what you get. No use looking for depth there. High maintenance and getting higher. Of course, we had a little fling some years back . . . I see you didn't know that? Well, notice how I'm cooperating by telling all, even though it has nothing to do with anything. She never married, oddly enough, don't you think? That rather aggressive brand of femininity usually attracts a certain spineless type of man. I have heard she was on the stage at some point – rep theater stuff as far from the West End as can be imagined. That career failed, or perhaps it would be truer to say parts requiring over-acting and scenery-chewing dried up.'

'Anything else you can tell me?'

Again the indifferent shrug. 'She seems to be over-flooding the market lately with her books. She needs to take a year off but instead she's upped production. People will start to notice: It's pretty much the same book she wrote the last time out. Womjep shit.'

'I beg your pardon?'

'Womjep. You know – woman in jeopardy. Lately she just cranks them out. They say you can't die of boredom, but reading one of her books, I came close. I don't know if Jay is to blame for the decision to publish more of her books, faster – more likely she's been telling *him* what to do. Whatever. I hear the bloom is off that relationship, and the rumor is the Americans no longer want her, either. As for Jay, he only wanted – or needed – Kimberlee in his stable.'

'She – Magretta – must have found that difficult to take.'

'Yeah. But Magretta, she was always wrapped in dreams. Reality could hit her hard.'

'And now Kimberlee's gone.'

'Uh huh. . .' The implication seemed to be seeping in. 'You don't think Magretta would do away with Kimberlee just so she'd get to keep Jay as an agent? Hey, Jay is good but he's not that good. Pretty far-fetched idea. Even for a crime writer, don't you think?'

St Just wasn't sure what he thought, but he wasn't going to sit here swapping theories with B. A. King. He shot his cuffs and adjusted his suit jacket, thinking.

'Nice threads,' said King. 'Who's your tailor?'

'The night you sat around with the Bracketts and Winston – what did you find to talk about?'

'When Kimberlee was killed?'

'That would be the night in question. Yes.'

'You know. Deals. Online bookstore rankings. Royalties. Rights. Which publisher was on the skids this year. Which agent.'

'That's all? No undercurrents of some kind?'

'You mean, did any of them get a crazed look in their eyes and rush out of the room, shouting "Fuck Chick Lit"? No. Strangely enough, we spent a lot of time talking about Winston's plans for a young adult book. I guess it came up in connection with Edith's success.'

St Just was a bit taken aback. He realized that, quite unfairly, he pictured those who could write for children as being . . . well, not scary looking. King surprised him by reading his reaction perfectly. St Just was reminded of the old joke: I'm not as think as you drunk I am.

'I know,' King was saying. 'It's like Boris Karloff wanting to play Tiny Tim in *A Christmas Carol* or something. But if you read Winston's books, you will see there is a wild and wooly imagination at work there. I can see him writing the next Harry Potter for the younger set, absolutely. And you can bet he'll be needing a publicist, so—'

Just then there was the sound of the heavy library doors being opened. A man's voice, quavering and thick with emotion, said, 'Could I have a word, Inspector?'

CHAPTER 20

Don't Be a Stranger

St Just turned. A dark, sleekly attractive head, presumably attached to a young and attractive male body, peered around the library door, which was held open in a white-knuckled clutch. He looked as if he might be a few shades paler than normal; his eyes were as red as Mary's in reception.

Like St Just, he wore an expensive suit from a bespoke tailor's, but it looked new and of an up-to-date cut. St Just felt he might have seen the man before, but then decided it was only his resemblance to any actor appearing in any recent movie having to do with high livers in London's Square Mile.

B. A. King, having looked up at the intrusion, had resumed his contemplation of the bottom of his glass. Suddenly he said, 'I heard a splash.'

St Just signaled the other man to wait for him outside.

'You what, Sir?'

'When I went up to my room to get some whiskey. I heard a splash.'

What now? Pink elephants frolicking in the moat?

'Time?' St Just asked.

'What? No. How should I know what time it was?'

How indeed. 'Yes, Sir. Thank you.'

'And another thing. . .'

'Yes?' St Just asked politely.

'Just out of curiosity, you might ask Winston what kind of hold he has over Easterbrook. Nobody reads serious "litrature" like Winston's any more, even when it's crammed with serial killers. So why does Easterbrook keep him on? I've heard rumors. Yes, rumors . . . an affair . . . Easterbrook's wife controls the purse strings – don't let him tell you otherwise. Oh, and what was Magretta doing skulking about the hallway up there? I saw her.'

'Time?' he asked again.

'Late. When I went up for the whiskey. I think. Must have been.'

'Late,' St Just repeated. Great. 'One other thing, Mr King. Stay away from the female staff of this hotel, and keep your hands to yourself. Or else.'

St Just left him. B. A. King, he thought, could stew awhile. Literally.

St Just first looked for the dark-haired young man in the lobby, then saw that he had taken St Just literally at his word and was waiting outside for him. He was leaning against an ancient tree nearest the falconry, apparently staring at the birds but with a distracted, unfocused gaze. St Just began walking across the castle grounds. Just then, Sergeant Kittle emerged from the castle.

'Sir, you should see this.'

St Just took two pieces of paper from him. Across the top was the time-and-date stamp of a fax machine. He read the contents, then raised his eyes to meet Sergeant Kittle's. St Just nodded curtly, then continued walking toward the outdoor cages.

He reached the solemn young man, and held out his hand.

'Detective Chief Inspector St Just,' he said. 'How can I help you?'

'You're not Scottish?' the man surprised him by saying.

St Just smiled, shook his head. Really, the man looked as if he hadn't slept; his handsome features were haggard, his jaw covered in steel-blue stubble. This might just have been a testament to the latest fashion, but only added to the impression of a man who desperately needed a good night's sleep. His dark hair was closely, neatly cropped at the sides, and he wore glasses with thick black frames of the type only 'nerds' used to wear, most often held together at the bridge with a sticking plaster. But his were the hip, trendy version. He had an athletic build that suggested regular visits to a spa with an iPod stuck in his ear rather than manly outdoor pursuits. St Just guessed he was what they called a metrosexual, without being entirely sure what the word meant.

St Just said, 'I happened to be here when . . . the incident . . . happened. I'm just helping out my colleagues from the local forces.'

The young man said, 'I'm Desmond Rumer, Kimberlee Kalder's husband. I came down from London as soon as I heard.' His voice had the solemn tones of a BBC announcer carrying bad tidings. It was a good, clear voice.

'Yes. I'm terribly sorry – I didn't realize who you were. I was just looking at your marriage license.' He turned the pages toward him. 'You're the Desmond whose message we found on Kimberlee's mobile, of course. Let's find some tea, shall we? It's colder out here than I thought it would be.'

Indeed, the short day had crept on, and a hint of darkness now stained the horizon. The two men turned and walked slowly back toward the castle.

'I am very sorry for your loss, Sir. How did you hear?'

'My God. How could I not? The news services have it now and they are making a feast of it. She wasn't royalty, but she was fairly well known. Better known, in a way.'

St Just, who had seen only the day's headlines and a few seconds of coverage by the exhilarated BBC announcer, again could only hope the media hadn't got hold of the fact the murdered woman had been found in a bottle dungeon: It was not the kind of news family and friends wanted to hear at all, let alone in that particular way. But what were the chances? That scabby little Quentin was behind the frenzy, he was certain, and it was doubtful he'd have left out the most titillating detail. He should have warned Quentin to put a lid on it – but too late now.

'I see,' said St Just, peering at the somewhat smudgy fax, 'that you have been married just two years. Perhaps you should start at the beginning, by telling me where you met Kimberlee?'

Desmond looked stricken by the question. He visibly took a moment to collect himself before he began to speak.

St Just waited quietly. He remembered the day he became a widower too well. All the pieties in the world were useless against such a loss.

'I'm sorry,' said Desmond. 'I was just stunned rigid when I heard.' He passed a shaking hand over his eyes. 'We met at a party. We often said that the odd thing was, it wasn't my kind of group, nor hers. An odd grab bag of staid academics and insurance executives. God knows how or why I was invited, or Kimberlee. Probably someone wanted something from one of us. She was highly, well, decorative, as you know. And I – I was fairly well off. Anyway, meeting her was one of those heart-stopping things, like finally seeing the Southern Cross. You feel you've waited all your life for this. Do you understand?'

St Just took a moment to reply.

'I believe I do.'

'Let me start by telling you,' continued Desmond, 'that I made my money designing trading software for stockbrokers and investors. I hold the patent on various of these designs.' He paused, brushing back the thick dark hair that had fallen across his brow. He adjusted his glasses. 'I guess what I'm really trying to say is I'm kind of a computer geek, Inspector, happiest with my fellows, discussing the cure for some computer virus or other. Kimberlee, as you probably know by now, was a vibrant, elegant, gorgeous creature. Just drop-dead gorgeous. I couldn't believe she'd stoop to even talk to me. Maybe if we hadn't been bored to tears at that party, she never would have done. Anyway, we were introduced. The world . . . well, the world stood still for me – truly. We were married six months later.'

'But, no one knew about it? Why all the secrecy?' St Just asked, although he thought he knew the answer.

'Her image, of course. You see, her career started to take off right about then. I remember one night she came home from some restaurant where some journalist or other had interviewed her. The subject of her marital status never came up. She told me she realized then that, of course, they had all made the classic mistake of assuming that because she wrote about some hip, ditzy single chick with a freewheeling lifestyle, she must *be* that person. The reality couldn't have been further from the truth. Kimberlee was frightfully bright, Inspector – well read, well educated. Certainly no ditz-brain. She worked hard – I saw the work that went into those books. In no way did they just fall out of the pen, as some of her reviewers seemed to think.'

The men had reached the castle by now, and began walking across the drawbridge. St Just looked up just in time to see five or six faces disappearing from the window of the sitting room. That left the sitting room off-limits as a spot to continue their talk. Just then his eye caught the flare of a flashbulb going off from somewhere in the surrounding woods. An emissary from the media world, no doubt – one of many. He signaled to Desmond to follow him upstairs. They'd use the incident room unless there was too much going on in there.

Moor looked up in surprise from an easy chair, where he was reading through another page of what was becoming a mountain of forms, reports, and witness statements.

'DCI Moor, may I introduce Desmond Rumer. He was, or is, Kimberlee Kalder's husband.'

Moor collected himself and stood up. He made the conventional expressions of sorrow, which Desmond stoically absorbed. Everyone accepted Moor's offer of tea.

'I saw the report come in and sent yon Kittle down with it,' said Moor over his shoulder as he fussed with the electric teakettle the hotel had provided to the police, probably tired of their endless orders of room service.

'Sergeant Kittle was almost in time. Please take a seat, Mr Rumer.' St Just indicated one of the upright chairs across from Moor's. 'Mr Rumer and I were just discussing the reason for all the secrecy about this marriage, the reason being Kimberlee's career. Or her "image". That would be the term most likely to be used these days, wouldn't it?'

Desmond Rumer nodded.

'She told me, when she came back from that interview I told you about, that she thought it would hurt sales to suddenly project this completely different picture of domestic bliss. Image was what Kimberlee Kalder was all about – you have to be aware of that. As I said, she was a hard worker. She wore pretty dresses and high heels and make-up when she went out, sure, but she was more often to be found at the computer in some tattered old tracksuit, her hair knotted back with a pencil holding it in place. I swear,' and here Desmond gave a small, reflective smile, 'I swear she would forget to eat when the writing was going well.' He sighed. 'I would cook for her sometimes, you know, just to keep her alive . . . Oh, God . . .'

The two inspectors nodded, whether in understanding or encouragement it was difficult to tell. But St Just was thinking: And you? Did she forget about you as well as dinner, Desmond?

'She was clever, I tell you,' Desmond insisted, as it were somehow essential for the policemen to grasp this point. 'Crisply decisive, businesslike. Did you know, she was selling posters and calendars of herself? There is even talk of a line of clothing, and a shoe design called the "Kimberlee". And some affiliation with a coffee store chain. So it's not just the books, you see. It's the entire Kimberlee package. And make no mistake – this was her doing. No one helped her. Not Ninette, not Easterbrook. She came up with these ideas herself, handled all the negotiations. No one else thought it would work.'

'What can you tell us,' said Moor, 'about her? Her background? Her parents, for example?'

'Her parents divorced when she was six. Her father, who was a British businessman – later a stockbroker – raised her. To be exact, a series of nannies and the occasional stepmother raised her. She only heard from her father when he wanted something from her, after she became successful.'

'He wanted money?'

'No, no. He had some book he'd written – *Naval Architecture in the Midlands: 1205–1538* or some such, you know the sort of thing – and he thought Kimberlee could use her connections to get it published. She told him that was doubtful.'

From what St Just thought he knew of Kimberlee thus far, he imagined she'd more likely laughed herself into hiccups and refused him point-blank, but Desmond was probably indulging the natural tendency to gloss over the worst failings of the deceased.

'You said "the occasional stepmother"?' he said instead.

'That's right. Her own mother ran off, back to America. Kim never, ever got over that.' He shook his head. 'She always needed – and, you could say this turned out to be a positive in her life – she always needed to prove that her mother was wrong to abandon her. If only because, in pragmatic terms, there would have been a lot of money and a bit of fame involved for anyone who showed loyalty and love to her. Becoming successful was how Kimberlee coped with being unwanted, or feeling that she was. And I think it also goes a fair way toward explaining her drive to succeed. Doesn't that make sense to you?'

St Just nodded. He thought in fact it was a generous assessment of Kimberlee's ambitious character, and probably accurate.

'Is this how she explained it to you?'

Desmond shook his head, a little sadly, thought St Just. There was a distant look in his eyes, as if he were trying to conjure the ghost of his dead wife.

'She wasn't given to introspection, Inspector. This was simply my own assessment.'

'This is a bit indelicate, Mr Rumer, so I hope you will forgive us – we have to ask. But was Kimberlee the type to make enemies, in your estimation?'

Desmond grimaced slightly, as if he'd been dreading the question. Finally he said, 'She was a bright, warm, loving human being, and I loved her. She could also make enemies among those who didn't know her – those who just saw the surface.'

'And were there a lot of those?'

'I wouldn't say a lot. A few. It was jealousy and spite, pure and simple. That's why . . .'

'That's why what?'

Desmond's words came in a rush, as if he were afraid he'd lose confidence before he could get the words out.

'When I heard she was killed at this conference, I knew it had to be one of them. These other writers. You've no idea how nasty some of them have been to her over the years.'

'Anyone in particular?' asked St Just.

'I don't remember the names, I'm afraid,' Desmond said. 'I don't follow the mystery scene – I read science fiction. But she'd come back from some conference or other annoyed or hurt, sometimes crying, sometimes angry, because of some snub or other. Mostly she was able to laugh it off. I see now that was dangerous. I should have pressed her for details.'

St Just paused, watching him. The castle's thick walls seemed to shield them from any sound but the faint electronic hum of the office machines. Moor broke the silence.

'Was she afraid of anyone?'

'Not that I'm aware. I tell you, she just shrugged it all off for the most part – eventually – and put it down, quite rightly, to jealousy. You have to remember, Inspector, that not only was my wife a successful author, she was a beautiful woman as well. No matter what she did, she'd make enemies, with a certain type of personality, without even trying.'

St Just asked, 'Did she talk about anyone at the conference? Anyone who was going to *be* at the conference?'

Desmond thought. 'She mentioned some guy named King. He used initials rather than his first name.'

'B. A. King?'

'That's right.'

'And what did she say about him?' asked St Just, as Sergeant Kittle's pen began flying across his notebook.

'She said if they gave out prizes for treachery, he'd win. She said he was a snake.'

The policemen exchanged glances.

'Any particular reason?' asked Moor.

'She just called him that in passing. There was no specific reason, no – it was something to do with some manuscript. I'm sorry, I really don't know the details. Again, I should have pressed her more.'

'Anyone else?' asked St Just.

'Not that I recall. And believe me, I've already racked my brains over this on the train coming up. She did mention some woman with an unusual name. Said she would be going head to head with the "raddled face of chick lit" and was rather looking forward to it.'

'Magretta Sincock?'

Desmond looked doubtful.

'I think that was it, yes.'

St Just gave Moor a questioning look. *You or me?*

Moor shook his head.

St Just inhaled deeply and said, 'Sir, I am sorry to be the one to tell you – but your wife was pregnant. Four weeks pregnant.'

Desmond Rumer's eyes widened.

'No,' he said, disbelievingly. '*No.*'

'I'm afraid there is no mistake. Obviously, she didn't tell you.'

Desmond shook his head back and forth.

'She might not have wanted me to know. Until she was sure. Maybe she didn't know herself. Only four weeks. *Jesus.* This is a nightmare.'

'We'll get someone to arrange a room for you here for tonight, Mr Rumer,' said DCI Moor.

'When can I . . . I want to. . .' The man looked weighted down – pale and very on the edge of tears, totaling the double loss. 'Has she been taken . . . somewhere?'

'Yes, sir,' said Moor gruffly, but with a surprising gentleness. 'Don't you worry. My men are taking care of her. You can see her tomorrow. We'll do all we can to help with arrangements for her . . . transport . . . once she's released.' He repeated, 'Don't you worry.'

Desmond nodded. St Just wasn't sure Kimberlee's husband had heard the words, but perhaps he had just registered the gentle tone. Moor got on the phone and a few minutes later one of his sergeants appeared to lead Desmond downstairs. Desmond stood and began shuffling slowly to the door. He turned in the doorway and said, 'Find whoever did this. For me. For her. Please.'

Once he'd departed, St Just and Moor looked at each other. Moor puffed out his lips and said, 'That's the part of this job I cannot take. The rest of these people don't much care about anything except getting out of here. The family, though. . .'

'Yes, indeed,' said St Just. 'Any luck tracing the parents?'

'Still trying to get a reply from the father. Can't locate the mother, as of yet. But I didn't get the impression they'd either of them much care, did you?'

St Just shook his head. 'Not overmuch. Listen, I'm afloat in tea and coffee. I need something to eat. Catch me before you leave if you can find me, will you? Oh, and listen. . .' He tilted his head in the direction of Desmond's departing back. 'Check him out, too.'

St Just again took the back way downstairs. If he were hoping to run into a blue-faced Portia again, he was out of luck. He'd just reached the door to the spa when Portia's agent, Ninette, emerged, however. Perhaps a different form of luck, because he realized he had a follow-up question for her.

'My second sauna of the day. I'll positively be a *shade* of my former self before this is over, not to mention, completely dehydrated,' she informed him. She was nearly unrecognizable when not wearing half the contents of her make-up kit.

'Ms Thomson, did you know Kimberlee Kalder was married?'

'*What?* No!' she said. Since either surgery or Botox injections seemed to prevent her lifting her eyebrows in surprise, she gaped at him, pop-eyed. 'Who to?'

'You worked with her a long time. You really didn't know about this?'

'We hardly sat around swapping recipes and referrals for wedding planners, Inspector. It was a business relationship. We talked marketing, and strategy – things like that. I took out my percentage, and sent the rest of the cheque straight to her bank.'

'You never heard one name come up consistently? You never visited her at home?'

She shook her head emphatically. 'All of our business was transacted in my office. But . . . you know, now that I think about it, I'm not terribly surprised to hear about the marriage, somehow,' she added slowly. 'Kimberlee *always* seemed to have a life totally at odds with her image. She was not out on the town hoisting Manhattans every night, by any means, so far as I could tell. She'd call me at all hours and there was no hip-hop or disco beat blaring in the background – nothing like that. If she went out, it was done rather more in a *strategic* way, depending on whether photographers would be around. Of course, books don't get written that way, do they, with the author out carousing every night? Anyway, no, I tell you I didn't know anything about it.'

He guessed he had to take her at her word, although it seemed an incredible ruse for Kimberlee Kalder to have pulled off.

'Look, Inspector, Kimberlee kept her own counsel. It was really none of my business but I can see why she kept it quiet. Bad for sales. Kimberlee did nothing that was bad for sales. If you don't mind, I have to run. Hot rocks massage in ten minutes, followed by eyebrow threading.'

Somehow he felt confident that Moor, with his long experience of esoteric beauty rituals, might know what she meant.

'Before you go – I'd like to say it was good of you to agree to look at Donna's manuscript.'

She gave a hoot of laughter. 'Goodness has nothing to do with it, to borrow a phrase from Mae West. From what I've seen so far, that bizarre little book of hers will sell like hotcakes, just you watch.'

St Just, who was beginning to realize he would never understand the whys and wherefores of publishing, waved her on her way.

CHAPTER 21

This Just In

On the next landing he ran into Quentin. Rather, he saw the posterior view of a man he took, from the narrow hips and low-slung, denimed covering exposing two inches of boxer shorts, to be Quentin. He was at the moment leaning precariously out of one of the windows, punching furiously at the keys of a mobile phone. No doubt texting in his latest breaking news item, thought St Just.

He sighed. It was getting on for well past dinner time. He was completely hollowed out, but wanted to wrap up as many of the interviews as possible, while there was still a chance of catching his suspects awake. He tapped Quentin on the shoulder.

'I'll have a word now, Sir. In your room.'

Quentin hurriedly – and with a guilty, furtive look back at St Just – hit the send button.

As Quentin led the way, St Just took a moment to size up the man. He seemed to the detective to be ridiculously young, but that, St Just imagined, was more a factor of his own middle age. He knew Quentin to be about twenty-five, an age when he himself was already happily settled in job and marriage, most youthful experiments safely behind him. Quentin, with his spiky, dyed hair – well. St Just felt it was time for Quentin to grow out of that kind of nonsense. St Just noticed he smelt powerfully of some musky, animal scent that for some reason seemed familiar. Then he remembered: The stuff was called

Ravage. St Just had accidentally ripped open a sample taped into a men's magazine. His flat stank of it for weeks.

Quentin, as it turned out, had been given one of the ground-floor rooms. While Dalmorton didn't offer any rooms that weren't in some way sumptuous, Quentin's was smaller and less sumptuous than the others, reminiscent of its probable origins as a castle storage area. Whether this reflected Donna Doone's opinion of Quentin or was simply what was convenient when everyone was stranded by the lights-out situation, St Just couldn't guess.

Quentin led St Just in and immediately flopped onto the quilted bedspread, hands behind head in a Queen-of-Sheba pose. St Just sat in a nearby wing chair. Quentin, despite his relaxed posture, gave every evidence of keen, bright-eyed interest, waiting expectantly, even eagerly, for the questioning to begin.

'The night of the murder,' said St Just. 'Where were you, what were you doing, when were you doing it, and with whom?'

'Well . . . hang on. Let me see . . . I had a bit of a wreckie that night, so I must tell you I don't remember a whole lot about it. I toggled back and forth between the bar and that lot sitting in the parlor. Sitting room, I guess they call it.'

'Tom's group?'

'I suppose that's what you'd call it. Although it implies the man has some kind of following, which I would roundly dispute.'

'Why?'

'Why what?'

'Why did you "toggle back and forth," as you put it? Why not stay put in one room or the other?'

'Boredom, Inspector? I don't really know. I was restless. If the conversation started to pall in one area, I'd head over to another. This lot don't half talk a load of crap. A man can only take so much.'

'Tell me who was in what we will call for shorthand "Tom's group".'

'That beaten-down wife of his. Winston Chatley and B. A. King. King wandered a bit, too, but mostly he was there.'

'Do you remember what you or they talked about at any point?'

'I was seriously rat-arsed, so the answer is no, not really. The usual writer stuff. They like to haver on about how their genius is going unrecognized.'

'No one remained in place the whole time, did they?'

'They all took turns fetching drinks. Except for Tom, that fucking tightwad. Edith, I'd bet you anything, was paying out of her own purse. Nice woman, but she seriously needs to grow a spine.'

'Tom remained there?'

'Yes, I – no, wait, he did go out once. Maybe to the loo. But in the library, where the bar is, those folk there seemed pretty stationary to me. Again, I wasn't paying attention and I wasn't in any condition to. Then the lights went out and it got really confused. Nearly came a cropper myself when I tripped over a coffee table.'

St Just sat back, having a think, picturing the group of four-point-five in the sitting room, and the group in the library: Portia, Joan Elksworthy, Annabelle, and Ninette. Winston Chatley and B. A. King, until they wandered to the sitting room. Donna, who came to the library a bit late. Kimberlee had been there a short while, with Jay Fforde. Magretta had flitted by early, only to say good night.

Then he said, 'You knew Kimberlee Kalder from before, didn't you?'

Quentin nodded readily enough.

'She came to my old newspaper as a temp – it was a maternity leave gig.'

'You didn't mention this when you were questioned previously.'

'Didn't I? I meant to.'

'Really? You meant to. Well, tell me now: How did you two get on?'

Quentin gave a brief, noisome snort. 'The name Kimberlee Kalder became a sort of shorthand among the other reporters for back-stabbing, self-promoting bitch, I can tell you that,' he said. 'Any of them still at that paper will tell you the same.'

'Really? Why is that?'

'It's hard to describe exactly what she did, really. A bit difficult to quantify, you know? But she'd cozy up to someone – you know, be their very, very best friend, go out to lunch with them, buy them little gifts – softening them up, you see. Then the next thing you hear, that person had got the sack. Happened three times in a row. One of the women involved – I went out with her for awhile – she told me she and Kimberlee would sit around over drinks and grizzle on about the boss. The way you do, you know, except this particular boss was such a paranoid little wanker, it wasn't a wise conversation to have, at all. Anyway, then Kimberlee got Karen – that was her name – to repeat something she shouldn't have said in the first place, in an e-mail. An e-mail that *somehow* the wanker boss got hold of. It was stupid of Karen, but Kimberlee had a way of making people trust her – when she chose. Reporters have to know how to do that, of course, but the idea is not to use your charm to destroy your colleagues. After awhile, when we all started to catch on, Kimberlee ate lunch alone. But as I say, it was a six-month gig so that solved the problem nicely. *And* she had bigger fish to fry about that time – a better job offer in London.'

'Why do you think Kimberlee did all this?'

'She was after their jobs, wasn't she?' said Quentin flatly. 'Just in case nothing better turned up. But mostly, I think she just liked to stir up the peasantry, which is how she seemed to regard her fellow scribes. It was the attitude that made you want to ki – I mean, avoid her. *Avoid* her. The rest of the staff were pigging it, but she would walk in, in her four-inch heels and her Chanel suit. She didn't half stand out, like a Viking at a luau. She obviously saw herself as headed for grander places than the *Sheffield Bugle*.'

'Which, as it happens, she was.'

Quentin shrugged. He said, grudgingly, 'Yeah, I suppose she was. Life, as Kimberlee would say, is so *totally* not fair.'

'Were you jealous of her success?'

There was a tiny pause. St Just might almost have imagined it.

'Don't be daft. I couldn't-a written that girly, gushing tripe of hers, now could I? *Dying for a Latte*. What *crap*.'

Quentin's brief assessment sounded remarkably like that of the other writers. But St Just wondered if Quentin wouldn't also be happy to write something that might make him a millionaire, as had Kimberlee. He had heard that many newsmen were frustrated novelists.

Also, was it possible that Kimberlee, in her race to better things, had made it clear that young Quentin – like the other peasants – would never stand a chance in the romance department?

'Nobody trusted her, you see, mate?' Quentin continued. 'And for a reporter, that's deadly. The whole place was like working for the fucking Borgias, mind, but Kimberlee had a real gift for mischief. There was a rumor . . . well, never mind.'

'Rumor?' St Just prompted.

His mouth twisted slightly with the effort of recollection. 'I don't know the facts, so I shouldn't say, right? Just rumor, you see? Something about her hounding some poor bloke to his death. But I'll tell you the real reason I wouldn't hurt her, leaving aside whether or not she might deserve it,' said Quentin. 'She was going to give me a blurb.'

'Blurb?'

'You know, a few glowing words about my first book. That

stuff they put on the back cover to convince a reluctant public to buy. My book's coming out later this year. I asked her and nice as pie she said she would.'

Which helped explain, thought St Just, that hagiographic write-up Quentin had given her in his paper – the one that had sent Magretta through the roof.

'Despite your history with her, you felt you could ask her that favor?'

'Man, you are new to this business, aren't you? For a blurb from a well-known author like Kimberlee, you develop amnesia about the past – real fast.'

'I am, as you say, new at this. Is it a crime novel you've written, then?'

'Yep. I'll let you read some of it sometime, if you like. It's awesome. I'll tell you this for free about her salad days, though. She was either a trustafarian or some bloke or other she was shagging was footing the bills. There is no way anyone was buying Chanel on the crap wages they paid us.'

'Had you seen her since she left the paper?'

'Nah. Of course, I kept up with her career after she left. How could I avoid it, really? She was news. Photos of Kimberlee gliding down the stairwell to Annabel's, or Kimberlee racing about Saint-Tropez in a convertible and a bikini. She was still always, of course, dressed to kill – ah, sorry.'

'Dressed to be killed, in this case,' said St Just. 'Let's go back to where everyone was, and when. Annabelle Pace, for example.'

Quentin shook his head.

'All I can tell you is every time I saw her, she was in the library talking to that Portia lady or that Mrs Elksworthy. Oh, hold on. I also saw her outside the ladies' talking with Kimberlee. But Kimberlee went her own way, headed for her room, presumably, and Annabelle rejoined the rest of the group.'

'Did it look like a friendly conversation?'

'Yeah. They were smiling, anyway. This was – nine-fifteen at a guess?'

'How about Edith Bean?'

'I don't recall. She's the kind of woman it's hard to remember she's alive, you know what I mean? I do remember at one point she spilled a drink and had to go right out and fetch another. It was Tom's drink, poor woman.'

'Where were you when we lost power?'

'In the library getting a refill. The fireplace was going, which helped a bit so we didn't all positively maim ourselves on the furniture. Like I said, I nearly lost it over a coffee table, anyway.'

'So there was enough light to see by? You could see clearly who was there?'

He lifted his shoulders in a shrug. 'No, not *clearly*, but more or less. It's more that I wasn't paying attention; I just was on a mission to the bar to get one for the road. Annabelle was there, and Mrs Elksworthy. Magretta wasn't there, or I'd have been able to hear her yodeling. At dinner she kept saying that her muse was calling her – you know the kind of shit she comes out with. I do remember one thing – but this was from before, when I was in the parlor with "Tom's group". B. A. King ran up to his room to get some whiskey he wanted us to try. Not that he or any of us really needed any more to drink at that point.'

'What time was that?'

Quentin shrugged again.

'So you were in the library when the commotion began over Kimberlee's body? Or were you in the sitting room?'

'In the library, once again. We heard the screams and we all kind of rushed the door. Tom came out of the sitting room, holding a lighter. He went off down the hall to investigate. He came back and told us someone was dead.'

So, Tom had lied about heading straight to bed, thought St Just. So had Edith. No doubt distancing themselves from the scene of the crime, but it was a foolhardy lie.

'You could see clearly it was Tom, I imagine – but you couldn't see the others?'

'Not once we were all in the hallway, no. Black as pitch it was away from the fireplace.'

'So you aren't sure who else was in the hallway.'

'Man, ask me who wasn't. I don't know. Just a big, jostling crowd at that point. Oh, wait, I do remember something else. Jay Fforde, he must have left the group early and gone to bed or something. I remember now because we all kind of shuffled our way en masse in the direction of the bottle dungeon. When we got there, Jay and Donna Doone were approaching, but from down the stairs. I could see them because he was carrying a candle.'

'Did you get the impression they were coming downstairs together? I mean, that they had not just run into each other by accident?'

Apparently struck by the idea, Quentin thought for some time before answering.

'Now you mention it, they *might* have been together. Yes.'

CHAPTER 22

I Know Why the Jaybird Sings

Wondering very much what Jay Fforde and Donna Doone had found to talk about – assuming Quentin was correct; St Just had had enough experience of reporters to know the profession was larded with unreliable narrators – he went in search of the literary agent.

He found him now reclining in the library, feet up on a pouffe, and brooding handsomely over a large, leather-bound book. The louche, Sebastian-Flyte pose looked staged, lighted as it was by the pale remnants of sunset merging with the moon. St Just suspected that the man went through life forever putting his best profile forward.

'Come on, Mr Fforde,' St Just said to him. 'I've got to find dinner somewhere, but you and I can kill two birds with one stone.'

Jay looked up from his book and frowned, as if trying to place St Just in his list of acquaintance.

'Dinner is over,' he informed him.

'The police, we have our ways,' St Just said. 'Come along with me, please.'

They found Donna in her office. Whatever was on her computer, she rather guiltily closed out the screen at their approach, but she cheerfully agreed to organize a cold meal for St Just.

'If you'll go to the small dining room upstairs, I'll send Florie straight in,' she said.

St Just soon sat in splendid isolation at a table for eight in a corner of the deserted, 'small' dining room, which belied its name by being the size of a minor cathedral. Jay remained standing, warming his backside at the fireplace. DCI Moor's men were nowhere to be seen; St Just assumed they'd finished their work for the day. He looked at his watch. They'd probably all long gone home, to families and pets and warm meals. Moor himself might be at the police station, or headed for home.

He looked across at Jay. It was difficult to credit him as a man in the middle of a murder investigation – a suspect in same. With his high color and thick, flopping hair, Jay Fforde looked the very picture of carefree relaxation, if not of innocence. Jay had too much of the Byronic hero about him to ever project innocence.

'So, Mr Fforde,' St Just said, easing into the interview. 'Tell me something I've always been curious about. What exactly is involved in being the British agent for an American novel? I assume you do have American clients.'

'Certainly,' replied Jay. 'Well, we don't do a *frightful* amount, actually. We find a buyer, of course. For the British edition we might help translate the American spellings – "correct" the spellings – that's our little in-house joke.' He offered a little heh-heh by way of demonstration.

Jay suddenly interrupted himself to turn and preen in the mirror over the fireplace. *What had Kimberlee seen in this self-absorbed ninny?* St Just wondered. *Herself reflected back?*

Satisfied that his hair remained artlessly tousled, and his expression set in its usual cast of petulant ennui, Jay turned back into the room and continued, with the air of a man humoring a dim but willing pupil.

'We might also help mess about with the cover art,' he said, 'although that's really the publisher's call.' Like Easterbrook, he had the strangulated, upper-class diction of a man reading a speech whilst being slowly choked to death. 'We witter through

202

all the little legalities, that's the main thing. Frequently, we help change the title.'

He arranged his mouth into a self-satisfied smile.

'Why?' asked St Just.

'Change the title? No one knows, really. It does add rather to the confusion.'

'So,' said St Just, 'your involvement with Kimberlee amounted to—'

'Who says I was involved?' Jay cut in, his voice suddenly losing its fruity overlay. 'Nothing of the sort. No. I'd brought some cover-art mock-ups for her to look at, that's all.'

He folded his arms defensively. St Just decided to circle around the topic for now. If Jay was going to go in for such a childish lie, it should be easy enough to arrange a later ambush.

'I see. And, when did you show her the cover art?'

Jay uncrossed his arms, relaxing as his interrogator apparently bought into his denials.

'Last night. Before dinner.'

'Where?'

'Where what?'

St Just heaved an exaggerated sigh.

'Where were you when you showed her your etchings?' he said, more nastily than he'd intended.

Jay's guard immediately shot up again.

'Oh, I say, no need to take that tone with me,' he sputtered. 'As a matter of fact, we were in the library.'

Professor Plum in the library with the candlestick, thought St Just. He thought, not for the first time, how strange it was that a game for children should be about death and the worst sort of mayhem.

It would make his life simpler if they were just playing Cluedo, he reflected. There were no bedrooms in Cluedo. Here there were dozens. A thorough search could take days.

'Did anyone see you there?'

Mrs Peacock perhaps?

'As a matter of fact, yes. That American woman with the gray hair and Native American jewelry.'

'Mrs Elksworthy. I see.' His voice trailed off. Something Jay had said just now sent a jolt of alertness through St Just – a tantalizing near-memory hovered, but he couldn't capture what it was.

'I see,' he repeated vaguely.

What the deuce was it? He slid down a few inches on his chair, stretching out his long legs. He shook himself mentally. *Best not to force it; it will come back.*

'Tell me more about your job,' he said. 'Do you do much editing?'

This, at least, seemed to unleash a deep wellspring of emotion. 'God, no. Do I look like I have time for that? Not that writers don't expect it. If it were up to them, we agents would do all the writing and their job would be to cash the royalty cheques. Lazy sods, writers. No, if I get involved, it is perhaps to suggest to an American writer that the expression "knock up" has quite a different meaning in the UK and that no one gets pregnant by answering the door. Well, not usually.'

What an opening, so to speak. St Just wondered whether it were to his advantage to keep news of Kimberlee's condition – if news it was – from Jay. He decided that, for the moment, it was also a topic best circled around.

'Your dealings with Kimberlee, then, were . . .?'

'Superficial, to say the least. We were negotiating a business deal. Perhaps mixed with a *little* harmless flirtation. I must say, I was a bit in unfamiliar territory, business-wise. Most British crime fiction of recent decades has been dark and stormy – *très, très noir*, you know. Makes Philip Marlowe look like Mary Poppins. The Kimberlee Kalder phenomenon took us all by surprise. Apparently the British public *does* like a change from kidnap, rape, and torture. They want to read endless descriptions of handbags and *haute couture* and whatnot.'

'When the commotion occurred, at the discovery of Kimberlee's body, where were you?'

'In the library with the rest, I would imagine?'

'You weren't coming downstairs at that point? With Donna?'

'I was n—'

'You were seen by a reliable witness, coming downstairs.' Well, thought St Just, he was sure that in certain circumstances, Quentin could be reliable. He probably never forgot Mothering Day. 'It would very much be in your best interests not to lie to me. Now, let's start again: What exactly was the nature of your relationship with Kimberlee Kalder?'

Jay stirred. He struggled through several expressions, finally settling on a lopsided, man-of-the-world smirk.

'All right. We were, erm . . . lovers – *potential* lovers. Not me and Donna, of course. I just collided on the stairs with her. Rather, Kimberlee and I were going to become lovers – *perhaps*. I went up to her room that night at about 10:30. I waited there for her. And waited. At some point shortly after I got there the lights went out.'

'How did you get in?'

'She'd given me a spare key she'd got from the registration desk. She told them she'd lost hers.'

'Go on.'

'That's it. I waited. There was a room service tray sitting outside the door. I brought it in. I didn't open the wine but I nibbled on some of the canapés. I fell asleep waiting. After an hour, maybe an hour and a half, I got fed up and left. I was a bit put out, to tell you the truth – until I realized later on, of course, why she didn't show. She must have been killed as I sat around waiting for her, or even earlier. Anyway, I was headed downstairs to the library again when the hubbub started. I ran into Donna on the way.'

'How did you find your way? In the dark?'

'Kimberlee had one of those scented candles – probably

bought from the spa store. I lit it using a bit of kindling from the fireplace.'

Despite St Just's distrust of the man, everything in his narration rang true. Everything except...

'When did this affair start?'

'I told you, it wasn't an affair, it was...'

St Just gave a great sigh of weariness. 'A dalliance, then.'

'A nice, old-fashioned word, that. It should be brought back into use. Very well, let's say a dalliance. My interest in Kimberlee, really – I have to be honest – was financial. She seemed to want... something more. Let's say we were exploring the possibilities. Or getting ready to.'

St Just wondered at this insistence on a chivalrous, or self-serving, relationship, when a paternity test might so easily prove him a liar. But... did Jay even know about the pregnancy? She'd apparently told no one about it; she might not have been aware of it herself.

If she did know, was she hoping to hold him responsible? Was that the reason she arranged their meeting?

And was any of that a motive for murder?

'When did you arrange to meet?' St Just asked.

'The night before. She invited me to come to her room to celebrate her award, to talk about joining my stable, and perhaps—' He shrugged.

'Perhaps, joining you in bed.'

'Precisely. Perhaps.'

'And she didn't show up.'

'She didn't show.'

'While you were in her room, did you notice a letter she'd been writing?'

'You couldn't find a giraffe in that room. You must have seen the chaos in there for yourself.'

The love letter was probably just a writing exercise after all, thought St Just. Practice. A sad thought occurred to him: Perhaps it was Kimberlee's way of practicing emotion and connection with another human being, something she didn't seem to be particularly good at.

'Did Kimberlee confide any – fears to you at any time?' he asked Jay. 'Any apprehension about anyone at this conference? Any worries? Any enemies?'

Jay shook his head throughout this series of questions.

'You really didn't know her, did you? If Kimberlee Kalder was aware she made enemies, and there is little evidence she was aware, she bloody well didn't care. She left dead bodies in her wake like a battleship. It wasn't even a form of confidence, not really. Just a supreme unawareness. All the world was a stage to Kimberlee, and she was playing the lead role. Everyone else was in the supporting cast.'

'You don't sound very fond of a woman you were entertaining launching a liaison with.'

This seemed utterly to baffle Jay. His forehead creased with a perplexed frown.

'Since when does fondness have anything to do with sex?' he asked. But he quickly added, 'I didn't dislike her, Inspector, not by a long chalk. I did feel she required special handling, especially given the business nature of our relationship. I didn't want the whole thing to blow up in my face if it turned out Kimberlee and I were . . . incompatible.'

'I see,' said St Just. And he thought he did. An entanglement with Kimberlee Kalder would give any man pause, and getting out of a relationship was always trickier than getting into one. Jay would not want to foul the nest of the goose that laid the golden eggs. In fact, Kimberlee's apparent interest in Jay – might it not altogether have been a mixed blessing?

And exactly how did her husband fit into all of this?

'You were aware, of course, that she was married. That must have added an extra element of—'

'She *what*?' St Just watched closely as Jay's expression changed from its customary bored sneer into a mask of bewildered alarm. His hand flew to his forehead in a dramatic gesture, pushing his hair on end above half-moon eyebrows, and his mouth flew open, exposing some impressive dental veneer work. 'She was married? Why in the – she never – I had no idea. No! *None*!'

St Just, having witnessed several displays of astonishment that day, felt he was becoming a bit of a connoisseur of the emotion. Even though he rated Jay's particular exhibit as a bit over the top, it might well be genuine. Full points.

They talked for another quarter hour, but St Just could get nothing more from the man than expressions of amazement and heated denial.

Later, after Jay had collected himself and left the room, rather less cocksure than he had entered it, St Just sat staring into the dwindling fire, thinking. The room was growing chilly. He was hungry to the point of madness.

He was at a loss.

St Just sank back in his chair in exhaustion. He often skipped meals in his job, or ate on the run, a fact of police life that had many of his colleagues fighting both the battle of the bulge and the bottle. In his case, the problem was more likely to be in reverse – the stress of an investigation often meant he had to struggle to keep from falling too far below his fighting weight. He longed for this particular investigation to end, for normalcy – in the form of a hot meal, maybe at St Germaine's – to return. If he were lucky, might it not be a meal that included Portia De'Ath sitting at his table? Might he not take her punting on the Cam, to The Orchard for tea? It would soon be June, Cambridge's magic time, the time of the May Balls, and anything could—

The entrance of a young waiter with a tray interrupted these halcyon daydreams. He placed before St Just a salad of chicken, almonds, blue cheese, and currants. The cold meal, rounded off with bread and wine, and ending with a selection of cheeses and port and a pudding, surprised him by being exactly what he might have ordered if asked – instead of the steak. Donna could have hidden talents as a mind-reader, he decided. He'd asked for lots of strong black coffee and someone – perhaps the missing Florie – had obliged with an enormous silver pot of the scalding brew.

St Just sat in the deserted dining room like a liege laird, happily tucking into his food, relieved to be alone with his thoughts for the moment. He turned over in his mind everything he'd learned, mentally running through a list of all the suspects. Apart from the staff, who tended to alibi each other – and it was hard to imagine some Area-51-type conspiracy featuring Florie and the *sous-chef* – some but not all of the castle guests did have what seemed solid alibis for nearly the whole time. Nearly. Anyone nipping out to kill Kimberlee would have to have gone about it sharpish. And would first have had to have known where to look for her. It was much easier to picture the publishing gang than the staff engaged in carrying out some Byzantine murder plot. Not so easy to picture them happily cooperating in carrying out a plot *together*, though.

Sighing, he pushed aside his empty plate, reached for his coffee, and pulled Magretta's 'alibi' manuscript from his coat pocket. Just then, he looked up to see Portia De'Ath walking toward him.

Tonight she was dressed in black – a high-necked, clinging jersey and slacks, and flat shoes. She looked like a slightly more voluptuous version of Audrey Hepburn. Since when, he wondered, had he become such a connoisseur of women's clothing?

'How's it going?' she asked.

He shrugged.

'We need a barrister-proof case,' he said. 'And I'm not sure we have one. Yet.'

'You think you know who did it?' asked Portia.

'When I know how it was done I'll know who must have done it. I have a small idea. . .'

'Well?' she demanded. 'Tell me.'

'Soon. I promise. Soon. And, Portia . . . Ms De'Ath . . . when all this is over . . .'

He let that hang in the air. When this is all over, what? We start calling the caterers? Book the college chapel? The thought that her answer might be 'no' made something dark and cold clutch at his heart. It was too soon, much too soon. He'd have to work frightfully hard and make sure that when he asked, the answer could only be 'yes.'

He was tempted to blurt out something about Nuncross, his weekend home, but, desperate as he was to impress her, he had what he recognized as a juvenile wish that she like him for himself alone, not for the status symbols he could bring to a union. He supposed he was testing her, which somehow did not seem kind.

God, but when did love get so complicated?

'Okay,' she said simply. Was she angry, resigned? He couldn't read her. Her eyes held her usual look of dreamy intelligence. 'When this is over. Maybe—' and he cringed inwardly at that hateful, tentative word – 'maybe, when this is all over . . .'

She paused, and when she began to speak again, the treacherous subject had changed: 'You remember what I told you when we met, about Kimberlee and her *roman à clef*?'

He dragged his attention back to the present. 'About how she couldn't spell?'

She smiled. 'That, and something else I was going to mention. You looked so unwell at the time I thought it best to wrap up the conversation.'

That point being when St Just was struggling, without success, to remove Cupid's dart from his heart.

Never, he vowed, *but never will I tell you why I looked like that. Not for at least, oh, thirty years.*

'What was it?' he asked.

'Just that what's interesting about her book is that they

210

published it at all. It was a book about the magazine publishing industry, rather than the book publishing industry, but there's a lot of overlap between those two worlds.'

'I don't follow.'

'The book she wrote. *Latte.* It was all about them. Trashing the people at the magazine, I mean. Airing laundry about affairs, back-stabbings, bankruptcies, and et cetera. Even after the lawyers got through vetting it, it was still not very nice.'

'So . . .'

'So, if Kimberlee was going to dish the dirt on the book publishing industry, and in a big way, it might have made someone here nervous. The people here are convinced she was writing another tell-all. But no one will admit to what she had to tell about *them*, if anything. No one, including Lord Easterbrook, seems to know a lot about what she was really up to.'

'Not surprising. He claims not to have bothered reading the first book.'

Portia hesitated. 'Do you know . . . Kimberlee was never going to found a leper colony or anything like that, but I hope you catch whoever did this. Dishing the dirt – all right, not a nice way to make a living. She was ambitious, far too ambitious, but I don't think she *herself* was capable of killing. Not like some I could name here.'

'Do you have anyone in particular in mind?' He could see her stiffen at the question.

'No,' she said.

St Just waited out the silence until it was clear she had no intent to elaborate.

'Why do you say no?' he asked at last.

She smiled wanly. 'I've started to think pretty much any of them are capable of killing, if pushed to it. I suppose that's true of anyone, though, isn't it? Do you really have no solid idea of who did it?'

'If I did, I wouldn't tell you. I'm too, erm . . .' Oh, golly effing Moses, he thought, half tempted to share with her his half-formed theories. *She's a suspect; they all are. I can't do this.*

'You do realize you are being condescending and chauvinistic?' she asked.

'Chauvinistic. Now, there's a word not heard much in the past thirty years.'

'If the shoe fits. . .'

'It's a police investigation. You are not the police. You are a—'

She folded her slim arms tightly against her narrow waist.

'Go ahead, say it. I'm a suspect, which is why you can't confide in me. Or won't.'

Of course he couldn't. Years of ingrained training didn't disappear just because. . .

She turned away. She was backlit like a Greek icon by the dim ochre light of the room. Just then, she turned her head back toward him.

. . . just because she actually glowed, damn it. The woman glowed.

Training! said the voice, the voice that might belong to either an angel or a devil capering on his shoulder.

He had once as a child seen lightning in a snowstorm, a dazzling sight that had filled him with wonder and a kind of dread, as he hadn't realized such a thing were possible. Akin to this sense of wonder was his reaction to Portia. Could she be real, or were his eyes and mind deceiving him? Had he simply, damn it, lived alone too long?

'Tell me how she died.' It wasn't a question.

'She was hit with a blunt object and thrown into the dungeon.'

'What, like a hardback book?'

He smiled weakly. 'Something a little deadlier.' A cosh, probably makeshift, was the best guess. A cosh long since dismantled, its parts scattered in the moat, or burned, or hidden where they might never be found.

'There's something I've been meaning to ask you. Why do all you authors seem to travel with your own books? It's rather coals to Newcastle, isn't it?'

'Sometimes the bookseller runs out of copies. If so, we provide them on commission, or come to some other arrangement. No one wants to miss the chance of a sale.'

'It's a funny business you're in.'

She sighed. 'It's a horrible business you're in. I'm glad I only have the academic side. Murder twice removed.' She paused, added: 'I don't think I could marry a policeman.'

That no one had actually asked her to marry a policeman needn't be said. It had been on his agenda almost from the beginning, probably from the first time he set eyes on her in the restaurant.

'I can't picture being anything else.'

'I know,' she said flatly. 'Well . . . perhaps we'll talk later.'

Perhaps? Which was worse – perhaps or maybe?

'Perhaps a meteor will destroy all life as we know it on this planet before noontime tomorrow,' he said. 'You and I will certainly talk later.'

Good, he thought. Manly, decisive – that was the ticket.

But she merely smiled, that wondrous smile that made him forget everything, forget his name, practically.

'Perhaps,' she repeated, but now he thought she meant, yes. Eyeing him thoughtfully, she asked, 'What are you? Originally, I mean. Not English. Welsh?'

'Not English. I'm Cornish.'

'Ah. Like the hens?'

'Like the miners. I need to talk with Annabelle.'

'I just saw her in the sitting room. I'll tell her.'

CHAPTER 23

Rumor Mill

'I want your impressions of Kimberlee,' St Just said a few minutes later to a duly summoned Annabelle. 'How did the other writers seem to like her?'

The contrast with Portia could hardly have been greater – Portia with her clear eyes and skin, indicators of rude health – and of a clear conscience? The opposite, at any rate, of the woman who sat before him now, a woman who seemed to be turning more parchment-like, her hair more drained of color, by the day.

'Oh, fine, fine. Great,' said Annabelle. 'Kimberlee was . . . hmm. Were you asking for an accurate assessment?'

'I was.'

'Well, then. She managed to piss off everyone who came in contact with her, high or low. I was the least surprised person in the world when I heard she'd been killed. Well, second-least surprised, after the killer.'

'Yes, but I'm trying to get at the "why".'

'Well, can you blame them, really?' Annabelle tugged idly at her stringy, nondescript hair, finally giving up and pushing it messily behind her pierced ears. 'A lot of these authors really sweat blood, fine-tuning each sentence again and again. Then along comes this little trixie who sort of vomits it up on the page – and makes a zillion pounds for her "efforts". It was bound to cause bad feeling among this crowd. You know, I heard her tell Magretta, "I've never read

214

Agatha Christie." I swear, I thought Magretta was going to faint. Kimberlee really did give the impression she could barely read and write.'

'Stupid is so often a perfect cover,' murmured St Just. 'Who were her readers, do you think?'

'I don't know.' Annabelle shrugged. 'The same people who care, 24/7, what Paris Hilton gets up to? I mean, it really beats me. But you know, in fact, now I come to think of it. . .'

Her voice trailed off, her gaze fixed on the room's ceiling medallion.

'Yes?' he prompted patiently.

'It's just that. . .' She returned her attention to him. 'Now I come to think of it, I wonder why she bothered. Why she was here at all. To boost her name recognition? Gilding the lily, surely. To lord it over the rest of them? More likely. I suppose that's the answer. Kimberlee never did anything, from what I could gather, that didn't involve the entertainment or further-ance of the career of Kimberlee Kalder, author.'

'You knew her well, then? I thought you'd just met her on this trip.'

'Knew her well? Oh, Lord, no. Just by reputation, you know. I may have met her in passing at one or two dinners or con-ferences before her career really took off. Most of us spend a certain amount of time on the circuit – one has to, these days. Also, she made her name rather infamous on a few mystery listserves for her blatant self-promotion. There were some anonymous postings about how fascinating and *brilliant* her book was – those postings were definitely suspected by some to have come from Kimberlee herself. Quite forbidden, that kind of thing. Got herself tossed off a few lists, I'd imagine. But I didn't know her personally. No. No, indeed. I choose my friends more carefully than that.'

Funny, thought St Just. The sudden claim to passing acquaintance. That was common in a murder case, of course. People either didn't want to know you at all, or they decided they'd always been your bosom buddy, once you were dead. The truth might be anywhere along that continuum.

He took a final sip of his coffee. It was cold now. He pushed the cup to one side.

'What was the topic of conversation after I left the library that night?'

'Much the same as when you were there. The usual stuff, which is why I don't recall it in detail. That and a few drinks – not good for the memory.'

'Give me some examples.'

'Oh, writers talking about platforms and hits and listserves and blogs and grogs and meager royalties.'

'I thought all writers *ever* talked about were sales and royalties. Please don't tell me what a grog is.'

'Yes, still, as in the good old days, meager royalties. Some things don't change. And it's a group blog.'

'I still don't know what it is. But hits – I do know what hits are. That used to be a term reserved for Mafia types.'

'Coincidence?' she said, smiling. She had a not-unattractive smile. He shifted in his chair.

'Kimberlee used to work in journalism. You aren't familiar with her from that time?'

She shook her head.

'I first became aware of her when she wrote for that fashion rag. She caused a publishing storm at the time that caused the magazine to drop, for the moment, its heated debate over whether metallic blue eye shadow really deserved such a bad reputation. This time, Kimberlee was rumored to be writing a tell-all about Easterbrook and his authors,' she said.

'So I've heard. . .'

'In fact, Kimberlee told Jay, I think it was, that the night before the awards dinner, she had put most of the finishing touches on the only copy of her manuscript and would be mailing a disk next week.'

So, thought St Just. Where there's a disk there must be a laptop. Where the devil was it?

'Mailing it to whom? Jay? Or Ninette?'

'I didn't ask.'

'Blackmail?' he asked. 'Do you think that was her game?'

'Could have been, but would she really need the money? I doubt it – not unless she had a well-concealed drug or gambling problem. The power? Maybe. Much more likely. But if we can indulge in speculation, word on the street, if you want to talk blackmail, is that it was Tom Brackett who was blackmailing Easterbrook – to get more publicity and promotion for his books. If I got wind of that bit of news, Kimberlee certainly would have.'

'Any basis to this speculation?'

'Tom gets nearly all the publicity out of Easterbrook, in comparison with the rest of us. Just take a look at that showy four-color ad for his latest book, in the conference program. Since when does a piece of dreck like *G-Man Ranger Danger* warrant that kind of splashout?'

'I thought he was a popular author.'

'Well, yes, he is – but with a lot of help from Easterbrook. That's what is odd, you see. It's not as if he's writing either great literature or great entertainment. It's not as if he has a *personality*, for pity's sake. It's hard to see why Easterbrook would back him at the expense of the others. Winston and Portia, for example, are far better writers, and far more personable. Even Magretta: Magretta writes – or maybe wrote, is a better word – popular entertainment, and God knows she knows how to put on a show.'

'Like Kimberlee Kalder.'

'Yes.'

'Only Kimberlee Kalder did it better.'

'Yes.'

'And you?'

'What about me?'

'How would you rank your work?'

'Entertainment, well forgotten within a decade. I have no illusions, Inspector. It's a job like any other, and it beats waitressing. There's something else – you've heard by now Kimberlee had some kind of tiff at the conference with B. A. King, haven't you?'

'How did *you* come to hear of it?'

'The rumor mill, of course, Inspector. But I thought nothing of it. No one can stand B. A.'

'So I gather,' said St Just. 'Now, you told the police you were in the library from after dinner until the body was discovered.'

'Yes, I was with Mrs Elksworthy. Portia De'Ath was also with us – both before and after we lost the lights. Well, they were all with us at some point, really.'

'Mrs Elksworthy remained with you the whole time?'

'Except for a brief visit to the powder room. Very brief.'

'What time was that?'

'I've no idea. I suppose we'd been talking for an hour since dinner.'

'And you remained in the library.'

'That is correct. I assure you Mrs Elksworthy had no time for . . . what you are suggesting.'

'You were seen talking with Kimberlee earlier that night. What was that about?'

She cocked her head, puzzled, then said, 'In the hallway, you mean? I'd forgotten about that. Actually, I was popping into the ladies and she asked me if I had a blank CD she could have. I couldn't oblige her – I'm still stuck in the stone age, using floppy disks. I guess she wanted to make copies of her *magnum opus*.'

He sighed. The more he learned, the more puzzled he became.

'Well, if you think of anything further—'

'Inspector, when are we going to be allowed to leave?'

'A matter of hours rather than days, I would say.'

He stood, giving his spine and shoulders a stretch. It seemed like days since he'd slept and exhaustion was creeping in – wearing cleats, apparently.

'Days? Good heavens, man. I have a plane to catch.'

'And I, a murderer.'

CHAPTER 24

Purple Prose

After Annabelle left, St Just turned at last, with palpable reluctance, to the document in which Magretta had captured her experiences on the night of the murder. It was written in purple ink on the castle's stationery, in a large, loopy handwriting that ran chaotically over the pages, at times running off the edge. Holding his head in his hands, he read:

Following a repast of pink salmon, plucked new that day from a sky-blue Lothian loch, and not too overcooked, I repaired to the library to announce my intention to retire for the night. It was indeed a dark and stormy night of the sort described by the deeply misunderstood and underappreciated Bulwer-Lytton and – dare I say it now? – shivers of apprehension raced up and down my spine, in formation, like jack-booted thugs. I knew, in the way a sensitive spirit such as mine will know (my mother was psychic), that Death had come to dwell at Dalmorton Castle.

Filled with a dreadful and eerie foreboding, then, I bravely went to my room to work on Madness and Love on the Moors *(working title for my much-anticipated new novel, which will soon be available online and in fine bookshops everywhere. It is the sequel to my best-selling* Death Be Not Plowed. *I am told my novels make the ideal holiday gift).*

Still, upon retiring to my chambers, the feeling of doom would not leave me. I also had a killing head, a migraine of the worst sort. Nonetheless, after laboring at my profession for nearly an hour against these terrible odds, I looked by chance out the window where the storm raged with the sound and fury of souls in purgatory – but I could see nothing amiss. No creature stalked abroad that cursed, cursed night.

But then! Then! At the stroke of ten I thought I heard a prowler trying to break into Kimberlee's room. I clothed myself in green velvet, the color of emeralds in sunlight, and out I crept into the hallway and over to Kimberlee's door. Hesitantly, I knocked. There was no answer. I knocked again. The silence of the dead reigned, apart from the crashing crescendo of the storm and the throbbing pulsation of my heart. Then it was that I felt a ghostly presence, an eerie sense of Someone or Something from Another Dimension. Turning, I saw a vaporous form, draped in white. It was – no more and no less – the Ghost of Dalmorton Castle. I now know it had come to warn me of Kimberlee's impending death.

But what could I do? The figure turned to depart. I called after it. 'Wait!' I cried. 'Wait!' But the dead need pay no heed to the living.

Quite exhausted now, minutes later I was asleep, sleeping the dreamless sleep of the just.

There was more, but apart from a dramatic description of her discovery of the body, in which she glossed over her shrieking fit of hysteria that had roused most of the castle, it amounted to a rambling promotional spiel on the inspiration for her books. He sighed, putting the sheets back in his pocket. He noted the 'killing head' didn't quite go with the dreamless sleep, nor with the fact she apparently felt well enough later to scamper girlishly about the castle.

Precious little real help there, he thought. Curious omission she'd made, though. He dallied awhile, a great weariness washing through him, but in the end he knew it would have to be 'once more unto the breach' that night. He still needed to talk with Mrs Elksworthy. Even though he felt he could rely on the thoroughness of the Scottish detectives' report of their interview with her, there was no real substitute for the face-to-face interview.

For now, he decided to skip Magretta, feeling somehow he had just spent many, many hours in her company. But the thought of Magretta and the desire to avoid her, of course, made her manifest. Her voice rang out as he crossed the lobby.

'There you are, my darling Inspector!' she cried. 'I have solved the crime! With a little help from dear, dear Portia. You simply must come with me and see.'

Latching onto his arm, she began to pull him toward the library.

'Wait until you see!'

Three women were in the book-lined room: Donna Doone, Mrs Elksworthy, and Portia, but he was surprised to find them crowded behind the small service bar with the bartender. They all stood staring raptly into what appeared to be a large storage room behind a door – a door disguised as a bookcase. The good-sized area – several meters square – held the overflow from the bar: cases of beer and cartons of liquor were stacked against the stone walls.

'Do you see what it is, Inspector?' asked Magretta.

'A storage room?' he hazarded.

All four of them shook their heads. Portia said, 'Look closer. Behind those boxes against the far wall.'

He stepped inside, stooping under a doorway clearly intended for shorter medieval-era frames. The area was illuminated by a single bare electric bulb overhead. Peering about, he saw that the boxes Portia indicated in fact stood some way out from the wall. Behind them was yet another wooden door. Opening it, he was startled to find himself in a large broom cupboard stocked with cleaning supplies. He twisted the inside handle of that door and ended up in the hallway outside the library. On either side of him were doors to the loos, his and hers.

There was something odd . . . He turned and looked from side to side. The broom cupboard didn't appear to be as wide as the bar storage room, as would have been expected. Then he realized there was yet another door to his left, disguised by shelving like the one in the bar. Behind it he found narrow stone steps leading down. A failsafe escape, in case the hiding place was discovered. He made his way back into the bar area.

'As you can see, you wouldn't realize there was a room behind that wall in the bar,' said Portia. 'There's a switch hidden in one of the "books" that you have to push to release the door. What it is, is a priest's hole.'

St Just addressed Randolph, the young bartender.

'Those steps lead where?'

'There's a passage runs under Reception. The exit is a door into the hallway near the bottle dungeon – the hallway guests take to get to their rooms.'

'How widely known is this?'

'Not widely.' Randolph had a shock of auburn hair that seemed to be standing straight up from his scalp at the sheer excitement of it all. 'We found more than one couple using it as, how would you say, a *trysting* place over the years. You know the sort of thing. Forbidden pleasures. There's still mention of the priest's hole in the castle's marketing materials, but staff have been instructed for some years to keep quiet about its exact location. The tunnel isn't mentioned at all.'

He added: 'The loos were installed when Dalmorton became a hotel . . . they weren't part of the original construction, of course. They just built them out into that wide hallway.'

St Just turned to Portia. 'How did you happen to find it?'

She tapped a thin, leather-bound volume sitting on top of the bar. The title, in Gothic script, read: *Dalmorton through the Ages*.

'There's a complete description in here – it's a family history written in 1925 by a younger son of the castle owners. I found the book misfiled on the botany shelf. I asked Randolph here about it.'

Magretta said, 'I think it has to be Lord Easterbrook.'

'I really don't follow that, Ms Sincock,' said St Just.

'He's the only one unaccounted for, isn't he? He went missing immediately after dinner. He could have positively *stolen* into the broom cupboard, nipped to the dungeon, and awaited his chance to attack Kimberlee.'

It was Portia who said, 'But what on earth would have been the point, Magretta? He could have come down from his room or anywhere else with little risk of being seen by anyone on his way to the bottle dungeon. We, after all, were all in here. What this really means is no one of us has much of an alibi now.'

St Just nodded. It put a whole new light on things. Anyone who knew about the underground passageway could nip out on the pretext of using the facilities, race over to the dungeon to meet Kimberlee, and scurry back, avoiding being spotted in the lobby. And all without the inebriated crowd noticing the absence.

Easterbrook was beside the point. Or was the point – for Magretta – to implicate the one person whose whereabouts were completely unverifiable, apart from her own? In any event, he'd have to get Moor's forensics team to have a look down there.

He turned at the sound of a grunt from across the room. B. A. King, who had apparently taken up a permanent position in the library, was starting to rally, or perhaps the exact phrase was, emerge from his stupor on the sofa. He staggered over to the bar with his empty glass.

'Just a splash more,' he told the bartender. 'Maybe two.'

St Just, turning to Magretta, said, 'Leaving aside your supernatural adventures of Saturday night, I'd like to ask you a few questions about your little alibi.'

'Oh, yes? What an enjoyable exercise I found that to be,

Inspector. My training as a mystery writer, of course, has made me frightfully observant. And to have the opportunity to express my deepest—'

'It might be truer to say your training as a mystery writer has taught you the art of invention.'

She inclined her head graciously. 'Quite true, quite true! I am renowned for my imagination! But I assure you in this case—'

'In this case, you've been feeding the police a pack of lies. The opacity of the document you handed us, that farrago of nonsensical invention, was designed to conceal your true whereabouts at the time, was it not?'

Gracious pose forgotten, she began to play nervously with the scarf at her neck.

'I beg your pardon?' Then, recovering swiftly, 'How dare you?'

'How dare you lie to the police?'

'I never—'

He decided to chance his arm with a bluff.

'Before you say anything further, I will warn you – you were seen.'

At that, she astonished him by turning and fleeing from the room. She was surprisingly fast on her feet and was already in the hallway by the bottle dungeon when he caught up with her. But she was no longer running by that point, merely waiting for him to catch up.

'Not in front of the others,' she said. 'I beg you.'

'Someone saw you that night.'

'It was that Florie, wasn't it? She should learn to mind her own business. You're right, I . . . left some things out of my account.'

'The laptop,' he said.

'The laptop.'

CHAPTER 25

Daughter of Time

The only thing about the case St Just would call a dead cert was that there was a remarkable amount of concealment going on – but whether related to the murder or not it was difficult to say. Obfuscation seemed to be second nature to mystery writers – an occupational hazard, like Mrs Elksworthy's writer's butt. They fantasized and lied and fabricated for a living, dreaming up improbable plots, seldom stopping off in the real world for more than a brief visit.

That, of course, was what made it all so damnably difficult. He had a sense they all concealed for the hell of it, to keep in practice.

Magretta had a slightly different motive for concealment, as it turned out.

'I know how it must look,' she began.

'No, I don't think you can begin to imagine how this looks.'

'Listen, I only wanted to destroy the manuscript. That's all. You have to believe me.'

'You went to her room that night to steal the laptop,' he said flatly.

She pleated her lips into a moue of distaste. 'No. I do not *steal*. I went there to *destroy* the laptop. You see, I saw her arrive with one – with a laptop case. And she told me she was just putting the finishing touches on her manuscript. The great artist, Kimberlee. She never shut up about it.'

It figured. There had to have been a laptop. It was unlikely in

the extreme that Kimberlee – nearly a poster child for her tech-
nology-obsessed generation – would not travel with a laptop.
He'd never thought to ask Portia about the bags Kimberlee
brought with her on the train.

'Why did you want to destroy her manuscript?' St Just
asked Magretta.

She took a step closer and said in a low (for her) voice,
'Now, this has to be kept in confidence.'

He shook his head firmly.

'You must be joking. Look, I'll go this far: If your information turns out not to be relevant to Kimberlee's death, I can
promise you it won't be needlessly broadcast.'

She stared at him in some distress for a moment, then sur-
rendered. 'Oh, very well. I may as well tell you. She'd heard
the story about my son. I do have a son; it's not widely known,
but. . .'

'Let me guess. He was bad for your image so you didn't
play up the fact.'

'Something like that. But, you see, it was far more than
that, of course . . . he was a troubled lad, always was, and
eventually he was sent away a few years for dealing drugs.'
A shadow stole across her eyes. 'I nearly went to gaol myself
over that . . . we had that rubbish all over the house and I
never knew it. This was when he was still at school. I was a
single mother. That isn't an easy life, I can tell you – his father
left us without a backward glance, and without a *sou*. Years
of barely scraping by . . . I guess someone at the newspaper
where she and I used to work told her the story. She came
along there after I had left. Anyway, somehow she got hold
of it and. . .'

'And she was putting this in her new book?'

'Yes. She barely bothered to change his description, or
mine.'

'And you know this – how?'

'She told me! Came sidling up to me at the conference, bold

as brass, the malicious little . . . Anyway, she said I wouldn't be able to do anything about it, said she'd chosen her words too carefully for that, but she said it was time the world knew the truth. As if she would know the truth if it bit her. Since when did Kimberlee Kalder care about *truth*, anyway?' Magretta was building up a head of steam as she spoke. 'Kimberlee cared only about herself.'

'And you didn't tell me this because you knew I'd like you for her murder.'

She nodded glumly. 'That's exactly why. I just wanted that piece of rubbish destroyed, not *her*. I was completely frantic – not really thinking straight, of course. My son paid his debt, kicked his habit. He's straightened himself out. And for her to come along and try to stir it again. . .'

'So you threw her laptop—'

'Out the window, yes. I knew from watching telly that if I just deleted the file, it could be recovered. The whole thing, laptop and all, had to disappear.'

'What made you think there were no other copies?'

'She was asking everyone earlier for a disk to make a back-up copy, whatever that is when it's at home. I'm not technically minded. Not in the least. Very agitated about it, she was – no one seemed to have brought a spare. More likely, no one was willing to help her out. I heard Winston, I think it was, tell her just to e-mail a copy to herself. She said – and she was quite shirty with him, let me tell you – she said she "couldn't get an effing signal in this mausoleum." The castle wasn't set up for wired, I think she said.'

'Wireless,' St Just said automatically. There weren't even computer ports on the phones in the guest rooms, either. Dalmorton styled itself as an escape from the pressures of modern-day life, and as far as technological gadgets went, it certainly was that.

He stood, appraising her. There was one rather large hole in her story. If not more than one.

'What made you feel so free to wander around Kimberlee Kalder's room?'

'What do you mean?' she asked slowly. Her expression didn't change but he saw a burst of panic in her eyes.

'If she came back suddenly, there would be no escape; she'd be sure to find you. There's only one exit from her room and you certainly couldn't jump through the window.'

This was greeted with silence, as Magretta studied the toes of her shoes.

'You knew she was dead already, didn't you?'

She looked up at him, appalled.

'Because you killed her.'

'No! *No!* You've got it all wrong. I didn't kill her. Indeed, I did not. I couldn't—'

'A woman threatens you and your child – threatens to expose his secret to the world. A secret you'd carefully kept hidden for years. Why couldn't you kill her?'

'I didn't. She was d—' Magretta paused, breathing heavily. Her eyes were wide with panic.

'She was dead already,' he finished for her.

Magretta, giving up at last, gloomily nodded her head.

He leaned placidly back against the cold stone wall, arms crossed.

'Yes. Yes! All right, I found her. She was down there – at the bottom of the bottle dungeon.'

'You mean you found her twice. The first time, you kept quiet about it. Then, when you'd done what you wanted, searched her room – you stole her key, took her purse, didn't you? – you let some time elapse and then came downstairs to "discover" her again. The maid tried to deliver a tray to the room while you were in there and you called out, pretending to be Kimberlee. I guess this is where your acting experience came in handy.'

Again Magretta nodded. 'I also left the water running a bit in my bathroom, so the maid would think I was in there

229

when she delivered the hot water bottle to *my* room. Anyway, Kimberlee's purse was there where I found her, near that balustrade where you look over into the dungeon itself. Yes, I took the purse; her key was inside. I thought someone else would find her, don't you see? When they didn't – you have to believe me, I wanted her killer caught. If it waited until morning or later, I knew the police would have more trouble determining the time of death. I wanted to *help*.' Even now, her appalling ego was at work; she couldn't forebear to add, 'That's part of my expert knowledge, you know, learned honing my craft as a crime writer. I know all about rigor mortis and things. So I did all I could to help the police, you see.'

'Help?' *For pity's sake.* 'Ms Sincock, you are in very serious trouble indeed for lying. You covered up a crime, tampered with evidence, even committed a theft of the dead person's effects. And then you proceeded to waste police time trying to butter it all over with ghost stories and God knows what-all sorts of nonsense. Ghosts, indeed.'

At this she raised her eyes from their study of the floor. 'But that was true about the ghost. It was *true*. Every word, I swear it. I saw her. It.'

He opened his mouth to speak and thought better of it. He would not be caught dead debating ectoplasm with Magretta. Realizing the unintentional pun, he smiled. Magretta smiled back, warily.

'Is something funny?' she asked.

He shook his head. 'Not at all.' He put on as stern a countenance as he could muster. Really, she was the most ridiculous woman. The deuce of it was, in spite of it all, he believed her story – excepting the ghost, of course. At least, he felt he'd gotten major parts of the truth out of Magretta at last.

'I'll let DCI Moor decide what to do about charges of obstructing this inquiry,' he said. 'What else do you know? It will go down better if you get it all out now. How did you happen to find her body?'

'That was pure chance, I swear. I couldn't sleep, I was that upset about this . . . blackmail or whatever you call what she was trying to pull on me. I hadn't seen the bottle dungeon yet, but from what I'd heard, it would make the perfect setting for the final scene in my novel. You see, my heroine is being held hostage – she's been kidnapped by white slavers – but she drops a glove and her fiancé who has a hunch where he'll find her anyway finds it and I—'

'Ms Sincock. . .' he said warningly.

'Oh, all right. Anyway, I just wanted any distraction that might take my mind off things. Besides, there was all this rackety traffic up and down the corridor. People knocking on Kimberlee's door.'

St Just unfolded his arms at that, pushing himself away from the wall.

'What people? Why didn't you at least tell me this?'

'I was supposed to be engrossed in my writing, wasn't I?' she retorted. 'But I heard two people come to Kimberlee's door and knock.'

'Who?'

'First it was Mrs Elksworthy. Kimberlee let her in. She only stayed about five minutes. Right after that came Lord Easterbrook. He stayed maybe ten minutes.'

'How did you know it was Joan Elksworthy and Easterbrook?'

'I stuck my head out the door to look, didn't I? They didn't see me, but I saw them clear as day.'

'And still you didn't think this worth mentioning until now?'

'They couldn't have killed her. I heard her voice – Kimberlee's – when she opened the door to them. And after Lord Easterbrook left, I saw Kimberlee herself leave. Before you ask, it was just before ten. I didn't tell you because I'm not a – what is it the Americans call it? A stool canary?'

He regarded her sternly.

'Is there anything else you saw that night that was suspicious. *Anything*? However minor? Let me be the judge of what's important or not.'

She shook her head.

'I don't think so. I think that's it.'

Oh, good. 'You think so? For your sake and mine, I hope so. Understand this: It's not up to me what happens to you. But from what I know of DCI Moor, he'll have your guts for garters.'

Her lip began to tremble. 'May I go back to my room now? I promise I've told you everything that could relate to this murder. And remember, I did try to help.'

St Just sighed.

'Go on. Keep yourself available. Moor will want to talk with you.'

'But, I tried to help!' she repeated, her voice shrill. She spun around in a whirl of green fringe and ran off, in floods of tears this time. Again he leaned against the wall, thinking through the new timeline Magretta had presented him. And about other concealments he didn't know about yet. If Magretta wasn't the killer . . .

He breathed deeply, and tried to will his ragged thoughts into some sort of order. Not for the first time, he regretted coming here at all – even though it meant Portia De'Ath was nearby, a thought that filled him with a fierce, bittersweet longing. Was he ever going to solve this case, get out of this castle, and be able to talk to her – not as a suspect, but as Portia? Solving the case, at least, was looking increasingly unlikely, despite Magretta's belated cooperation. He trudged upstairs for what felt like the twelfth time that day.

He was surprised to find Moor and Sergeant Kittle working late in what they had taken to calling the Incident Turret, poring over a novel's worth of computer printouts.

'Ah, good. It's you, Cambridge,' said Moor. 'Some interesting things are starting to turn up.'

St Just pulled up a chair.

'Yes, they certainly are.' He filled them in on both the priest's hole and Magretta's revised version of her activities the night of the murder. 'We're going to have to get men to check out that underground passageway, and into that moat to retrieve the laptop. What do you say we find out if any of these people have stayed at the castle before? The chances are against anyone just stumbling across that priest's hole. Good Lord. How much more thinly stretched can we get?'

'The priest's hole says to me, "Inside Job",' said Moor.

'You're thinking one of the staff, of course. Yes, I suppose we'll have to look at all that much more closely now. Oh, and before I forget, Moor. Whatever you do, don't let someone get the bright idea of trying to dry out the laptop, if you find it. Tell them to put it dripping wet into an evidence bag and get it to the lab ASAP. It's the only hope of retrieving any data from it.'

One of the uniforms was dispatched with instructions.

'You believe her? Magretta?' said Moor, turning to St Just.

St Just settled his long back against the worn leather chair, his handsome face a study in frustration.

'Strangely enough, I do. She's still lying about something – when she opens her eyes wide as she talks, she's lying or deliberately leaving something out, I've noticed – but I don't think she killed Kimberlee. I really don't. By the way, I've told her they still use the rack up here in Scotland. A little fear of God won't hurt her a bit. What do you have?'

'Well,' began Moor. 'First we have Tom Brackett's armed forces record. Sparse info, cautiously worded in impenetrable government-speak. He did do top secret work; this is where the rumor of a CIA affiliation comes from, I imagine. His specialty was interrogations. Reading between the lines, he became something of an embarrassment and had to be muscled out. Operated as sort of a freelance Torquemada after he left the service, and also served as an instructor, of all things

– just imagine the PowerPoints for that course. We'd have to clear a lot of bureaucratic hurdles to get the full details, and I'm not sure it's relevant. Anyway, there's a more "unclassified" report that talks about his aptitude for the work, and not exactly in glowing terms. Geneva Convention be damned, seemed to be his motto. What's more a surprise is that Edith was CIA.'

'What?'

'Yes. Officially she was a clerk-typist, but there are hints of undercover work in her CV.'

'Well, I must say, it's a great disguise.'

'Apparently Tom saved her life a few times, and she his. I suppose that created whatever bond those two managed to form.'

'Even though the bond seems to be loosening a bit now, with her success. Or more likely, the thrill of being a punching bag is just gone.'

Moor nodded, 'Too bad we can't at least apply for an ASBO against Brackett.'

'Anti-Social Behaviour Order? Yes, too bad. Even though his wife seems to bear the brunt, it would still be fitting.'

'We also have a report from New Mexico of suspected embezzlement by Mrs Elksworthy.'

'You're not serious.'

Moor nodded. 'It was never prosecuted; she was just quietly let go by her employer. Apparently they were sympathetic – and besides, she paid back every penny. She has – had – a lover who came down with a terminal illness, and didn't happen to be covered by health insurance. Of course, she wasn't covered by Mrs E.'s insurance at work, either. So Mrs E. embezzled to pay the hospital bills, which were enormous. Her partner had no family – or rather, they had turned her out for her . . . inclinations, long before. I got all this straight from some gabby old cat who still works at the firm. Anyway, Mrs E. took it all on as her responsibility, and the employer let her pay them back in increments. Luckily, her books started to sell about then. She's still poor as a church mouse – just take a look at her financials over there – but she owes no one a penny. This was ten years ago and there's not another spot on her record, before or since.'

Was that the reason for her insistence on the 'Mrs?' St Just wondered. She was from a generation where keeping up appearances about that sort of thing mattered very much. The fear of reprisals was always there. And of exposure. Blackmail. . .

'The power of love is. . .' he said aloud, without intending to.

'Is what?'

'Nothing. Go on. I was just wondering if Kimberlee some-how got wind of this for her little book.' And he filled them in on Kimberlee's threat to Magretta.

'Probably did,' said Moor. 'Our Kimberlee didn't seem to have a strong sense of self-preservation, did she? I thought novelists were supposed to make things up – it certainly sounds like that would have been the safer route to take. Anyway, then we have B. A. King. His real name, apparently. I guess his parents couldn't afford anything but initials. He has one or two drunk and disorderlies in his file.'

'You astonish me.'

'Here's something that really will astonish you. He writes romance novels. Well, he wrote one. That book you found in Kimberlee's room, it was his. He's Leticia-Anne Deville.'

'I find it really, really hard to picture B. A. King writing that heaving-bosoms kind of thing, sober or not.'

'You're not the only one. Anyway, not much motive there in either case – or is there? A case could be made that Mrs E. was pushed too far – but would she have the physical strength for this murder, I wonder?'

'I'm not certain about that myself. But never underestimate the power of an adrenaline surge,' said St Just. 'Well, the only constant motive across the board seems to be rivalry. Fear of what Kimberlee might have been writing in her new book is certainly, to me, the stronger motive.'

'Agreed. Then there's Ninette Thomson.' He jabbed a finger at the report. 'A real scofflaw, this lady. Overdue parking tickets all over London and New York.'

'But nothing really dodgy.' It was a statement rather than a question.

'Afraid not,' said Moor.

'How about Rachel Twalley?' St Just asked. 'Her alibi check out?'

Moor nodded.

'Straight home to her husband, a pillar of the church. I can't see any problems there, or with the other people Donna let out of the castle. The timing pretty much puts them out of it, and they swear they all hung together until the moment they left the premises, anyway.'

'Even if they'd hung around, motive would have been a problem.'

'Agreed. Young Quentin Swope, now, might have the type of personality we're looking for. According to his employer, he spends most of his time in the penalty box.'

'How so?'

Moor chewed thoughtfully at the corner of his mouth, twirling one side of his mustache, then said, 'Nothing too serious, apparently. I'm reading between the lines here again. The employer marks it down to youthful idealism. A few complaints of "aggressive" tactics used in landing an interview.'

'Hmm.'

'Donna Doone has a possible connection to the case, though.'

'*Donna?*'

'She had a brother who committed suicide. He was a teacher, living in Sheffield at the time – the same time Kimberlee was working for the paper. There were some allegations – unproven

– that his relationship with one of his students wasn't all it should be. There was a lot of press coverage – you know the kind of thing: hint, hint; nudge, nudge – but nothing written in plain language that could land the paper in trouble. I gather the man had always been a bit unstable, and the notoriety seems to have pushed him right over the edge. They're looking back at Kimberlee's columns now; she seems to have led the crusade against him.'

'Poor Donna. Certainly there's a motive there. Good old-fashioned revenge. Although I wouldn't have said that was her style. She's more the type to agonize endlessly, trying to forgive the unforgivable. How about Easterbrook. Anything on him?'

'Not really. Nothing at all, really. Born in a house the size of the Vatican. Public school background, Oxbridge, yada, yada. One of the few aristocrats to escape the rolling tumbrels of inheritance taxes and make enough money to maintain his stately home by himself, without having to turn it into a theme park. Doesn't appear to have ever held an ambition beyond the family business. He's apparently honest, as far as businessmen go.'

St Just was not overly surprised. Easterbrook's cold mind may have been forged in the dank, unheated dormitories of a Gulag system like Eton or Gordonstoun, but that wouldn't necessarily have turned him into a criminal. If that were the case, the gaols would be filled to over-crowding with bluebloods.

'Married?'

'Yes.'

'And?'

'She grows tulips.'

'Anything else? Anything on her?'

'No.'

'Tulips.'

'Yes.'

St Just stood and walked over to one of the arrow-slit

windows. Far below, Portia was sitting on a garden bench, wrapped tightly against the cold, the light from the castle windows gleaming faintly on her dark hair. Winston sat beside her, his head close to hers in urgent conversation – closer than St Just felt was strictly necessary to convey an opinion, however urgent. His heart did something he didn't know hearts could really do – a triple-axle followed by a somersault. He had to get this woman out of his mind; she was making him ill.

He realized Moor was speaking to him.

'I'm sorry, what?'

'What we don't know is why it was done, then.'

'Or how. Not to mention, by whom.'

Moor nodded. 'And we won't know who until we know why. Sod this for a lark. Practically any of them could have done it.'

St Just turned deliberately away from the window view. It was like removing a sticking plaster with one pull. He wanted to be down there with Portia, dragging her away from Winston's doubtful charms, not stuck here discussing this damned case.

He felt somehow like a traitor, but he had to ask. In a voice as casual as he could manage, he said, 'Anything on Portia De'Ath?'

Moor shook his head. 'Not on her, no. Her only connection with crime is that her American uncle was shot by an off-duty policeman. Killed. Turned out the man was unarmed. That kind of thing can queer you on police the rest of your life.'

Oh, God.

'Let me see that report.'

Moor handed it to him.

'Winston comes up clean, too,' said Moor, as St Just scanned the pages. An untested cop, an uncle who looked like a wanted suspect, stopped at a traffic light. He'd reached for his wallet to show his identification and. . .

St Just willfully pulled his mind back to the case. Time enough to learn Portia's story later. Her uncle's death couldn't be connected to this crime – he only hoped to God it wouldn't end up having anything to do with the pair of them, himself and Portia. It certainly explained the 'I could never marry a policeman' remark.

'Magretta Sincock did see something helpful that night,' he told Moor, 'but not a ghost. It was Kimberlee, probably on her way to the dungeon, "to meet her fate", as I'm sure Magretta would put it. It's odd, but . . . Winston thought he saw Kimberlee, too, later, but that's unlikely. As did Portia, although she's even less sure. Maybe it was someone wandering the stairs in one of the hotel's white robes. But by the time we lost the lights, Kimberlee was almost certainly already in the dungeon – and probably dead.'

St Just went on. 'They all claim alibis but none that are reliable – or completely verifiable, for that matter. There was a lot of wine with dinner and drinks all around in the hours following. And they say no group, on average, can go through drink like a group of writers.'

He couldn't help himself. He looked back into the garden. Portia had gone, leaving Winston sitting alone again. *Good*.

He turned back to Moor.

'By the way, we really should have someone hanging about the spa. There are some conversations going on in there that we should be privy to, and that might prove useful.' And Portia could use watching if she's going to play detective, he added to himself.

'Good idea,' said Moor. 'Sergeant Kittle, I've been noticing you've been letting those enlarged pores of yours get the upper hand.'

Kittle, stung, said, 'What enlarged pores?'

'Get on with you, man. See what you can learn from our friends, the murder suspects.'

'Sir, one of the WPCs would surely be a better—'

'Don't argue with me. Go.'

As the door closed on Sergeant Kittle's back, stiff with outrage, St Just said, 'We come back to why she would be in such an unlikely spot, at such an unlikely hour. I doubt very much she was looking for inspiration for her book, as Magretta claims was her own mission. That's just silly enough to be believable where Magretta is concerned, but Kimberlee – I'm not so sure. So the question is, which of these people would Kimberlee agree to meet? We assume her lover. Why? Why not meet Jay in her room as he claims they had planned?'

'So many "whys." Someone met her at the bottle dungeon and that's all she wrote. Literally. We—'

Just then they heard a scream, followed by a low, keening wail.

'It's coming from outside,' said St Just, already running. 'Let's go.'

CHAPTER 26

And Then There Were Fewer

It was a small body, nearly as short as a child's, but then Florie Macintosh in life had been a small woman.

Magretta had found her, a fact suspicious in itself. To find one body – fine, okay. Two bodies shot a person straight to the top of a suspect list.

Florie was floating facedown in the moat, in an unlighted area to the rear of the castle. A large gash to the back of her head gave him the hope she'd died quickly, unawares, even before she'd hit the water. A mace, no doubt taken from the castle's extensive collection of weaponry, lay on the ground not far from where she floated. Magretta, sobbing hysterically, was crouched at the edge of the wide ditch, staring in disbelief into the dark water.

St Just exchanged a few words with one of the constables hovering nearby before angrily stalking away, leaving Moor and Kittle to organize the forensics. There was nothing to be done until they retrieved that little form. He'd seen enough drowning victims to know Florie was past mortal help. And he didn't dare trust himself around Magretta.

'Have someone keep an eye on her – constantly,' he told Kittle before he left, with a nod in Magretta's direction. 'And get her away from the body.'

Damn. Damn it all to hell. How could he have been so stupid? He'd as good as told Magretta that Florie was the one who blew her 'alibi' apart. Could she really have raced right out to exact

241

revenge? Had Florie been killed only because he'd bluffed Magretta into thinking Florie was a witness against her?

Was Magretta insane? Or just panicked into carelessness? Kimberlee's death showed signs of careful planning – the murderer had to have lured Kimberlee somehow to such an obscure part of the castle. Florie's death – it was madness for the murderer to have taken such a risk.

He tried to turn all his prior thinking on its head. Everyone had kept assuring him that Kimberlee Kalder had everything going for her – and yet Kimberlee Kalder had ended up dead. Now he wondered: Had he been wrong from the start not to recognize her as a victim – as someone whose looks and success would attract jealousy wherever she went, almost – as Desmond had said – no matter what she did?

His footsteps led him unseeing, far past the range of the castle floodlights, towards the outdoor cages of the falconry. A snowy owl was the only one at home at the moment. He had read somewhere there was a word for a group of owls – a parliament, that was it. A funny word for such a typically solitary creature. St Just stopped in his tracks to stare at him – or her. The company of a creature that killed for food was infinitely preferable to that of a creature that killed for love or money – the usual human excuses. Love or money, sometimes with a little revenge thrown in.

The owl stared back at him with its great golden eyes – eyes that might have been lined with kohl. It seemed to say both, 'Hello? What's all this, then?' and 'I could have you for breakfast if I felt like it, you know,' but all in a supremely indifferent way.

'Boo,' said St Just, experimentally.

The owl, not surprisingly, had no time for this and looked peevishly away: *There must be better prey out there than this fool.* St Just stared at its downy, silken back. As he did so, a thought seemed to come from the remembered depths of the creature's eyes.

'What if?' he said aloud. 'What if it was something else she'd seen? Someone else?'

He walked slowly back in the direction of the hulking gray bulk of Dalmorton.

Florie's body had been removed from the water. Sergeant Kittle stood respectfully back inside the scene shield, watching forensics do its job, his melancholy expression even bleaker than usual. Moor was on the phone, giving somebody hell.

'They found the laptop, sir,' Kittle told him.

'Good. I'll be wanting a word with your IT man.' St Just turned away as the examiner began to practice the intimate, violating rituals of his trade. There was no dignity to be accorded the victim of foul play. 'For one thing, depending on what's on that laptop, we might need it at trial. Listen, can you get a search-and-rescue dog out here?'

Kittle, momentarily taken aback, said, 'I guess so, sir. Who are we looking for?'

'I think I've already found the one I'm looking for, actually. How long will it take to get someone out here?'

'An hour. Two at the most.'

'You're certain?'

'For a high-profile case like this? With a serial killer on the loose? Yeah, I think so, sir. Besides, Robert, the handler, is one of my mates. I'll get him here with Rob Roy. That's the dog, sir.'

'Good. Once they've arrived, I want you to get the suspects together in the library. All of them. Tell them the castle is offering free drinks all night. That will get them there with bells on. And when you talk with Donna about the drinks, tell her I want a word with her.'

'Well, I don't know about—'

'Don't worry, I'll clear all this with Moor. Oh, and one more thing,' he added. 'Find me a good local bookstore, one that's willing to cooperate with the police, no matter the time of night.'

And he told Sergeant Kittle exactly what he wanted.

They were clustered by the priest's hole, whispering, the whole job lot of them. They jumped apart as St Just, Moor, and Kittle came into the room, precisely like a gang of old lags caught trying to break out in an old gaol movie.

He did a quick head count as they turned to look at him. They were all there, and looking only slightly mollified by the free drinks, crisps, and snacks the sergeant had arranged via Donna.

St Just was carrying a small carton, which he placed carefully on the seat of one of the chairs. He turned to address the group. Good, all eyes front. Rather, all eyes were trying to get a closer look at the carton behind him, which happened to be labeled 'Olive Oil – Imported from Greece.'

Annabelle Pace broke the silence.

'Any progress yet, DCI St Just?' she asked. Her voice held a tinge of exasperation. Annabelle still seemed to be auditioning for a role in newsreel footage of wartime shortages, this time wearing a gray, loose-fitting dress that might have started life as a slipcover.

'Well, I've determined that many of you are lying. That's progress of a sort.'

There were splutterings of protest at this, but not as much, he thought, as one might have expected.

Mrs Elksworthy said, 'Perhaps you will explain what is meant by lying?' But her voice was tentative. He might only have imagined that her eyes held a pleading look.

'First, would everyone please take a seat. Make yourselves comfortable. This may take awhile.' He waited until they'd settled in. Jay, he noticed, took his usual position by the window, so as to be highlighted to best advantage. Did the man never give it a rest?

'I say, Inspector, it's a jolly late time of night for this,' said Easterbrook.

'Certainly it's too jolly late to help Mrs Macintosh,' St Just replied curtly. His anger at himself for not foreseeing the danger to Florie was still bitter, even though he recognized that it was her death that had pointed the way. Hands in pockets, he began pacing the room. 'Now, in any murder investigation, things are uncovered that a suspect – however innocent – doesn't necessarily want revealed.' His eyes slid of their own accord in Mrs Elksworthy's direction. 'We, the police, are perfectly aware that most of what is uncovered may have nothing to do with the case. Still, we need all the pieces of the puzzle so we can start throwing out the pieces that belong to a different puzzle altogether.

'For example, Mrs Elksworthy. You never told anyone you spoke with Kimberlee that night in her room. I had to learn that from someone else.'

She answered, in a slow, tentative voice he had never heard her use before.

'Yes. Yes, I – Oh, what difference does it all make now? I had a friend of many years. Her name was Laura. But I suppose you know all about it. About . . . everything?'

He gave a slight nod of his head.

'We don't care about the particulars, Mrs Elksworthy. But I need you to tell me yourself why you were in Kimberlee's room.'

'Kimberlee came over to me after dinner the first night and said, "Writing about Laura was such a challenge, but I think you'll be pleased with the result." Of course I asked why she would write about her at all. It was "such a fascinating love story," she said. I told her she didn't have my permission to write about Laura. But of course she didn't need my permission. "You're a crook, aren't you?" she said then. And she gave me this triumphant, this *gloating*, little smile. I think the devil probably smiles like that. Anyway, God knows what she was writing exactly, but I was not going to have her treat Laura's life, and mine, as fodder for some trashy '*Latte*' sequel. I went to try to talk her out of it. I could have saved my breath, of course. If I hadn't been so angry and frightened – I was just *shaking* with fear and anger – I'd have known that. She just laughed at me. Called me an old – well, never mind. I should have known better than to even try with her.

'The real joke is, Kimberlee owed me. She wanted a blurb from me when her book first came out. I was glad to help. Well, I did write something innocuous rather than glowing – I think the marketing people pulled out a single word like "intriguing" for the back cover. It was that, all right. *Intriguing.*

'Oh, what difference does it make now?' she said again, in a voice pitched to a wail. 'If I expected gratitude, I wouldn't have helped her in the first place. I just didn't expect that kind of betrayal. But Kimberlee was very much alive when I left her, Inspector. Alive, and laughing.

'As to the rest – I can't say I'm sorry for any of . . . what happened . . . as difficult as it made my life. If left to the US healthcare system, Laura would have died on the streets, too ill and broke to care for herself. I had to do something to help her.'

The rest of the group looked at each other, mystified by this narration.

'Who in hell is Laura?' demanded B. A. King.

Somewhat melodramatically, St Just turned and pointed in the direction of B. A. King, who stared mulishly back.

'As for you,' said St Just. 'You're one of the finest liars in this collection.'

'That's just not true,' said King. 'I told you everything. Practically solved the case for you, I'd bet. I saw them dredge up that laptop from the moat. That must have been the splash I heard. I told you about seeing Magretta—'

'Why didn't you tell me about "your" book when you had

the chance? Instead, you dredged up some nonsense about how you'd lost Kimberlee's pen.'

'I'm sure I don't know what you mean.'

'I'm sure you do. We checked out the copyright on *When Summer's Passion Lingers*, a simple enough thing to do. The copyright holder is Thistlegrove Enterprises. An "enterprise" registered to B. A. King. You changed the title of the book, of course, an elementary precaution. But Kimberlee found out, didn't she? She stumbled across a copy somehow, and she of course recognized her own writing. She began threatening you, probably with legal action. And there is only one way to silence that kind of threat forever, is there not?'

'No!' King shouted. 'You've got it all wrong. It was nothing. Just a little fiddle. She didn't care . . . The book didn't make much money, anyway. She wasn't . . . I didn't think—'

St Just cut across the blether. 'You didn't think there was any way for her or anyone else to find out, did you? She'd moved on to the mystery field, she wasn't writing straight romance anymore. You made up a name, and you submitted her book to a publisher as your own, didn't you? Leticia-Anne Deville, indeed. Now, how did you get hold of the book? I think that was the simplest part of all. Kimberlee's manuscript came in unsolicited when she was looking for an agent, back in the days when you were still working as an agent, before you became a publicist. She must have been just a kid. What could be simpler than to decline to represent her but to steal her book as your own? No wonder she was angry – I'd have been angry, too.'

'You're crazy,' said B. A. King. 'I'll have you up on slander charges.'

'Be my guest. I'll look forward to that day. Now, another liar is Jay.'

Jay uncurled slowly, cautiously, from his languid pose. The blue eyes beneath the tousled blond hair held a startled, wary look.

'Those were stupid lies you told me. The platonic, hand-holding, love-at-a-distance lies. At least you admitted you went to her room the night of the murder – that admission was a wise move on your part. As it happened, you were seen by Quentin, coming downstairs. But you met Kimberlee some time ago, didn't you? You had an affair – a sexual relationship?'

Jay shook his head, all his arrogance returning. 'You couldn't possibly know that. And I really fail to see how it's any of your busi—'

'Three little words.'

'No. I didn't love her.'

'Two words, actually. DeoxyriboNucleic Acid. DNA. Kimberlee was pregnant. Naturally we'll be testing to see who the father was.'

'Good God. But I—'

'This would really be a good moment to tell me the truth. Your story of chaste, courtly love may not hold up.'

Desmond Rumer, meanwhile, was looking at Jay with a steely hatred. He made to cross the room toward his rival, only to find Sergeant Kittle had stepped nimbly into his path. Reluctantly, Desmond backed away, but he remained standing, fists clenched at his sides.

'Oh, all right, all right!' Jay bellowed, then, collecting himself, said more equably, 'We had begun an affair. But I didn't kill her and it's a far leap to try to claim I did. I was just afraid if you knew how far I was involved with her it would look bad for me. The situation had altered when she turned up, you know, dead.'

'This admission at this late date is what looks, you know, bad. Just for your future reference. Sir.'

'All right, I said. But I told you everything that was salient to your investigation. I went to her room at ten-thirty to keep our prearranged rendezvous, but she wasn't there. She'd given me a key – I told you that.'

St Just nodded. 'She was probably already dead by then.'

St Just still thought Jay had rather a wonderful motive, but he decided not to waste any more bullets on him.

'Just tell me,' said St Just, 'one thing. Where did you meet her for your little secret get-togethers?'

'We always met at my place. Once or twice we went away for the odd weekend, met up in the Bahamas. I didn't even know where she lived, except in the vaguest terms. Kimberlee was evasive, always. It was part of her nature, I thought. I didn't know about . . . him. I didn't know he was the reason.' He stole a glance at Desmond, who returned the glance with a glower of scarcely controlled loathing.

'That's what I thought,' said St Just. He turned, assessing each of the suspects, one by one. Eeney, meeney, miney . . . His eyes settled at last on one face in particular.

'But for the real liar, of course, the prize goes to the one who killed Kimberlee, and the one who killed Florie.'

CHAPTER 27

Witness for the Prosecution

St Just had once sat through an interrogation training course in analyzing facial expressions. Looking about, he saw nearly the whole gamut arrayed before him: Fear, guilt, puzzlement, annoyance, anger. Pretty much everything but joy and lust.

'This would have been a simple case to solve if so many of you hadn't lied about so many silly things,' he reiterated. 'Stolen books, love affairs – none of the secrets some of you have been hiding holds a candle to murder. Even in the case of Donna Doone, who has a sadder connection with Kimberlee. But Ms Doone, we needed to have heard about that from you.'

Donna nodded miserably. 'She killed my brother. She was *directly* responsible for his death.'

'And there is a case to be made that she was. Unsubstantiated allegations, cleverly worded – that poisonous type of writing was Kimberlee's specialty.'

'I never knew,' said Donna slowly, 'what it was like to actually want to *kill* someone. But that's how I felt about Kimberlee. For a very long time. But I'd put it all behind me for the most part – I have my writing, you see. That helps me forget.'

'Donna,' said Winston. 'You really shouldn't say any more.' St Just was more than a little surprised to see a look of stricken tenderness on his face. When had this connection sprung up between them?

She shook her head, returning his look with one of deep

affection. 'It's all right, Winston.' She turned her eyes to St Just. 'When she came here, it just stirred it all up for me again. I hated the sight of her face. Hated . . . And then – she didn't know who I was, you see – I showed her my book, she asked to see it, and she laughed—'

'Donna,' said Winston again. 'Please. You need to take advice.'

'But you didn't kill her, did you.' This, also gently, came from St Just.

'No,' she said sadly. 'And I guess you'll just have to take my word for it.'

'Ms Doone, I think I can do better than that.' He turned again to the rest of the room. 'Now, others here have far less serious secrets they've been at pains to hide. For example, this staged animosity toward Kimberlee. . .'

His eyes were on Magretta now, who gave him her patented 'Who, me?' look of innocence.

'That really worked against you once she was killed, Magretta, when it became a dangerous game – for you. You should have helped us get a clearer picture from the start. The whole thing was a publicity stunt, wasn't it?'

'We-e-ell, not the whole thing,' she said. 'Kimberlee and I discovered by accident that press about bad blood between us made sales figures for both of us go up. You can track this kind of thing online these days, you know. Any newspaper article we could engineer, debating the worth, or not, of chick lit books – making it look like a spitting feud, you know – that caused quite a spike in both our online visitors and sales. So we went about deliberately stirring things. As Oscar Wilde said, "There is only one thing in life worse than being talked about, and that is not being talked about." It certainly worked to my advantage over time – if they, the press, mentioned Kimberlee, it got so they almost had to mention me. It was harmless.'

'Let's let me be the judge of whether or not it was harmless, shall we?'

'How did you guess?' she asked.

'Partly because you overdid it. You overacted – how did B. A. King put it? You chewed the scenery. Yes. I gather that was the stamp of your previous career in the theater.'

'Well, really,' huffed Magretta. 'I—'

'And you—' St Just added, turning, '—you might also have told me, Quentin, that you were in on this little scheme. So much for high journalistic standards. You did nothing but create more little lies for us to clear away, before we could begin to see the larger truth.'

'It's got nothing to do with anything . . . I told you, Kimberlee was going to give me a blurb. What was the harm? One hand washing the other.'

'Yes, I wondered at that, Kimberlee *promising* you a blurb. She had to be getting more out of it than what you let on. The open-handed gesture was never in her repertoire, according to all of you, and your history with her hardly suggests she would be nursing some wistful nostalgia for an old friendship. Why on earth would she go out of her way to help you – unless there was something in it for Kimberlee? Let's see, who else? Oh, yes, Winston Chatley.'

'Me?' His gaze flitted automatically toward Donna.

'It was B. A. King who suggested to me Winston had blackmailed Easterbrook, in order to get his books published. He implied Easterbrook had been having an affair and since it was his wife who happened to control the wealth . . . But I didn't believe a lot of what B. A. King told me, and I certainly doubted this. If Winston was such an excellent writer, as I've heard, why would blackmail be necessary to get published?'

The writers looked at him, stunned.

'You must be joking,' said Magretta. 'Haven't you learned anything in the past few days? Writers would *kill* to get published – just using a figure of speech there, of course,' she added. 'But would they stop at a spot of blackmail? No. *Heavens* no. Talent or a lack of it has *nothing* to do with getting published. That's why we're such *desperate* creatures.'

They all nodded their heads in agreement.

'Yes, you've already told me the lengths you, personally, would go to in order to get what *you* wanted. B. A. King told me he heard a loud splash – something being thrown out of Kimberlee's room. I tended to dismiss that – he was so busy implicating everyone and dragging red herrings about the place. Plus, he was drunk and rambling half the time.'

'Look here, that's uncalled f—'

'But by your own admission, Magretta, you did throw the computer out of Kimberlee's window. It would just fit through the medieval arrow slit, wouldn't it? It's almost as if the stonemasons had planned for future technology. You had found Kimberlee dead when you went to the bottle dungeon, wandering about, maybe a little drunk. You stole Kimberlee's purse, with her key, from the crime scene. This was, of course, how you knew you had the free run of her room. Kimberlee was dead.'

All heads turned to Magretta.

'What?' she said. 'I had my reasons. He knows.'

'Perhaps what you really wanted, Ms Sincock, was to end the reign of Kimberlee and her pink handbags. Did you imagine killing her would put an end to the chick lit trend?'

'That's preposterous. Of course not.'

'Yes,' said St Just. 'I do tend to agree. Be all that as it may, B. A. King told the truth about the splash he heard. But he got the wrong angle on the blackmail, didn't he? Winston wasn't the blackmailer. According to Annabelle, that was Tom Brackett, a much more likely scenario. He was holding Easterbrook's feet to the fire so he could get expensive publicity and more promotion for his "spy" books.'

This earned Easterbrook a few reproachful stares, and a few wistful ones as well: *Why didn't I think of doing that?*

'Of all the nonsense. . .' began Tom. But he stopped on seeing the look on Easterbrook's face.

'You can find yourself a new publisher now this has all spilled open,' Easterbrook told him. 'That little game is over.'

St Just continued, 'King did get a couple of things right. You see, it's so hard to tell when you're dealing with someone who deals in half-remembered gossip and innuendo. He also claimed to have seen Magretta skulking about when she claimed she was asleep or in communion with her Muse.'

'I don't skulk,' said Magretta. 'I told you what I was doing. I helped your investigation, remember?'

'After first sabotaging it almost beyond repair, yes. Thanks so much. But let me come to the point. Someone here at the castle is not what they say they are.

'And that someone would be you, Desmond, the "devoted husband."'

CHAPTER 28

Something Wicked

There was a long pause. The others exchanged puzzled glances, then settled their eyes on Desmond. He kept his gaze stolidly fixed on St Just.

'Tell me something, Desmond,' said St Just. 'Satisfy my curiosity, let's say. Have you ever set foot inside the priest's hole?'

'What? No. No, never. *What* priest's hole?' he asked, in a voice loud and hoarse. He might have been shouting against a sudden influx of noise.

St Just smiled in satisfaction. It was all he could have hoped for.

'Then why did forensics find strands of short dark hair in there? You're the only one we've got who would have any earthly reason to hang about the priest's hole that night. The rest of them had rooms.

'We can easily test hair for DNA, too, you know,' he added.

The room fell into a hushed silence, the muted ticking of the clock on the mantelpiece the only sound. But St Just thought he could almost hear the two minds that most concerned him communing telepathically across the room.

'Let me tell you how this happened,' said St Just. 'You, Desmond, killed your wife, Kimberlee. It had to be done before she got around to filing divorce papers. My conversations with both her agent and her publisher elicited a portrait of Kimberlee as a steely woman of business – the type of person who could annihilate you in a divorce action. So the question, of course, is why she would want a divorce. Did she find out you'd been unfaithful? Or did she just want out herself? I gather she did have rather a short attention span for relationships. Either way, you couldn't have her suing you for divorce, quietly or otherwise. You'd become accustomed to the lifestyle her money provided . . . far more money than you'd ever made in your lifetime.'

He looked at the man, closely watching his eyes, eyes that glanced nervously about the room, as if deliberately avoiding . . . a certain person. 'You didn't arrive *after* the murder. You've been here all along. You hid in the priest's hole, and you returned there after you killed Kimberlee.

'But you left the castle the next morning, after Kimberlee's body was found. You changed clothes somewhere at a safe distance from the castle, and then you returned much later in your business suit to talk with the police, wearing your distraught-husband face.'

'But,' said Portia. 'There were people crawling all over the place by then, and police guarding the only entrance. There's no way he could just walk out.'

'Ah, you've come to the heart of the matter, Portia. I'll get to that in a minute,' St Just replied. 'No, there was no way, Desmond, you could walk in or out as you pleased. You'd need help from an accomplice. An accomplice here in the castle.

'Let's trace it back, shall we? The drawbridge went up just before dinner and stayed up until Donna released Rachel Twalley and some of the other guests. She closed it behind them. The drawbridge opens only from the inside, and it makes a tremendous racket. We'd all have heard someone letting you in. You had to have come in *before* dinner, when it stood open.

'But here's a curious, related thing. We checked all the hotel's files going back years, and only one name appeared. And it wasn't yours, Desmond. Now, no one could just wander in and start looking about for the priest's hole. A stranger asking the staff about it would be sure to be remembered. No. It took someone who had been here, someone who knew the layout, someone to make sure the entrance to the priest's hole hadn't been sealed or obstructed at some point.

'It also needed someone to help you escape the next day, someone to act as lookout, someone to give you the all-clear signal.

'And that someone was . . . your lover, Annabelle Pace.'

At this, the silence was broken by a collective gasp of disbelief.

'I told you,' said Magretta.

'You did no such thing,' said St Just.

'You're mad,' Annabelle said stoutly. 'I'll not stay to listen to this.'

At a nod from Moor, Sergeant Kittle lightly stepped over to block the door.

'I think you will. So, we have Desmond hiding in the priest's hole, and maybe taking a little nap there after the murder. Murdering one's wife is so fatiguing, is it not, Desmond? But . . . why not just plan to kill her and leave? Why? *Because the drawbridge would be heard*. You might also be seen fleeing across the grounds.

'At first I thought the original plan was that you would wait, hiding, until everyone was asleep and then slip out, risking the noise. Maybe stay in a hotel in Edinburgh that night under an assumed name. But now I don't think so. I think the plan all along was to sabotage the drawbridge – literally, throw a spanner in the works – so the castle would be sealed all night, providing you an airtight alibi, so to speak. There would be no way a "stranger" could enter unheard. The storm and power outage allowed you to skip that little sabotage step. That part, I am sure, was to have been Annabelle's role. She was free to walk about, after all; you were not.

'You – you only had to sit tight in your hidey hole until the time was ripe. You were Annabelle's alibi. She didn't make a move that night without being seen by someone. She couldn't have done the killing, and she did not. By the way, where's your mobile, Desmond?'

'I left it at home by mistake, I was that upset,' he said. His face was flushed. A thin, bright sheen of perspiration had appeared on his forehead.

'No,' said St Just. 'Not a mistake. Your own alibi was that mobile message you supposedly sent to Kimberlee's phone from London.

'Only you didn't really send that message, did you? At least, not directly. You knew the police could tell from where the call was made. So you left your mobile at home in London. The simple thing would have been to bribe an accomplice to send the message from London for you, but that was a risk in itself. I think you – clever, technical genius you – programmed the mobile for a delayed send of a friendly message you'd written to Kimberlee. And then you headed for Scotland. Her mobile shows the message was sent at ten the night she died. Almost the exact minute you were killing her – the time you had planned in advance to kill her.

'You invent software for investors, Desmond – you told me writing these programs is how you made your packet. You must have taken this as a small challenge, to adapt the delayed-order-placement feature you'd invented to a mobile phone message. We'll be taking a close look at that mobile, you can be certain.'

A smile began to play about the edges of Desmond's mouth. St Just added, 'We'll be taking a closer look, even if you designed a program to remove almost all traces of itself, and then cause the device to restart, eliminating the last little bit. But certain controls would have to be defeated first, and that in and of itself would leave a trace.'

The smile disappeared.

'But back to Annabelle's role in this. She was here in the first instance to show you the hiding place.'

'You'll have to do *much* better than this,' said Annabelle.

'I shall. You had another role, which was to get Kimberlee to the bottle dungeon. You were seen in the hallway outside the ladies' room, talking with her. You passed her a message, didn't you, purportedly from Jay Fforde, that there had been a change of plans and she was to meet him earlier than planned, and in a different place than planned. I doubt Kimberlee would question this, your being enlisted as go-between. That was part of her nature, wasn't it? The love of intrigue. Remember, her first book was a romance novel. Her second was all about the mating rituals of the sexes. It was the perfect ploy to get her where you wanted her.'

Annabelle looked at him contemptuously.

'And this passes for evidence these days, does it? So I was here at the castle, over two years ago, during the Edinburgh festival, as you can easily find out by going through the castle records. So what?'

He had to hand it to her; she wasn't just going to give it up. She, he suspected, had masterminded the whole scheme. Desmond didn't have the starch. St Just paused, a knight looking for the chink in the armor. There was always one.

'Yes, I think the credit for this elaborate charade must go to Annabelle,' he said aloud.

'Do tell.'

'What was it?' he went on relentlessly. 'A plot for a new book, one that you decided to apply to real life? Or did you from the beginning address your demonic creativity to the little problem of how to get rid of Kimberlee Kalder? Either way, it worked – or nearly did.'

'Nonsense.'

'It is most assuredly not nonsense. You, as you say, were here during the Edinburgh festival. And you are the only one in this room who has ever been a guest here.'

'I repeat: You call this evidence? What about the staff?'

'Ah, yes, speaking of the staff: The bartender, having been

shown a certain photo, remembers you well as the lady who showed such a keen interest in the priest's hole. Combined with a few other inconsistencies, yes, I think we can put a seal on this nicely.'

'Inconsistencies . . . such as?'

'Such as this.'

He reached into the box behind him and pulled out several books. He held out one, its back cover facing his audience. He turned slowly, so they could all get a good look.

'Your author photo.' He held up another book, then another, all with different photos of Annabelle through the years, but all of them glamour shots of a woman unrecognizable as the frumpy, haggard-looking Annabelle that sat before them. The woman in the photo was coiffed and buffed and highlighted to within an inch of her life, and even allowing for the photographer's art and skillfully applied make-up, her beauty could not be denied. Her blonde hair fell in graceful waves to her shoulders; in one particularly ravishing photo she wore a low-cut dress of red satin. At her neck and throat were diamonds. She was a stunner.

'This is why you got rid of all the copies of your book you could lay your hands on at the conference booksellers, isn't it? Your disguise was to play the frump, the woman of no sex appeal whatsoever. Especially once you saw me browsing the bookstore at the conference that day, you realized you had to buy up all the copies of your book and destroy them or throw them away. They couldn't be found in your room by the police, could they? Because your deadly game with Desmond was already, if you will forgive the expression, afoot. You could not have the police noticing your disguise.

'What did you do with the books?' he demanded.

'What books?' she snapped. 'This is madness, I tell you.'

'The first day of the conference I saw you carrying a bag that had to have had a dozen books in it. The bookseller will have a record of that purchase, of course. But we only found three books in your room, all by other authors. What did you do with your own books? Will we also find them in the moat – or did you just find a handy trash bin somewhere?'

'I really don't know what you're talking about.'

'You're the only author – the only one – who isn't traveling with at least a few copies of her own books. Dozens, in some cases. Why is that, I asked myself? Humility? A lack of vanity? Not ruddy likely. That's an unheard-of modesty for an author. But there are practical reasons as well: All of you keep your own books about you in case the bookseller runs out of copies, in case a fan asks to see the cover – whatever authorial reasons. Then I remembered: All of the authors had a big, smiling photo – in some cases, a scowling photo – of themselves on the backs of their books.

'It was the *photo* you didn't want us to see, wasn't it?'

'Disguise.' She fairly spat at him, fixing him with arrow-slit eyes, a brief flare of temper beneath the ice. 'Don't be absurd. I've just not been well.'

'That is make-up on your face,' he replied, 'but you've painted yourself almost gray. You've painted yourself *old*, haven't you? No woman wears make-up so that she can look *worse* – unless she's playing a part, like an actress in a play. I would've said you wore no make-up at all, but there were in fact the usual little pots and bottles in your room. And baby powder – possibly used to dull your hair. That's an old actor's trick. Something you learned as a photographer's assistant, perhaps? There were also tissues in your bathroom waste bin with lotion and traces of make-up on them. I thought nothing of it – all the women's waste bins were like that.' The women exchanged looks at realizing how thoroughly their privacy had been invaded. 'With the exception of Mrs Elksworthy,' he went on, 'who really does wear no make-up.'

'Allergic,' Joan barked, traces of her usual staunch self returning. 'I could have told you that. No need to snoop around my room.'

'And the clothes – all wrong, all cheap and ill-fitting, nothing you would normally wear, nothing like what we see in these photos. Yet all the clothes looked brand new, bought especially for the occasion – the occasion being this farce you were about to play. Also, you have pierced ears, but I've yet to see you wear a single piece of jewelry. I was reminded of this when someone said something about Mrs Elksworthy's jewelry, but I couldn't put my finger on the memory then.'

'I did tell you Annabelle looked changed somehow—' began Mrs Elksworthy.

'Yes, I missed the significance. You didn't even recognize her at first. I started looking closer and asked myself again what woman would work that hard at looking fat, bloated, and ill – especially a woman speaking before a conference audience. Especially a woman who had been involved with B. A. King – a man who would never waste a minute on a woman like the Annabelle we see before us. I could not for the life of me see how someone like B. A. King – a man of all flash and no substance – would ever have taken up with someone like Annabelle, and vice versa. It was a complete mismatch. He would go for youth or sparkle, every time. Another inconsistency.'

She gazed at him from hooded, predatory, eyes. He was reminded of the falcons in the aviary.

'This is all pretty insulting, and yet I fail to see how my personal dress and make-up choices have anything to do with this. I've been unwell, I tell you. Maybe I've gained a few pounds. The stress of deadlines can do that. So what?'

'Do you know what I think? For one thing, I think a woman must be very sure of her man to allow him to see her looking like that. Not to mention, letting your fans wonder what train ran over you. There had to be a reason for the sudden lack of author vanity. And the reason was this: You couldn't be seen as an object of desire – a girlfriend, a mistress. There was too much money riding on it. Kimberlee's money. No. It was best the police believe you'd never had color in your cheeks, that your hair was always drab and stringy, that you dressed like a bag lady.

'That is why you didn't join the other ladies in the spa, even though it would have been a natural indulgence, a way to pass the time. You didn't *want* to be spit-polished. Your disguise was the frumpy hair and clothing.

'I also started to notice, Annabelle, that you had quite a good brain, and could generally be counted on for the sharp observation. But your sharpness, your apparent savvy, your confident way of speaking – that didn't match your appearance, either.

'Now, which one of you two killed poor Florie, is what I want to know?' He had a sense just then of energy flowing between the pair – but mainly of energy flowing from Annabelle to Desmond, bolstering him up. 'She had to have been killed because of something she saw, something she knew. Then I remembered those four men standing around, "repairing" the drawbridge. Florie saw them, too, and made a comment about how typical that was. Three men supervising while one worked, something to that effect.'

He turned to Donna.

'How many men on your repair staff were called out that night?'

'There are only three, as I told you when you asked just now. We called them all.'

'*Not* four?' St Just eyes glanced across the assembled group, collecting their attention.

'No. I saw them myself when they first arrived.'

'So somewhere along the way, they added a fourth man. That man was you, Desmond. Florie must have seen you later in the castle and recognized you as one of the "repairmen". But you were supposed to be the victim's husband, the one who'd rushed up, weeping all the way, from London. So what were you doing there, dressed in baggy jeans, pretending to be a workman? No one else thought anything of it – the work-men you chatted with took you for one of the friendly guests. You just walked out of the castle – anyone watching would have thought you were going to get something from the lorry. And you kept walking. Later that day, you came back, this time playing the widower.

'I congratulate you, Annabelle. It was a good plan, and it nearly worked.'

Still, she stared at him insolently. Time to go for the weakest link, he thought. He turned to Sergeant Kittle, and nodded.

The policeman turned and opened the library door. A dog – a black and cream German Shepherd – came tumbling in, attached to his handler by a leash. Kittle's friends Robert and Rob Roy had arrived.

'Everyone remain seated,' commanded St Just.

The dog made an exploratory circle around the room, sniffing as he went.

He came to Desmond, and lay down. Desmond recoiled, as if the dog were going to take a bite of him.

'You're all witnesses to that. He's following the scent he found in the priest's hole.'

The dog stood at Robert's command and resumed his circle around the room.

The next place Rob Roy lay down was at Annabelle's feet.

Epilogue

St Just had an hour until his train to Cambridge, and no desire to sit in the waiting room, reading yet another newspaper, or resuming his copy of *Baudolino*. The case was closed, or as closed as cases ever get, via a combination of high- and low-tech means. Man's best friend meets the age of technology.

'You did all right by us, Cambridge,' Moor had told him, dropping him off at the train station. 'Even if you're not from Scotland Yaird.'

St Just had smiled. He was going to miss Moor and Kittle. They'd walk their days under Scottish skies, and he'd probably never see either of them again.

Portia he'd not seen again. He'd spent most of what was left of the night at the police station and slept until noon the next day. By the time he awoke, all his former suspects had departed.

Including Portia, who had already claimed a prior, urgent appointment. That was probably even true. She'd said she would call him. There was . . . a 'situation'. . .she needed to sort out first. She didn't elaborate. He hadn't dared ask. He clung with hope to the word 'first.' He'd give her a week, he'd decided, and then call her.

A wedding party was arriving as he and Moor left the castle. He hoped it was an omen.

Desmond, the weakest link, had indeed broken down under interrogation, as St Just had known he would. Once the pair of them were separated, he'd described in detail Annabelle's role in the crime.

She had remained steadfast, loudly proclaiming her innocence and demanding a lawyer. He'd let the Scots work on her. Not his pigeon.

Walking aimlessly now about the streets near Waverley Station, he came to an antique shop. On closer inspection, it seemed to be more of a junk shop. In the window was a teddy bear that looked like the survivor of some horrible nursery experiment. Several experiments.

He'd had a similar toy as a child. Hadn't everyone? It was hard to imagine growing up without that small comfort, but of course by the many thousands there must be children who went without.

What next caught his eye in the window was a set of pastels. The wooden box was labeled 'Sennelier Landscape Wood Soft Pastel Set.' It would be years before he would come to realize they made another set in a different range of colors called Seascape, and yet another called Portrait. But he was drawn to these Landscape ones – with their rich, deep range of color, the deep blues and bright reds – like a bird drawn to a bright object.

There were fifty of these little crayonlike objects laid in two rows in their specially made wooden box. None of them appeared to have been used. Wait – the blue drawing stick, the one of the deepest shade of blue, the one nearly a match for Portia's eyes and her velvet dress – that was a bit worn at one end. He walked into the store and, leaning into the display, picked that one out of the box.

Who would buy a fancy set of colors like this and give up after trying only one? Intrigued, he picked up the entire box, looking for the price. Seventy pounds they wanted. Good Lord. But the set was nearly new, he told himself. And the colors, such amazing colors. . .

Drawing was something he'd always done instinctively,

usually when sitting, half-listening, in some interminable meeting, or otherwise held captive. He drew to record scenes the way another man might use a camera to take snapshots on vacation. He'd not had formal training, apart from one evening course, and he hadn't repeated the experience – he told himself his gift didn't amount to a major talent and he didn't want to start taking it all too seriously.

He'd never had the least inclination to pick up a paintbrush. Black on white was his métier. If he saw this, as others did, as support for his reputation for lucid, cut-and-dried reasoning, he would be the last to acknowledge it. He'd leave the Freudian interpretations to those who liked that kind of thing.

But . . . he'd have these pastels. He carried the box to the aged man behind the antique desk that served as a checkout counter. Black and white had its place, but until that moment St Just had not known how much he felt the need of color in his world.

He felt a surge of confidence. He would see Portia again and, this time, he'd win her over.

He'd return to Cambridge and he'd call her right away. Who had a week to waste? Maybe he'd try to call her from Waverley Station.

Or maybe he'd write. Anyway, he'd woo her, the old-fashioned way, no matter how big a fool he made of himself in the process.

Whatever it took.

As St Just was handing over his credit card to the store owner, Elsbeth Dowell, Florie's replacement at Dalmorton, was carrying a stack of freshly laundered sheets down one of the labyrinth hallways of the castle. Elsbeth, only months out of school, was proud of this, her first real job, and determined to do well. She liked stately Dalmorton, with its proud history and glamorous present; she knew Donna Doone to be a fair employer.

The door to one of the turret rooms – in fact the police's 'Incident Turret' – suddenly opened of itself.

That's odd, she thought. Those doors each weigh a ton.

She peered inside.

Suddenly she dropped the sheets, and screamed.

Her screams seemed to have no effect on the two women in gauzy white dresses who stood before her, smiling, and beckoning her towards them. The women were both as transparent as cellophane. 'Just like they was sweet wrappers,' as she told Donna later, handing in her notice. She could see through both of them to the gray castle walls behind.

One of the women wore a voluminous gown, medieval in style, with long sleeves and a veiled headdress; the other a modern dress with spaghetti straps, short and clinging and low-cut. It might almost have been a white silk slip.

She had long, flowing, white-blonde hair.

It was well over a year since the Dalmorton murders, with Cambridge heading into an unseasonably warm June. As St Just walked along Trinity Street past Heffer's, his eye was caught by the name Joan Elksworthy on a book in the display window.

He stepped inside for a closer look. He hefted the book off the display; it was a good-sized hardback with a glossy pink-and-black cover, edged in a tartan pattern of similar colors. A dark, looming castle dominated the illustration. Joan's name appeared in large, bold type over a title in still-larger type: *Death at Dalmorton*. Leafing through the pages, he saw what Joan had written was a nonfiction, 'eyewitness' account of Kimberlee's murder. One of the store clerks, just walking past, told him it was one of their more popular items.

Of course St Just had to have a copy. He remembered his last conversation at the castle with Mrs E., just before he left for the police station with Moor and Kittle.

'Poor Kimberlee,' she'd said. 'I'm sure she never saw it

coming. We all need to protect ourselves – some more than others – from knowing what our nearest and dearest *really* think of us, don't we? How could we go on living otherwise – without those blinders on?'

'A bit cynical, that, don't you think?'

'Not at all, Inspector. I'm just a realist.'

Taking the book to the checkout desk, he also noticed that *What Jesus Ate* by Sarah Beauclerk-Fisk, a name from one of his previous investigations, was apparently still selling briskly, judging by its prominent display. He picked up the book and smiled, deciding to buy it, if for no other reason than old times' sake. He'd never get around to reading it, but maybe he could give it to someone as a gift. Or maybe he could start a collection: books by murder suspects. It was then the name Magretta Sincock on yet another book on the best-seller table caught his eye. Another hot pink-and-black number. He picked up the book and turned it over to read the jacket copy: 'A refreshing and daring departure for the Queen of Romantic Suspense: hip, witty, irreverent. Most of all: *cool*. This season's must-have accessory for your beach bag.'

Really. Somehow, that didn't sound like Magretta, and, as he scanned the pages, he began to recognize pieces of the manuscript the Scottish police had managed to retrieve from Kimberlee's sodden laptop. He turned the book to look at its spine, and saw the distinctive Deadly Dagger Press logo.

He barked out a laugh, causing nearby browsers in the sanctuary-like atmosphere of the store to turn their heads and frown at him in disapproval. She'd stolen it from Kimberlee, of course. Magretta must have copied the computer file onto a memory stick or a CD – despite her poor-little-me claims of no experience with technology – and only *then* thrown the laptop out of the window, thinking that would destroy it.

As it was, it came so very near to being lost.

The police only cared about the will they'd also found on the laptop, not the manuscript. The will in which Kimberlee had left everything to her husband, Desmond. The will she hadn't yet had time to change, despite advice from her solicitor – in a document also on the laptop – to do so as a preliminary step to divorce.

And now Magretta was claiming the novel – minus, of course, the parts she didn't want to see the light of day – as her own.

He wondered what, if anything, he should do about it.

Portia will know, he thought. I'll ask her.

THE END